TELLING ONLY LIES

Jessica Mann was born and went to school in London. She studied archaeology and Anglo Saxon at Newnham College, Cambridge. Her husband is an archaeologist. The have two sons and two daughters.

TELLING ONLY LIES

Jessica Mann

ARROW

First published 1992

1 3 5 7 9 10 8 6 4 2

First published in 1992 by Hutchinson

Arrow edition 1993
Random House, 20 Vauxhall Bridge Road, London SW1V 2SA

Random House Australia (Pty) Limited
20 Alfred Street, Milsons Point, Sydney,
New South Wales 2061, Australia

Random House New Zealand Limited
18 Poland Road, Glenfield
Auckland 10, New Zealand

Random House South Africa (Pty) Limited
PO Box 337, Bergvlei, South Africa

Random House UK Limited Reg. No. 954009

A CIP catalogue record for this book
is available from the British Library

ISBN 0 09 914761 0

Printed and bound in Great Britain by
Cox & Wyman Ltd, Reading, Berkshire

'If you write fiction lying is perfectly moral and acceptable. You don't expect to write a novel telling only truths.'

Mario Vargas Llosa.

PART I
1990

1

You write well.

That is what reviewers say. It is what friends tell me.

Why, they ask, don't I write a real book?

A real book: not a mystery, nor a historical novel; not a story of action or suspense nor one in which writer and reader alike are insulated from feeling by irony and wit. I should write more about emotions, less about exciting events. The characters' anguish should be mental not physical, the appeal to the readers' hearts as well as their minds.

You write well, my agent says, but not as well as you could. Not as well as you want to yourself.

Mark Bissenden is a man who knows what he is talking about. He knows books and book people, he knows writers, publishers, critics, readers. He knows me. He knew me.

In every sense.

But that was nearly twenty years ago. I had just been taken on as his client after publishing a couple of quite successful historical mystery novels.

Mark praised the manuscript I had brought him.

'The mixture as before,' I said, self-deprecating but avid for reassurance. He delivered it punctually and then proceeded to a disconcertingly acute analysis of my work so far and yet to come.

'You'll make money, we'll see to that. And a reputation.' He held my gaze in his brown-green eyes. (The satirical magazine of those irreverent days referred to him by the name Bunny, which was an arcane reference to a rabbit called Hazel in a cult book of the period.) 'But to write a good book, you'll have to let it all hang out,' he said. It was the jargon of the time. So was his next remark. 'You are too up-tight.'

What made him think so?

Crime writers, he said, are like that. Inhibited. Secretive. Protected by the armour of objectivity. That's why they choose the

3

genre, to erect a barrier between themselves and exposure. Nobody could suppose them to be writing from personal experience.

Did he really think I would do better to perform one of those autobiographical stripteases on the page that gave women novelists a bad name? Did he want yet another saga of angst and adultery in North London?

Why not? he said, thinking of one of his most profitable authors. But all he really meant was that I should dig a little deeper.

I said if I could I wouldn't and if I would I couldn't. I made him a speech about privacy. He made me one about truth. Anyway, I told him, that's just the way I am, repressed; what did he expect me to do about it – spend the next ten years on a shrink's black leather couch, or what?

Mark's prescription was a wild, passionate affair. It was his panacea, his updated version of the hoary old theory that a virgin's singing voice or acting powers or painting style or even literary fluency could only be released by a man. The formula did not vary, whether the woman was inexperienced, exhausted, hysterical or merely irritating. It was expressed as 'What she needs is a good fuck'.

I did, as it happened. My husband had been away in Hong Kong for months, junior counsel in a case that kept prolonging itself. I was stuck in London with two of the children at day school and one still at home, an incompatible au pair girl and builders in the house.

So Mark and I had an affair. It was not wild and passionate, but friendly, enjoyable, almost innocent, which is a less inappropriate word than it might seem. It meant nothing except that I was lonely at the time. Gerry would have understood and forgiven, if I had ever told him.

The episode left both Mark and me unaltered. He got married within the year and we have remained excellent friends ever since, which is some kind of achievement, even if not exactly the one he had intended.

Unfettered sex did not free me from the bonds of literary artifice. Reviewers went on calling my books intelligent, dispassionate or elegant. They still do, damning with apparent praise, seeing little merit in disengagement.

Are they right?

Yes.

Detached. Dispassionate. Uninvolved.

That is how I write.

That is what I am.

If I were a character in one of my own books it could only be as the victim or the criminal.

Chapter One: Anne Medlicott, early fifties, married, prosperous, still quite good looking, with blue-ish eyes retreating into folds of slackening skin, a pale complexion and regular features, short and a little too fat. She lives in an expensive house which is too big for her and her husband now the children have left home.

The setting for her first appearance: a kitchen whose designer has managed to combine convenience and cosiness. Through the windows she looks out into her conservatory and, beyond it, a large walled garden. Once a week contractors come to maintain the plants and lawns.

In a moment she will go into a drawing room full of antiques and elegance. It has been redecorated this year under the guidance of a neighbour who runs an interior design company from her home. A Portuguese woman comes every day to clean the house.

She is smug. She has things easy.

I would make the sky fall in upon her.

It happens.

I am always conscious of the gulf beneath our feet. That is why I write the fear of it out of me in the form of fictional fantasies of cruelty and deceit. My books are set in the last century, that era of illusory stability. They concern an inescapable aspect of any age. It is human iniquity. My characters fall through the thin ice of civilisation.

It happened.

Among many others, to my own family. My grandmother, Hanne Silberschmidt, was exactly the same age as I am now when she fled from her own country into exile. She left the home in which she and her husband and three generations of the family before them had lived. Until that bitter end, they had faith in their future.

I have always tried not to think about it. I do not wish to know. I hide my eyes, guilty of failure in courage and humanity and it is no wonder that readers detect it in my books.

5

My latest one is published today. Mark takes me out to lunch to celebrate. I face him across the table.

Mark has aged perceptibly but well. His lips are still full, smooth, unexpectedly warm. His hair, once glossily black, is now stippled with equally shiny silver, there are fine white stripes in the tan of his face where he has wrinkled his skin against the sun. He is noticeably heavier. I look at his monogrammed shirt, his dark wool suit, his lettuce-green and salmon-pink striped tie, and speculate about the body beneath them. Is the crisp hair that grew to a point between prominent nipples now grey, is the skin above the coccyx still freckled in a leaf shaped pattern, does he still smell, under the laundered sea-island cotton, of fresh bread?

I wonder what he thinks of me. I have dressed carefully as women always do to meet their former lovers, in case they wonder what they ever saw in one, to remind them of regret that the affair ever ended. My artfully auburn hair is expensively ruffled, nails pointed and polished, face painted and powdered, body clad in silk that is meant to be at once simple and seductive. I am, like my prose, in disguise.

We are at one of the four clubs whose membership Mark lists in his *Who's Who* entry. To reach the dining room I have followed him up and down a maze of dingy staircases and corridors. I have a good sense of direction. 'You are taking me round in circles,' I say.

'Ladies aren't allowed to go up the main staircase.'

'But this place has female members.'

'Even so.'

Some of those female members are already in the ladies' dining room. I recognise the principal of an Oxford college and a governor of the BBC.

'They don't let women into the library either,' Mark says. He is embarrassed and so am I, knowing that its victims should never cooperate with discrimination. I feel as I do at parties when some unwary old buffer utters an anti-Semitic cliché, which he probably does not mean and certainly would never have said if only somebody had warned him that Gerry Medlicott's wife is of Jewish origin. When it happens Gerry always glances at me warily, as though I were an animal of uncertain temper; is she going to make a scene?

6

I am too often pusillanimous. I tell myself that if the head of a house and a pillar of the establishment can bear the anti-feminism it is not for me to protest.

Mark and I have run dutifully through the children and spouse conversation; how, where, with whom and what next? My sons are doing all right, I say. Flora is keeping her head above water.

Mark's sons are both at university but he has started all over again with an actress and they have twin daughters. He is at once boastful and rueful about sleepless nights and produces snapshots of babies on beaches. From that we progress to the obligatory though enjoyable gossip and guesses about writers and publishers.

Then, in the manner of a very superior private doctor moving smoothly from generalisations about the weather to intimate discussion of his patient's symptoms, Mark says,

'Turning to your next book, Anne . . . ' and I reply,

'I'm trying to write something different.'

'Goodbye Amy?' He sounds nervous. Amy Swift has been profitable for us both. My heroine's name was carefully chosen, twelve books before, to imply that she was lovable and quickwitted. She is a creature of certainties, not given to sitting and agonising over her next step. She is a photographer, which is historically plausible, and a free woman, which involves a certain suspension of disbelief, but her expertise provides a means for me to take her to places and let her meet a variety of people in a way that few women could a hundred years ago. She has solved murders on the north-west frontier of India, in Prussia and inside Windsor Castle (my third, sixth and seventh books).

'I'd like to see if I can manage something more serious,' I explain, but to my horror water wells up in my eyes, a spontaneous, quite involuntary expression of misery that I never knew I was feeling. 'Oh! I'm so sorry. Some allergy . . . What's in this salad? Scallops. Perhaps it's the mussels . . . '

Mark shakes out and hands me a freshly laundered white handkerchief. It smells of Floris Essence of Limes. Cautiously I wipe mascara from under my lower eyelids.

'What's really wrong?' he asks.

'I don't want to go on being successful, superficial, commercial . . . you know the adjectives. I've done it now, it's time for something new.'

'We always believed you had the Great Novel in you,' he says politely.

'But I haven't. I've been trying for months. The upshot is that I'm incapable of writing about things that matter. My mind slides away from them like mercury.'

'You must persevere.'

'I simply can't do it. As soon as I go along the road of thinking about real people with real problems and emotions, No Entry signs start popping up in my mind. Observe them, and I can trundle along with my damned elegant and intelligent trivia. Go past and I crash.' I wipe my eyes again. 'But there's no point in discussing it, you aren't here to be a psychotherapist. I don't want to talk about it anyway.'

I must look a wreck, on the very day when it is important to look my best. After lunch I am to go to the television studios to take part in a live programme called *Only Connect*. Those words are a quotation from E.M. Forster and indicate, to those who recognise it, that this chat show is of a superior kind. But in the end it is, like all others, an opportunity for self-advertisement. My duty is to mention the full title of my book at least once and preferably more often. Publishers' publicists compete to have their authors invited to participate, though this particular coup was my agent's.

I take out my compact and try to effect a quick repair. Mark says, 'Perhaps we'd better talk about this another time.'

'I'll have to be off in a moment,' I say in a bright, social tone. 'But do tell me before I go how you managed to arrange this wonderful opportunity. I'm really very grateful to you for it.'

'Pure luck, I'm afraid. No damned merit in it. I happened to meet a researcher on the show and mentioned you among others of my clients. Her job is to find connections between the guests, and one of them today is Perdita Whitchurch, the painter, who was at the same school as you. Do you remember her?'

'That's a tenuous link, I must say. We can't have met since we were children. I hardly remember anything about her, just that she was Lord Blanchminster's daughter.'

'There's another connection for you. This was their London house. The club took it over and knocked through the wall when old Lady Blanchminster died. She must have been one of the last private people to live in Pall Mall.'

'Perdita's mother, do you mean?'

'No, the old chap's stepmother, I think. That portrait over the chimney piece must be her predecessor, his own mother, but genealogy always defeats me.'

The picture shows a moon-faced blonde, her fair hair held by a tiara, a plethora of pearls on her white bosom, the white tulle of her dress wreathed with roses and pearls, wide, naive blue eyes under their semicircle of brow fixed in madonna-style adoration on a lace-enfolded baby on her lap. On her left a young officer stands at attention to the painter in his scarlet and gilt, his brown hair in flattened little curls, his expression arrogant. He is the archetype of the white Anglo-Saxon Protestant male, undoubted heir not only to acres and millions, but also to lifelong influence and power.

'The portrait of a hereditary legislator,' I murmur, and Mark says he was killed in North Africa, actually. The younger boy, on the mother's right, is fair, pink, unformed, the profile not yet hooked, the eyelids not yet hooded. He dangles a gold repeater watch in its chain towards the infant's chubby fingers. I fumble for my spectacles and read the label: 'The Viscountess Blanchminster with her children, the Honourable Cassian, Julian and April Whitchurch'.

'Julian is the present one, your chum's papa,' Mark says, and the name lodges itself disastrously into my mind.

2

TRANSCRIPT OF *ONLY CONNECT*
13 SEPTEMBER 1990
PRESENTER: JONTY SOLOMON
GUESTS: PERDITA WHITCHURCH, ANNE MEDLICOTT,
  PROFESSOR SIR HANS HAHN
PRODUCER: NELL WHITEHOUSE

OPENS:

SOLOMON: Good afternoon and welcome to *Only Connect*. Today's links in the chain of life will be forged by the painter Perdita Whitchurch, whose new show opens in London this evening, her old school mate Anne Medlicott, whose book *Swiftsure* appears this week, and Professor Sir Hans Hahn of King's College, Cambridge, writer, historian, board member of such august organisations as the British Council and the Arts Council, who has a collection of Whitchurch paintings and is a crime fiction enthusiast – and is about to publish his own account of potential British quislings in the last war.

(Eleven minutes chat omitted from transcript.)

SOLOMON: Now, turning to you, Sir Hans. You're holding that notebook as though it were a time bomb. I know some of the names are too sensitive to mention, but tell us the implications of its contents.

HAHN: Well, this may look like a small notebook with marbled paper covers, not much of a weapon at first sight, but contained in it is enough to blow a lot of reputations sky high.

SOLOMON: It concerns the period of the war. World War Two, right?

HAHN: That's correct.

SOLOMON: And what's in it?

HAHN: A list of members of what we now call the Establishment.

They are the names of men who could be expected to cooperate with the Germans if and when they occupied Britain.

SOLOMON: And who collected them?

HAHN: It is one of the lists known to have been made in the period before the war by Nazi sympathisers in this country and by the Germans themselves.

SOLOMON: You say 'one of the lists'.

HAHN: That's right, because there were others, such as the Black List, of those people, anti-Nazis, who were to be arrested immediately.

SOLOMON: So the names in that notebook are of collaborators with the enemy?

HAHN: Yes, potential and actual traitors, the so-called Fifth Column.

SOLOMON: Weren't such people called quislings?

HAHN: Yes, after a Norwegian collaborator.

SOLOMON: Of course, many of them are dead, but there must be people watching this programme now in terror of what your little notebook will reveal. This is a really sensitive document.

HAHN: That's right.

SOLOMON: So how do you come to have it in your possession? Where has it been all these years?

HAHN: I can't answer that question. It was sent to me in Cambridge, perhaps because I have recently published a work on the pre-war Right Club, the discovery of whose membership list in nineteen forty led the War Cabinet to frame regulations that permitted internment of enemy sympathisers without trial.

SOLOMON: But this comes from a different source.

HAHN: So I suppose. I do not know.

SOLOMON: Well, it happened before I was born. I wonder what my other guests think of this raking over old bones. You were born before the war, Perdita Whitchurch, but surely can't remember it.

WHITCHURCH: I was and I can't.

MEDLICOTT: Actually it sounds more like the plot of a thriller than real life. May I have a look? Thank you. The writing's very faint.

HAHN: Yes, there's a good deal of work to be done on this document, but there are still many people who would prefer it never to be done.

SOLOMON: I suppose that having one's name in here would be evidence of something pretty shocking. When you think what these men might have done if the Nazis had won, or even what they did do during the war.

HAHN: Yes. Some are the names of known traitors or their families.

SOLOMON: Are they afraid of other people learning about it? Embarrassed?

HAHN: The damage to a reputation would cause more than embarrassment.

SOLOMON: Sounds like good stuff for a libel action.

HAHN: Yes, I have received warnings of that and some threats.

SOLOMON: But I wonder, Perdita Whitchurch, whether you can really feel quite unconnected to the subject. After all, your mother was a famous war correspondent. You must have grown up with war talk across the breakfast table. The men listed in this little book would have betrayed their country – maybe even did betray it. Men who would probably have been shot as traitors or convicted of war crimes if their secret had been known. Men who might kill now to keep their identities secret. As a journalist's daughter, don't you feel concerned?

WHITCHURCH (hesitation): No, I don't.

MEDLICOTT: Goodness, I've just noticed. Look, Perdita, your father's name is on the list.

3

hers. She says, 'I do
you remember, I do re
me

The producer disappears immediately after the pr̶̶̶. Perhaps she realises, as I do not, what I have been a̶̶̶̶̶ ̶̶̶̶̶nd
done.

I would have liked the chance to speak to Sir Hans Hahn, whom
I had not seen for many years. He reminded me that he had
known both my parents and there is hardly anybody left who
did. But he arrived in time to greet everyone efficiently with a
personal word to each, performed and then left the studio even
before the credits finished rolling.

Perdita Whitchurch came up from Penzance and arrived late,
panting her apologies for locomotive breakdowns and signal
failures near Slough. She was hustled into the make-up room and
on to the set just before we went on air.

Afterwards we greet each other in unison: 'You haven't changed at all! I would have known you anywhere.'

It is not true. As pupils at the Abbess of Whitby's Academy both
of us were small, skinny girls with straight dark hair and nervous
dispositions.

Now Perdita's bobbed hair is grey and her clothes flamboyant.
She is still thin, has a gap in her discoloured teeth and obviously
neither gives a damn what anyone else thinks of her nor spends
any time or money on her appearance. I, who do, am irritated to
realise that I look no younger or more attractive than she.

The moment we leave the studio she lights a cigarette, holding
it in dirty fingers. We exchange information about our adult lives.
Anyone who ever sees a newspaper must have read about Perdita's numerous relationships but I pretend not to know that she
has a grown-up son and is divorced. I tell her that my husband,
Gerald Medlicott, is a barrister specialising in intellectual property, that we have three children and live in Saffron Walden.
Perdita says she lives alone near Land's End.

She asks after my mother, who died many years ago. I ask after

13

n't see my parents. But I never did much, if
...

...member. It was the first thing the new girl had said to
.. Miss Pinnell had chosen me to conduct Perdita round the
mysteries of the Abbess of Whitby's Academy. I was eight and in
the second form; she was seven and a half. Her mother lived in
America, her father was always away. She had been brought up
by her father's old nurse and never been to school before. On
mentioning her nanny, Perdita's eyes filled with tears. I warned
her never to let the others catch her crying.

Although only six months older than Perdita, I was a year
ahead of her at school. We did not see very much of each other
there once she had graduated from her status as 'new girl', but
at the end of one term I was told to take charge of her on the train
journey south and she stayed at my home for a few days. Another
time I was given a lift back from school in her family's chauffeur-
driven Daimler. Once I even went to her home, whose grandeur
made a great and lasting impression on me.

My mother seemed sorry for Perdita and wanted us to be
friends, but little girls are age-snobs and I did not care to spend
my time with someone in the form below mine. After I left the
Abbess of Whitby's for Cheltenham Ladies' College we lost
touch. If we met again, I don't recall it.

We have outworn our welcome at the television studios. The
programme assistant does not quite turn the lights off and on in
the inhospitable 'hospitality room' but the message is clear.

Perdita must go to the gallery for the opening of her exhibition.
She invites me to it. Gerry is due home late after a day in court
in Manchester and I feel overexcited, on an adrenalin high after
the performance. I agree and we walk to Cork Street together.

I feel curiously familiar with the woman at my side, as though
we had always known each other, and, at the same time, as
though she were a complete stranger, known to me only from
newspaper gossip. We talk easily about my books and her painting, about gallery owners and publishers, about art critics and
book reviewers.

The private view is well attended. I recognise a few of the
guests – the odd novelist who buys paintings and the odd artist
who reads books. One or two people have seen us on television

14

but nobody behaves as though the programme had been especially interesting.

There are three rooms of large, larger and largest canvases. I never know what to say to artists about their own work, but the catalogue calls the collection an advance in Perdita Whitchurch's intensity and vehemence, so I venture to remark that en masse the pictures give the impression of rage.

She replies, 'I know. I paint feeling perfectly happy and calm and then they come out agitated and angry. I suppose I must think at the tips of my fingers. As a matter of fact, before I started painting I don't believe I ever thought at all.'

Some of the pictures seem almost vicious. They would not be comfortable to live with.

'My own venom goes into murder plots,' I say.

'One of the critics said my work showed anguish, but I don't think I feel it.'

'Have you ever been psychoanalysed?'

'Oh no,' she says quickly. 'I wouldn't dare. I might never be able to pick up a brush again.'

Perdita Whitchurch is doing well. About a third of the pictures have red tabs beside them already, though the prices seem extremely high especially for work that, though furious, is also extremely feminine. That is a quality which usually depresses values in the art world. I am not tempted to buy one myself, except to prove to Perdita that I can afford it.

The gallery's owner and the director of an important American museum are to take Perdita to dinner. We say goodbye, steering a tactful course through the shallows and rapids of lunch suggestions, both knowing the code in which 'we must have lunch' means 'I don't care if I never see you again', and 'can you have lunch with me this Thursday?' means what it says. I say, 'Do let's make a date for lunch.'

Perdita says, 'I am not in London much, but you must come and see me in Cornwall some time.'

'I should love to,' I reply, but do not really expect to see her for another forty years, or to think about her either.

I go home to bed and hardly stir when Gerry joins me in the small hours. The next morning I totter downstairs in my usual pre-coffee daze and scoop the papers from the doormat on my way to the kitchen, but I have not read the headlines when Gerry

15

exclaims, 'Oh my God!' He never gets excited, never uses profane, obscene or exaggerated language. I turn round.

'Whatever's happened?'

'What have you done?'

'Me?' I look around the kitchen, as tidy as Mrs Carvalho always leaves it, check Gerry's clothes for stains on his shirt or tie, and can see nothing wrong anywhere.

He holds out the *Independent*.

It shows a grainy photograph of me holding Hans Hahn's marble tablet rather close to my short-sighted eyes. I look ugly, elderly and open-mouthed with surprise. My words are quoted.

'Look, Perdita, your father's name is on the list.'

4

Gerry does not scold me. He is kind enough to say that this sort of thing is to be expected on live television programmes. Someone should have taken precautions.

Someone did, but I missed the warnings. I was in the make-up room when Sir Hans Hahn was reminded not to mention the name of anyone who was still alive.

He had been careful not to do so.

Why did I pick the little book up from the table? Why had I leafed through the pages? What made me blurt out my rash and, I now realise, slanderous remark?

Because I felt too comfortable. I had not fluffed or forgotten what to say, I had given fluent answers and even made a couple of jokes. We had been told to relax and behave as though we were just having a convivial tea party with friends. That was the format of *Only Connect*. 'Be yourselves, join in the conversation, we want you to show everyone that you're having a nice time,' the producer insisted. I should have known better than to take her at her word.

I had relaxed and spoken without thinking.

'Look, Perdita, your father's name is on the list.'

That was what I said.

The Honourable Julian Whitchurch's name was written in spiky script, faint, mauve indelible pencil on checked paper between two other names I did not recognise and which did not pop out of my mouth.

He is now Viscount Blanchminster, the old, distinguished and well-known chairman of Blanchminster's Bank. I have effectively described him as a potential quisling, traitor, even perpetrator of war crimes. My words are undoubtedly capable of lowering him in public estimation, of causing him harm: they are, by definition, defamatory.

The news broke overnight. On the Tokyo stock exchange there

17

has already been a dramatic loss of value in Blanchminster's shares. Worse is expected to follow in London and later on in New York.

Surely the market is absurdly hysterical, I remark.

Gerry explains that a firm such as Blanchminster's depends on Trust and its Good Reputation. I can hear the capital letters in his voice. If you can't trust its figurehead, he says, you can never be sure of its probity in other matters.

I turn on the news. A spokesman for Blanchminster's Bank and its chairman has announced that a writ will be issued.

'I wonder whether one could justify,' Gerry mutters.

I snap at him not to talk lawyer's jargon.

'It means proving the truth of your statement,' he explains, and would I pass the marmalade.

'What if I can't?'

'Then there will be damages,' Gerry says calmly. 'I should think they will be simply enormous.'

A familiar sensation. The thud, almost physical, in the stomach at the moment of hearing bad news; a car crash, sudden death, infidelity, or any of those lesser tragedies that cloud a day such as an exam failure, a bad book review, a rejection slip. The ice may show cracks at such times, but so far in my life it has not ceased to support me. I do not know how one endures a true disaster.

Perdita rings during the afternoon. Her voice sounds like the Queen's, higher and crisper than it seemed face to face.

'Anne? It's me. Perdita. Listen, I thought you ought to know you'd better lock your doors. I'm under siege.'

'Where are you?'

'At home. In Cornwall. Actually, I'm sitting on the stairs because they keep looking in through the windows.'

'Who do?' I interrupt.

'Reporters. There's even a camera crew. Listen.' She stops speaking, and I hear the distant sound of doorbells, a chiming bell and a monotone buzz. 'Hear them? Back door and front door, knocking on the glass, ringing up – this is the first time I've been able to use my own telephone all day except when Niall called from his carphone. He's on the way down.'

'Your husband?'

'Ex-husband. He's worried about the bank, of course. He runs Blanchminster's, but I'm supposed to be a majority shareholder or something and apparently what we said on that programme yesterday has caused . . . Stop it! Bugger off!' I hear the sound of a crash. 'Sorry, Anne,' Perdita says. 'I had to throw my ashtray at the letter box. There was someone looking through it.'

'Perdita, are you in trouble? Ought you to call the police?'

'No need for that. It's only a question of sitting it out until the cavalry comes. Niall has his uses.'

'But all on your own – '

'I like it on my own. That's why I live here. My family think I'm crazy. Adam won't even stay with me any more because he hates a mattress on the bare floorboards. Nowadays he stays in a hotel in Penzance and brings his own hampers from Harrods . . . which reminds me, there's the last one under the stairs still. I wonder whether there's anything left.' Rustling sounds come down the line. 'Damn. The mice found it first.'

'Do you mean you haven't anything to eat in the house?' I ask.

'Oh, there's food in the kitchen but they'll take pictures through the window, Niall says. He thinks it's my fault for living this way, but it's how I like it. After years doing what other people thought I should, now I can please myself. I can't tell you how lovely it is to think that I'll never have to placate another cleaning woman or plan another three-course meal.'

'Perdita, is there anything I can do? Do you want Gerry to get hold of someone or – ?'

'No, I'm OK, honestly, but I thought you ought to know what's happening.'

'I suppose it's all my fault. If I hadn't – ' I stop speaking. What would Gerry say if he could hear me beginning to admit that I might be liable for any damage or distress? Instead I say, 'It sounds very unpleasant, Perdita, but if you don't want me to get in touch with – '

'Oh, God. There's Niall now. I'd better ring off. I expect he'd say you're the last person I should be talking to.'

'Well, thank you for – ' The call is cut off mid-sentence.

The evening news bulletin announces the drop in value of Blanchminster shares. It shows photographs of Sir Hans Hahn, of Lord Blanchminster, of Perdita and even of me. Then we see

19

Niall Ross staggering into a small white cottage, apparently isolated on a wintry moor. I wonder whether he realises how incongruous an impression is given by the bottle of champagne protruding from the side pocket of his well-filled navy-blue suit and the packages of food in a Fortnum and Mason carrier bag. In publicity terms, at least, he has made a tactical error.

I progress from horror to apology to self-justification. By the end of a week, much of which is spent on the telephone, I feel better and more combative.

A writ has been issued against me and the television company in Lord Blanchminster's name.

'What do you mean, in his name?' I demand.

By this time the affair is being dealt with by our solicitors. I have met Mr Paxton of Wootton Hardman. He is often at the same lawyers' parties I go to with Gerry. His professional voice is unexpectedly crisp. 'The old man had a stroke last year.'

'Do you mean he's incapable?'

'Completely paralysed, I'm told, voice and all.'

'Then how can he – ?'

'He's still alive, he's still capable of being defamed.'

'But who speaks for him?'

'You know his daughter, don't you? I believe she and her son, Adam Ross, are jointly in control of Lord Blanchminster's affairs. And of course the young man's father, Niall Ross, Perdita Whitchurch's ex-husband, is the managing director of Blanchminster's. They all have an interest.'

'So what happens next?'

'You can try issuing an apology.'

'But his name really was on that list,' I protest.

So it was; but by the time I read it aloud, the list had already been defined by Hans Hahn as consisting of quislings, traitors, potential collaborators and fifth columnists. To be associated with it is bound to be defamatory.

'Perhaps that is what Julian Whitchurch actually was at the time,' I say. 'He wouldn't have been the only upper-class Englishman to think the Germans had some sound ideas.'

But to defend any action, we would have to be able to prove it.

'Well then, why don't you?' Mark Bissenden says.

He has taken to working from home, making forays into the middle of London to see publishers and clients but otherwise shut up with an array of electronics in the attic of his house in Islington. Somewhere below us his daughters are rampaging around and from time to time Mark opens his door a crack to shout commands: 'Please keep those children quiet!' or 'Girls, shut up!'

He comes back to his chair. I cannot keep still. I pace from the mansard window overlooking the road to the French doors on to a balcony above the garden. I knock over a pile of manuscripts and kneel to replace them.

'Don't bother about that. I wish I understood why you can't simply apologise.'

'Do you know anything about my background, Mark?' I ask.

'I don't think so. I have met Gerry, of course.'

'My family were German refugees. You know, bourgeois, prosperous, settled, assimilated. The sort of men who won Iron Crosses in the First War, more German than Jewish.'

'I never knew you were Jewish. You don't look it.'

'No, I feel English through and through. Anyway, my father was killed in the war when I was a baby and my mother sent me to proper English schools. I don't even speak German. For me persecution and the war and fascism and all that are old history that I know almost nothing about. I've always avoided reading books or watching films about them. I haven't wanted to know and my mother wouldn't ever talk about it. But the facts exist. If Julian Whitchurch was one of the people who might have been part of it, if he was even tangentially to blame for what happened, then . . . '

'Then you're damned if you'll apologise to him?'

'Yes.'

'So why don't you prove it instead?'

'Me?'

Mark comes over to where I am crouching beside the spilled papers. 'You look so worried.' He puts his arm round my shoulders and I turn my face on to the scratchy comfort of his fisherman's jersey. Then we hear the little girls pounding up the last flight of stairs and I stand up and move away from him.

'Daddy, Daddy!'

'Not now, girls. Vicky, can you come and get the children? Vicky – oh, goddamn it, I'll take you down. Back in a moment, Anne.'

When he returned it was with a bottle and glasses. 'Wine? I brought this one back from Bulgaria, you'll like it.'

'Thank you.'

'You were saying the other day that you wanted a change from Amy Swift. Why don't we move further into this century? You could start on a new series of novels set between the wars. It's good in commercial terms just now, the Yanks like it . . . do your research and centre it on Julian Whitchurch. What made somebody put his name in that notebook in the first place, even if it was a mistake? There must have been some reason. They wouldn't have written down every obscure younger son of a backwoods peer. You could talk to his wife.'

'Is there one?'

'I looked him up. He was only married once so your friend Perdita's mother is the one to see. She's a very interesting woman, a former war correspondent.'

'Not that Blanchminster!'

'Didn't you know?'

'I hadn't connected the two. Silly of me. I've always admired her,' I say.

'You could talk to her about her young days and collect material, and by the time you know whether you need to apologise or fight you should have the background for a new series of stories. Two birds with one stone.'

'But I meant to write a serious novel.'

'Well then, do. Serious and contemporary are not synonyms, Anne. Anyway, I thought it wasn't going so well.'

'The nineteen thirties,' I say. I sip the wine and look out of the window into the garden, where the two girls are now playing in a sandpit. After a while I murmur, 'I could even write non-fiction. A biography.'

'Of Lady Blanchminster? You could, at that. It ought to do very well. Why don't you start looking her up? There's no great hurry. Any legal action takes ages to be heard and you're going to be quite busy this year with the filming of Amy Swift.'

I had been so thrilled when four of the Amy books were bought for television. Now I am excited about a new direction.

Possibilities churn about in my mind. I kiss Mark goodbye with absentminded gratitude. Our embrace is slightly more than decorous and less than intimate. 'You have made me feel much better.' As I come out of his front door, an empty taxi turns into the street. A good omen. I tell the driver to take me to St James's Square. I shall go to the London Library and look up the contemporary memoirs.

I feel a familiar, welcome well-being, the physical manifestation of creative excitement.

The jacket of my new book is one of those pinned on the notice board in the entrance hall of the library. For once I have been allowed some say in its design and the illustration reproduces an engraving of London seen from Hampstead Heath during a balloon ascent in 1893. In one corner there is a gathering of painters and their easels, in another a couple of photographers, heads hidden within folds of fabric, which fall in such a way as to hide their trousered legs. My detective can be seen as one of them.

Suddenly I know that she has left me. Amy Swift's presence, for years a vivid image in my mind, fades from technicolor to sepia. Her companionship is over and done with. She is gone.

I shall put away the archives assembled over the years, the box files, the folders, the cuttings albums, alphabetical notebooks and scrapbooks of contemporary fashion plates. I shall live in a new period, with new companions.

It is a reprieve.

I shall set aside the abortive novel. I am let off introspection and may pull the cloak of ignorance and anonymity around me again. For a while longer I may remain impersonal and uninvolved. I shall again defer that examination of my own thoughts and life without which I can never become a good novelist.

Agreeable vistas of objective fact open before me: lists of informants, shelves of newspapers and magazines, fashion journals and gossip columns. I shall order stacks of books from university libraries and spend happy days in them making notes, résumés, references and cross references. I shall even, at last, read my own parents' diaries and letters.

From the formless mass of collected material a shape will emerge: fiction, faction, fictionalisation?

This is the moment of conception; of mystery. The books I have written have never been those I had planned. Not one of

23

them has turned out to match the initial idea. I can no more visualise the finished book than, twenty-nine years ago, I could have imagined the adult who is the eventual result of my first pregnancy.

5

After the initial flurry of drama, discussion and dissension generated by the showing of *Only Connect* and the issuing of Lord Blanchminster's writ, silence ensues, if only because it is contempt of court to print comments about a legal action in progress. Gerry assures me that letters, telephone calls and arguments are flying between solicitors' offices and barristers' chambers. On the home front all is disconcertingly quiet.

Meanwhile I am buoyed up by the excitement of starting a brand new project, shuttling between the newspaper library at Colindale, the London Library and the occasional, self-indulgent day in the Cambridge University Library. The period I am studying has been exhaustively discussed and written about. My ignorance of it is astonishing. I used to think I would go mad if I knew.

At last I have started to learn about that past, but I still know that what happened happened to others. I still do not empathise. I do not try to imagine it.

On Sunday I break off. Gerry is at home after a fortnight away. Jonathon is coming for lunch. Christopher is in America. We do not, of course, expect Flora.

The boys are settled now. Jonathon has followed his father into the law. Christopher plays the drums in an American band. We have and have had our worries. Many's the night have I passed in anxiety about the use of illegal substances or the misuse of legal ones, about all the predictable miseries that are milestones on the way to adult life. If we had our way, our children's lives would be monuments to deferred gratification and taking thought for the morrow.

Jonathon is dithering about a career move; he cannot decide whether to change from commerce to crime, a branch of the law which – at least in the small world which he and his father inhabit – seems less respectable.

Though I do not speak German, I remember one phrase my

mother used. *'Deine Sorgen möchte Ich haben,'* I say aloud. 'I wish I had your problems.'

How merciful it would have seemed to the mothers of the period I am learning about if their only problems had been those that my children, absent or present, pose this peaceful Sunday.

Not all my research is done in libraries and the next day a package arrives from a survivor.

'Don't take it too seriously,' the woman had shouted on a crackling telephone line. 'When I look back on the young woman I was it's impossible to believe it's the same person. I saw everything through a personal filter.' The voice grew faint. 'I didn't keep much of a diary and most of my letters disappeared but I've looked out what there is.'

'It's very good of you,' I shouted back, and had meant it.

'It's years since I looked at it myself. But I tell you she's a stranger to me, too, that girl who arrived in Berlin in August nineteen thirty-six.'

PART II
PRE-WAR

6
Berlin, 1936

They had cut down the trees in Unter den Linden.

Celia Roget came up the steps from the underground railway and stood gaping at the once-familiar avenue. It was festooned with banners and flags where the eponymous lime trees formerly cast their pleasant shade.

That was the first difference.

The second was that Frau Silberschmidt did not recognise her.

Scurrying along the pavement with her head down, the woman clutched a large bag against her chest so tightly as to tear the thin fabric of her gloves. Before, every appurtenance elegant, every possible attention paid to her appearance, she had hardly seemed middle-aged; and surely she had been taller than this? Now, huddled into a coat too thick for early August, she looked shrunken. Her skin was as colourless as the hair that straggled out from a tight cloche hat.

The Silberschmidts, old friends of Celia's parents, had been her hosts when she came to Berlin to learn German after leaving school and before going up to Cambridge. In Celia's mind Frau Silberschmidt had epitomised the security and dignity of the prosperous Jewish families whose business alliances and networks of family connections crisscrossed Europe. Her home was always full of cosmopolitan visitors entertained by sophisticated conversation and perfect food. There was luxury without ostentation in their house in Berlin. They spent holidays in their little French-style château in the Thuringian Forest. Every summer they cruised in the Mediterranean.

Today Frau Silberschmidt looked like a charwoman; though the charwomen who worked for her had seemed more prosperous than this.

Celia held out her arms to greet her old friend.

With an awkward twist of the shoulders Hanne Silberschmidt slipped out from under Celia's embrace and scuttled away without a word.

'They aren't allowed to speak to foreigners, you know.' An Irishman's voice. The speaker was a small man in a ginger tweed suit. He raised his hat, revealing strands of sandy hair across a balding dome a few inches below Celia's eyes.

'I beg your pardon?' she said.

'Jews. You want to take care.' He replaced his hat and went along the Wilhelmstrasse.

Celia stared after him, as much surprised as irritated. Frau Silberschmidt had disappeared. Celia glanced again at the main road and its rows of patriotic decorations, symbols of might and history stretching as far as the eye could see. Then she turned her back on them to follow the strange man. The Führer lived in the Wilhelmstrasse. A small crowd of people stood waiting to catch a glimpse of him, but nobody was allowed to walk directly in front of the house, and the guards, in black breeches and boots, motioned passers-by to cross to the other side of the street.

Further along, the Union Flag flew alone outside the British Embassy. Celia was standing beside the windows of the Academy of Art. They were too dirty to show her reflection, but she knew that her appearance ought to inspire confidence. Hat, bag, gloves and shoes had been bought on her mother's account at Marshall and Snelgrove, the coat and skirt made by her father's tailor and the discreet regimental brooch in her lapel was a present from Peter Hoyland, the man she had refused to marry.

'Irreproachable,' her mother had murmured gloomily when Celia modelled the complete ensemble before packing it into her cabin trunk.

'Don't I look nice?' Celia wheedled.

'Oh, nice,' Mrs Roget said contemptuously. 'What do you care about that?'

Celia did care – quite; enough to have spent the regulation number of hours in front of her looking glass, trying to see her own profile, wondering whether a stronger perm would be the answer, even going through a phase of measuring her eyelashes in competition with other school friends. But she had forced herself not to repine over the undoubted fact that she would never be a beauty.

'You're a *jolie laide*', one girl had told her, but even that was not much comfort to a mousy, small girl with toffee-coloured eyes who yearned to be tall and blonde. At least there was no doubt about her brains, but that was not much comfort to Mrs Roget, who had never wanted a serious daughter nor expected to rear a bluestocking. The departure platform at Victoria saw the final disappointment of her hopes, because it was not a bride going on honeymoon but a career woman to whom she waved good-bye.

Celia knew that even if Mrs Roget ever became the mother of the first woman ambassador she would still have preferred to be the mother-in-law of some obscure and boring man. She had displayed incredulous disapproval of every step her daughter had taken, beginning with Celia's early insistence on leaving the schoolroom and governess behind and going to boarding school. Her mother would never forgive Celia's progress from Roedean to Newnham, from Cambridge to the Civil Service, from a job in London to Berlin.

Celia had been propelled by a determination to prove she could reach the top. Her semi-official posting to the Foreign Office (for women were not permitted to become proper diplomats) was her chance to show what she could do, to vindicate herself in the eyes of everyone who said she was mad to apply for this job, to make those who assured her that she could climb no further eat their words.

It was less than twenty years since women had won the right to vote. The diplomatic service was only one of many professions they could not enter.

Any ambitious woman was familiar with the varieties of ob-struction and opposition endemic in an imperfectly emancipated society: the warnings, the forebodings, the endless reminders that she would have to resign if she married, and that the despised status of spinster would inhibit her promotion if she did not; the implicit and explicit signs that men could not take women seri-ously, that her first-class brain was inferior to a man's second-class one, that unlike them she was bound to be at the mercy of natural physical phenomena.

Celia knew them all. Prejudice and tradition were old enemies and so far she had won against them.

Straightening her shoulders, raising her chin, she strode along the street. The attendant, at attention between the Embassy's gleaming brass plates, wore an unyielding expression. Celia walked briskly up to him. I'll show him too, she promised herself, and waited for him to open the door under her cold gaze.

7

'Achtung, achtung!'

The harsh, bass voice resounded over Berlin as though the city were one mighty ear. All day long loudspeakers attached to trees and lamp posts relayed a running commentary on the Eleventh Olympiad of modern times. In the intervals between races patriotic music boomed over the flag-draped streets.

Someone at the British Embassy had recommended Celia to lodgings with the widow of a municipal judge in Charlottenburg. Celia had a sitting room with a piano and a desk, and a bedroom furnished with a huge walnut bed, its posts carved with soppy cherubs. Framed tapestry samplers quoted pious exhortations. Both rooms were dark with brown paintwork and thick lace curtains, but they looked out on to lime trees and roses and a garden the old woman could not afford to maintain.

Celia's landlady was ruined, like most of her friends, and spoke often of the happy days of Empire before the war, before inflation, before the world turned upside down.

'But things are getting better at last,' she said. 'We have hope again. For my grandson, there is a future.' A deprived diet had made her stout and breathless. She panted through her house in her old clothes, feet tapping on the passage tiles, leaving a slightly sour smell behind her so Celia could tell that her belongings had been examined while she was out at work.

Frau Eberhart could ill afford to go on living in her turreted and tiled house; the linen was patched and darned with conventual neatness, the carpets were threadbare, the bath water tepid. Nonetheless she treated her paying guest with disdain, on account of her being English and female, for failing to be married at the advanced age of twenty-three and (even worse) for impertinently usurping a man's job. How privileged such a person was to lodge in so respectable a house in so exclusive a district!

Even in this tree-lined suburb the daily broadcasts resounded

33

inescapably from early morning until long after most people's bedtime. Nobody complained.

'I don't have time to do anything but work and sleep,' Celia wrote to her parents.

'I hardly even manage to mend my stockings. The Embassy is very busy and I have been pitched right in. Luckily the job is fascinating, but I still haven't had a chance to go and see the Silberschmidts or any other of my old friends. I simply rush between lodgings and work, and totter back exhausted through the crowds. You wouldn't believe how many people have packed themselves into this town for the duration! But en route I have managed to see something of the changes since I was last here. Everything looks a lot better. There is some talk at the Embassy of things going wrong with the new regime but you know how careful diplomats must be not to criticise the internal affairs of a sovereign state. All I can say is that Berlin, which used to be so dingy, is quite transformed, clean, tidy, well-organised – and the local people go out of their way to be helpful to the foreign visitors.'

One hundred and fifty thousand foreigners were expected in Berlin for the Olympic Games, and everything possible had been done to ensure that they were impressed by the new national purpose and prosperity. A series of government directives issued over the last months had exhorted Berliners to plant brightly coloured flowers in their window boxes and to find tenants for their empty shops, even if it meant accepting artificially low rents. Only the weather was uncontrollable. Heavy clouds hung overhead and an unseasonably chilly wind twitched at summer hats, flapped the bunting and sent eddies of dust into watering eyes.

'We have been very busy here since the games began [Celia wrote]. Lots of English people have arrived so we have distinguished visitors to entertain at the Embassy for luncheon and every evening. Being stationed here is completely different from working in London and I feel much more part of what is going on. Yesterday I met the MP for Southend and Count von Bismarck. The staff of the Embassy are taking it in turns to go to the games, and I shall be there in the stadium this afternoon. Perhaps you will hear my voice cheering on your wireless.'

This was an opportunity to put on one of the frivolous dresses that Mrs Roget had insisted must be part of Celia's wardrobe, but the weather was not suitable for chiffon or crêpe de Chine so Celia wore a tussore silk suit, made for her by her father's tailor from a picture in *The Lady*, with a saucer-shaped hat. Looking at herself before leaving, she realised what had made her choose this particular shade of light sea green. It was exactly the colour Frau Silberschmidt had worn on the day the whole family, and Celia, went to a *thé dansant* in a grand hotel and Michael had danced with his mother, round and round, reflected endlessly in high mirrors. Celia had watched jealously, not expecting Michael to take any notice of his little sister's English friend. And then Michael asked Celia to dance, and on the way home in the car Frau Silberschmidt had given Celia the aquamarine coloured scarf as a reminder of a happy day.

The Olympic stadium had been written about and photographed so many times that its size and grandeur were hardly unexpected, but it was thrilling to go in for the first time and see the vast bowl completely filled. Spectators were crammed together like worshippers at the shrine of sport.

Celia's ticket was for a row near the front and she sat down in the only vacant place before noticing that she was beside the man she had encountered in the street that first morning. He half rose and held out his hand.

'You'll be Miss Roget. Pleased to meet you again. Leary's the name, from the Consulate.'

'How do you do?' Celia was civil but distant. Mr Leary might outrank her now, but he must be over forty, a man who would rise no further, and she intended to be his superior in the not-too-distant future.

The British Embassy's block of seats was close to the Führer's official box, so Celia had a good view of the notables. When a fat man in white uniform came down to the front everyone in the stadium stood up and shouted '*Heil!*' in unison, the noise like a thunderclap. The man saluted in response.

'Goering,' said Mr Leary, his own arm, unlike those of most other foreigners present, firmly at his side.

'Yes, I know,' Celia said.

The crowd roared once more, and a voice from the amplifiers called out, 'We want our Hermann!' Goering bowed and saluted again, like an operatic tenor receiving plaudits, before sitting down as a sign that the games might proceed. Almost at once a German hurdling team won its heat. The entire audience surged to its feet and sang first the German and then the Nazi anthems.

Celia shivered. The wind was very chilly.

'Scared?' Mr Leary murmured in her ear. 'Oh, oh, look who's here.'

It was the leader himself. Frequently photographed and caricatured, he looked exactly as Celia had expected – square, stocky, in a brown uniform and with a Charlie Chaplin moustache. The crowd was electrified, hailing him with rapture. He was followed by several men in more glamorous uniforms than his own and by a few plain, dowdy women; one, stout and middle-aged, was ceremoniously conducted to the seat beside his.

Mr Leary continued his commentary: 'That's the old Kaiser's daughter, the Duchess of Brunswick. Have you heard the talk about restoring the monarchy?' The Prussian princess behaved like reigning royalty, bowing and smiling to both sides.

After some fussing and rearranging, the official party sat down and the hurdling heats continued.

A little short-sighted but reluctant to wear her unbecoming spectacles, Celia could not see the contestants well enough to concentrate on the games. For a while she watched the VIPs. She was not the only person whose attention was diverted to Herr Hitler. All around him men, women and children gazed with sometimes tearful adoration. A high, English voice floated across from the official box. The speaker was one of the women Celia had seen at the Embassy, perfectly dressed, languid, supercilious. 'It's too, too thrilling, darling. It's more exciting than when we met the Pope.'

A group of late arrivals was edging into the seats in front of Celia. Polite applause from some of the spectators greeted them. 'The Beowulfs,' Mr Leary hissed. 'He's one of their polo team.'

Baron Hubertus von Beowulf was in his black and silver uniform. Beside him was his sister, Marianne, like her brother tall, thin, and so fair and light-eyed as to seem almost sun-bleached.

36

She was famous for her own success at the Winter Olympics but seemed serenely unconcerned by the stares she attracted.

'That's Viscount Blanchminster's son with them. The Honourable Julian Whitchurch.' Even through the whisper, Mr Leary's disapproval was audible.

Anyone who had ever read an illustrated magazine would recognise the name and the face, which was long, secretive and indefinably English. Julian Whitchurch was a rich dandy, a sportsman, a playboy, an eligible catch – the description varied depending on the editor's prejudices. Celia's mother subscribed to publications which Celia herself was ashamed to enjoy and only looked at in the privacy of the bathroom, telling herself that it was for purposes of sociological research. She had often seen that hawk-shaped profile, that ready smile, photographed against the ski slopes of Garmisch or the sails of Cowes, relaxed at Monte Carlo or sharing a joke in a ballroom, frequently with Baroness Marianne von Beowulf. In three dimensions and in colour, both looked different: less stereotyped, more approachable. The baroness's eyes were huge, a pale ice grey, her lips glossy and pink, presumably naturally so since cosmetics were disapproved of to the point of prohibition in this country. Her hat almost certainly came from Paris. She reminded Celia of the girls who appeared in Cambridge for May Week, exotic creatures shipped in to entertain and be entertained, a different species from the women undergraduates.

As she used to in those days, Celia felt her confidence dissipating in a familiar wave of social inferiority and of resentment against the fate that had not made her tall, fair and beautiful. She drew around herself the psychic armour forged during those Cambridge years. Brains and industry, she reminded herself, would outlast good looks.

Marianne Beowulf's voice was husky but penetrating. 'Don't giggle, Julian, you have to take this quite seriously,' she said in English.

'An undertaker's m-m-mute, I swear it.'

'It's the women's relay race now.'

One of the uniformed stewards brought a note to Hubertus and handed it over with a click of the heels. 'From Fräulein Riefenstahl.'

'One of Leni's royal commands?' Marianne asked.

'She wants us to stay put here while she films us,' Hubertus replied aloud and added, in a low tone, 'damned impertinence.'

The film-maker was well known to be the Führer's protégée.

'Our Leni wants to turn you into a movie star, Julian.'

'California here I come.'

Bending forward to conceal her own actions, Celia took out her compact and gave herself a rapid dab of powder and a smear of lipstick.

The hubbub inside the stadium and the military bands outside, the continuous broadcast commentary, the eddies of dusty wind, were all exhausting. There was a pervasive smell of onions, garlic, cigars and of sweaty humanity. Flower girls in dirndl dresses edged their way between the blocks of seats, handing out posies of daisies and roses. Celia bought a bunch and buried her face in the cool petals, but they were odourless. She fanned herself with her programme.

Marianne Beowulf went on chattering vivaciously to her companions and greeting other acquaintances as they passed within her view.

The press box, equipped with seats for a thousand reporters, was almost full.

'Look, Julian, someone is waving at you,' Marianne said.

'It's D-Duggy Dugdale. Do you remember him, Hubertus? He was at the House.'

Celia turned to look at the young man who was coming down the crowded aisle.

'Someone you know?' Mr Leary asked. Celia pretended not to hear. She wondered how she could indicate that their proximity as colleagues was not an invitation to intimacy.

'Hullo, old man, I had no idea you were here,' Julian Whitchurch said, shaking hands.

'I'm here as a scribbling hack, writing up the games for the *Illustrated London News*.'

'You remember B-B-Beowulf from the House?'

'Of course. How do you do? You were a Rhodes scholar.'

'Let me present you to my sister. Marianne, this is Sir Douglas Dugdale.'

'I saw you win at Garmisch, Baroness,' Dugdale said. 'Marvellous. You really wiped that Yankee dame's eye. And I supose you're competing here, Whitchurch, are you?'

'Not me. I've hung up my foils.'

Marianne laughed. 'Except in private. Julian and Hubi were hard at it yesterday.'

The journalist's eyes rested on Hubertus von Beowulf's face, neatly marked by the crisscross scars which were the honourable evidence that he had undergone the bloody rite of passage of the fighting German. 'Who cried pax first?'

Hubertus said, 'A German never surrenders.'

Stepping back, Dugdale's eyes fell on the row behind. 'Miss Roget! What on earth are you doing here?' He shook her hand warmly. 'Baroness, Whitchurch, do let me introduce – '

There was a polite confusion of introductions and greetings. Celia, having named 'Mr Leary, of the Consulate', explained her posting to Berlin and Duggy explained his assignment. The two young women eyed one another cautiously. Hubertus said he believed he had the honour of knowing Miss Roget's brother. 'Of course you know him,' Duggy said. 'So do you, Whitchurch. He was there that time we decorated the Martyr's Memorial with . . . well, anyway, he was there. I'll never forget when we saw the Dean coming up Beaumont Street . . . ' The conversation degenerated into reminiscences of juvenile lawlessness. Then Duggy said, 'We must get together properly. You must all dine with me. Are you here for the month, Whitters?'

'I'm staying for the sailing at Kiel. Until then I'm imposing on the Beowulfs. What about you, Duggy? Are you out at the Olympic village?'

'No fear. Doberitz is too far from town and too near the competitors for me. I'm at the Adlon. It's packed with people we know. I saw Michael Silberschmidt there yesterday.'

'Did you!' Hubertus exclaimed. 'The man's nothing but an agitator.'

'P-P-Poor old Silver? He's harmless enough, surely,' Julian Whitchurch said.

'Did he speak to you?' Hubertus demanded.

'He walked right past me, but I grabbed hold of him for a bit of a chinwag. Interesting new light on affairs. I managed to make a few notes. Always thought he was a good chap in the old days at Oxford, though he's changed. Jewish, ain't he?' Dugdale said.

Marianne said, 'He should go away. There's no place for him

here any more. I remember him at Oxford, too, that time I came for one of your regattas. He was a communist.'

'Ah well, the indiscretions of youth . . . Anyway, he's still here, living with his old mother at Dahlem I gathered. Of course, how much longer he'll be able to . . .'

'Not much, I assure you,' von Beowulf said.

An excited voice announced the women's four by one hundred relay race, in three languages.

'I'd better get back to my desk,' Duggy said.

No longer ignoring the girl behind them, the von Beowulfs and Julian Whitchurch sat at an angle, arms over the back of their seats, making Celia part of their group.

Marianne said, 'This is one we should win.'

The loudspeaker shrilled another sentence – not, this time, translated.

Julian Whitchurch said, 'What did he say?'

'That this team represents the flower of German femininity.'

The girls in the German team were paler and thinner than the current Aryan ideal. They looked solemn, knowing it was their patriotic duty to defeat the world's competition. A full-throated roar from the whole stadium encouraged them. People were on their feet, including the party leaders, who grew increasingly jubilant as their favourites drew ahead. Even in the area reserved for important foreign visitors the tension affected diplomats and dignitaries alike.

Julian Whitchurch left his seat at the end of the row and disappeared from the stand.

The last leg. The German girl was being impelled towards a new world record by the willpower of the crowd.

'Deutschland Über Alles!' Hubertus shouted.

Then the German runner dropped the baton.

The Duchess of Brunswick fell to her knees, her hands clasped in prayer. Marianne von Beowulf covered her eyes. Julian slipped unobtrusively back into his seat as the party leaders, frozen-faced, resumed theirs. The stadium fell silent except for the commentator's voice broadcasting to the crowd outside. Then shouts and cheers began again. A minority of the audience would be happy to see a non-German win.

'Idiot!' Hubertus cried.

'Anyone can t-trip,' Julian Whitchurch said.

'It was unforgivable.'

Subdued clapping greeted an American victory and attention turned to the next race, a heat for the five hundred metres.

The Kaiser's daughter was helped back to her seat. The party leaders chatted quietly, waiting for some national achievement to restore their pride. A South American runner won, to desultory applause.

Hubertus von Beowulf stood up and gave first Celia and then his sister a stiff little bow. 'I have a few arrangements to make before this evening, if you will excuse me.'

Mr Leary also stood and jerked his body forward in a Prussian-style bow. 'I must go too,' he said, and then leaned forward to mutter in Celia's ear: 'That's a useful contact, you should cultivate him.'

8

Celia had been very busy at work. It was not until the Saturday that she went to visit the Silberschmidts at last; Duggy Dugdale's mention of Michael had been an additional spur to obey the call of duty.

She walked the last part of the way, passing first through monotonous streets of looming grey apartment houses with pot plants and patriotic symbols in their windows. Here, in a poor district away from the town centre, some of the roads were in as bad a state of repair as they all had been during Celia's previous visit to Berlin. Passing this way at that time, she would have had to run the gauntlet of shabby men who lounged about on the streets hating her for being healthy, well-fed, for having some occupation to fill the days, above all hating the fact that she was English.

Five years on unemployment was still prevalent back home, but Germany had solved the problem and now Celia's footsteps tapped along the pavement uninterrupted by catcalls or snide comments.

It was a hot, heavy day, and many people had left town in spite of the Olympic Games as the shuttered, deserted houses in the more prosperous districts showed.

Neither neglect nor even aerial warfare, Celia reflected, could alter the large, almost fortress-like mansions in which the merchant dynasties had established themselves in the last century. The Silberschmidts' house looked quite unchanged.

Dignified but without ostentation, it had been built in the days of Prussia's expansion at a time when the Jews, first emancipated by Napoleon, were completely assimilated and as patriotic as the haughtiest Junker.

Celia's host, Sigmund Silberschmidt, had served throughout the war in charge of a field hospital. His brother Max, a pilot, had been awarded the Iron Cross, second class. After the war Sig-

42

mund's clinic for the treatment of nervous disorders had become famous all over Europe and Celia's father became friendly with the Silberschmidts when he came over to study Sigmund's methods.

The clinic itself was not profitable, and many of its patients were treated without charge, but the old family business was carried on by Max with the drive he had brought to leading his squadron, and it provided more than enough to keep the extended family and to maintain their home as a welcoming, hospitable base.

As Celia approached the house she saw it was closed up. There were no red eiderdowns airing on the window sills or white muslin curtains fluttering in the breeze. The Silberschmidts must have been about to leave town when Celia saw Hanne but one or two of the servants would still be here as caretakers. Celia went up the steps to the familiar double grey doors with their baroque-shaped panels and iron railings to one side.

Who would answer? Minna, the housekeeper, or Gerda, the cook? Not Lydia; wherever Frau Silberschmidt went, her maid went too; nor Fräulein Bleichroeder, the secretary, who always spent August at one of the nudist colonies in the sand dunes by the Baltic Sea. During the other eleven months of the year she behaved like someone who did not know what a naked body looked like.

Nobody came to the door.

Celia knocked again, slow, slow, quick, quick, slow. The foxtrot rhythm did not sound cheerful, as she had intended, but menacing.

Where was everyone? Suddenly the silence felt eerie. The sun was shining brilliantly for the first time in days, the chestnut trees rustled pleasantly, the heavy scent of late-summer flowers hung in the air, some unidentified bird was singing, but Celia was shaken by a violent shudder and the tiny hairs on the back of her neck and her forearms rose to make her flesh creep.

Aloud she said, 'Someone walking over my grave.' The meaningless nursery expression was oddly comforting.

There had never been many passers-by in this street; nursemaids with prams, of course, and delivery boys, but at this time of year most families were away and so were the Silberschmidts. Nothing was wrong, nothing to worry about.

Celia turned away, thinking that she might go to the Tiergarten, which she used to visit with little Lotte Silberschmidt. She would see whether any of their favourite animals were still there.

The front door of the neighbouring house opened a few inches. Someone was staring at Celia. Two elderly sisters lived there, Fräulein . . . what was their name? They were a soldier's daughters who had never married, and devoted their lives to preserving mementoes of their family's greatness. They lived comfortably while complaining that the war had ruined them, a frugal, self-satisfied, inquisitive pair whom the Silberschmidts dutifully invited to their larger parties.

This was the younger of the two. Celia began, 'Good day, Fräulein . . . ' No good; the name would not come.

The old woman seemed agitated and jerked her head from side to side as though she feared she was being watched. 'You are seeking someone?'

'Don't you remember me? I'm Celia Roget. We used to meet sometimes when I was living here a few years ago. I suppose the Silberschmidts have already gone away?' Why did she look so frightened? Why had she gasped at her neighbours' name? 'Is something the matter, Fräulein?'

'Wait.' She left Celia on the pavement. The curtain of her front room twitched; the other sister was behind it. Celia saw their two grey heads together. The old woman came out again, peering up and down the street, and moved to stand very close to Celia. Behind her hand she whispered, 'They came for them this morning.'

'Who did? I don't – '

'They took them away.'

'Took the Silberschmidts away?'

She nodded vehemently, her eyes a terrified glaze above the spotted, wrinkled hand. A jet mourning ring dug into the flesh of her third finger. 'At dawn. They came at dawn. We were woken by the knocks and banging. My sister blocked her ears, she forbade me to take any notice, but I watched from behind the shutter. I felt . . . I couldn't . . . I didn't . . . ' She seemed surprised by the strength of her own reaction.

'But, Fräulein – ' The name came to Celia out of the blue. 'Fräulein von Noltke, what do you mean? Are you talking about the police?'

'They came to arrest them. They took them away in their black van, Frau Silberschmidt and her son. They took them away.'

'Then where are the others? What about Charlotte, what about the doctor?' Celia asked, aghast.

'You don't know that Doctor Sigmund died last year, you had not heard it? He was taken to . . . taken to a place and he never came back. It was a heart attack.'

'I had no idea. How dreadful, how unbelievably dreadful! But Fräulein, where's Lotte and the servants? The house is quite deserted.'

'The maids had to leave. They couldn't stay, it was not allowed. It is not permitted to work for Jews, you understand.'

'No, I don't understand. I don't know what you are talking about. What's happened to Lotte? To Charlotte Silberschmidt?' Celia's voice, rising above the whisper which had answered the old woman, frightened her into flight.

'I don't know any more. It's nothing to do with me. I can say no more. I wish you a good day.' Bang. The heavy door slammed on the sanctuary. Celia found herself staring at another silent, shuttered house.

She backed slowly away. Frau Silberschmidt arrested? The doctor dead? And Michael! Celia pressed the back of her hand over her mouth. I mustn't be sick in the street, she thought, but a wave of nausea made her shake uncontrollably.

Michael Silberschmidt.

He had been twenty-one. Celia had her seventeenth birthday while she was in Berlin. He took her out to bars, cabarets, clubs, cafés. He showed her the stretch of the Kurfürstendamm where life was really lived. Some people called it the Babylon of modern times. They sat together in his friends' smoke-filled studios discussing the world and re-making it in their own free image. And when the friends left them alone, he taught her about adult life. Adult love. Love and life – a hackneyed expression but nonetheless meaningful.

When Celia went up to Cambridge she assumed a mask of innocence and ignorance. Then and ever since she had pretended to know nothing more than was expected of an unmarried English virgin. Michael would probably have killed a man who gave his own sister the lessons he had taught Celia.

Celia adored him, of course, and although she grew out of that immature passion she had never come across another man who managed to make her feel as Michael had, or who had even tried to. But her priorities had changed. Her life plan precluded emotion or physical passion. She must never risk ruining her career. Michael was a fond memory now, nothing more.

But his arrest, his mother's arrest . . . what was she to do? I must pull myself together. I'm not helpless. I shall go to the office and make sure enquiries are made, protests from an official source . . .

A black car followed by a black closed van, both driven at high speed, rounded the corner with squealing tyres and came down the road, jerking to a halt outside the Silberschmidts' house. Four men, all in black uniforms, jumped from the car and another two in brown from the van. They ran to the door and banged on it long and loud. The noise echoed along the street.

Another thunder of knocking. Then one of the officers made a gesture and the two men in brown flung their weight against the door, once, twice, and it burst open. The men ran in, shouting.

Nobody appeared from any of the other houses in the street to see what was going on. There was a curious hush as though everyone within miles had retreated to cower under the bedclothes, ears blocked, hoping that if they took no notice the terror would go away.

Celia took several deep breaths. She firmed her palms, damp through the gloves, on to her handbag and stood so straight that a book would balance on her small hat. She walked towards the car, beside which one of the officers was waiting. He held a leather stick in his black-gloved hand and slapped it regularly against his boot. He stared at her and said, 'Komm.'

Celia paused and looked at him with as much disdain as she could muster.

'Papers. What are you doing here?'

'Can't you speak English?' she said. Very slowly she opened her bag and drew out her passport, holding it in the tips of her white-gloved fingers. The man snatched the little book.

'English? This is nothing to do with you. You shouldn't be here,' he said, but Celia allowed no sign to show that she understood.

The other officers came out of the house. One said, 'Gone.'

'Escaped? Hiding? Are you sure?'

'We have searched the whole place. The birds have flown.'

The senior officer, his sleeve bristling with silver badges, came out of the house last. He glanced first at Celia and then at his subordinate, who said,

'She's English. I didn't like to deal with her because of the orders about not letting foreigners see – '

'We must not cause distress to our honoured guests,' the older man said with heavy sarcasm. He took the passport, returned it to Celia and saluted her, his arm as stiff as semaphore, then turned away. 'Back to headquarters now. There will be trouble about this, our orders were exact.' He and his men got into their vehicles and drove off.

Celia stood watching as they rounded the corner. Her hands were trembling, and she pushed them tightly together.

The front door had been splintered and broken from its hinges. The street was still as empty as a disused film set. Slowly Celia went up the steps and into the house.

The decoration and furniture were exactly as they had been. There were the imported brocade, the inherited antiques; there were the practical pale grey paintwork, the polished floorboards, the jewel-bright Persian rugs. When Celia, a cold, travel-tired, tongue-tied stranger, first saw the house its atmosphere said, 'Welcome'. Very soon afterwards it said, 'Welcome home'.

Now the rooms showed signs of neglect. The cosiness and home-liness had vanished. There was dust on the mantelpieces and skirtings, the carpets were wrinkled on dulled floors. A cloth had been dragged from a table, carrying on to the floor with it some Frankenthal porcelain figurines that now lay in fragments on the ground. The chairs had been overturned, their delicate fruitwood and light striped silks suddenly absurd. The great gilt-framed mirror above the marble mantelpiece had been cracked right across. The glass doors of the cabinets were hanging open, the green pleated curtains that kept precious contents in the shade torn away, the Dresden tea services and ancient glassware scattered. Even the doors of the porcelain stoves were hanging ajar.

Vandalism. The urge to call the police was almost irresistible. In domestic emergency, one summoned the established authority.

A vision of her own home flashed into Celia's mind, the comfortable house, which had been the village doctor's for generations, that used always to suffer in comparison with the luxury and elegance of the Silberschmidts' establishment.

I want to go home.

Celia shook herself. Next thing, she thought, I'll be wanting my mummy. She was still holding her passport and her eye fell on it. How proud she had been to receive her diplomatic papers. What status and promise they seemed to represent – and did represent. You're a big girl now, Celia. You can cope.

She put the booklet into her bag, and bent to pick up a tiny cup which had rolled, unbroken, on the floor: a Meissen demitasse with a gold and pink background to the miniature painting of nymphs and shepherds. She stood listening to the house.

She could not remember it ever being so quiet before. The sound of family life should be humming in the background, Charlotte practising the piano in the music room, Frau Silberschmidt working her way down the daily list of telephone calls, Dr Sigmund giving instructions to the gardener in the conservatory or chuckling quietly over a Grosz cartoon.

Pleasant smells should be leaking up from the kitchen. The housemaids should have rubbed beeswax into the marqueterie commodes, the laundry woman should arrive with baskets of clean linen. Outside in the garden, where the lawn sloped down to the lake and drifts of blossom blew from the thick trees, Franz should be marching up and down with his mowing machine. Upstairs the sewing woman should be treadling away, turning shirt collars and putting sheets sides to middle before they were given away to the needy.

The house was not completely silent. A tap was dripping. Boards creaked irregularly, their wood shrinking or expanding in the hot air. A curtain was sucked in and out of an open window.

Celia turned the tarnished brass handle of the glass door that led from the salon on to the terrace. On other summer mornings coffee would be brought out. On the tray would be a silver pot with a swan neck and the Dresden cups with the dragon design. Lotte always had to be given the blue one, and to humour her Celia had made a personal choice too – for the red dragon with its fiery tongue. Cakes would be served on stacked stands, and the ladies would sit in the leafy shade while the fat pug panted under the sundial.

Now the grass was ragged, littered with debris from overblown flowers, and weeds were growing between the flagstones of the terrace.

Celia walked across the grass, down the slope to the water.

48

Berlin was surrounded by natural lakes and ponds. This one had been tamed and tampered with; a bridge crossed the narrow point and rushes and waterlilies had been planted in careful design. One of Monet's paintings of his pond at Giverny used to hang in Frau Silberschmidt's boudoir.

The waterlilies were unaffected by neglect, their flat pads and red, pink and white petals covering the surface of the water so that one might imagine it was solid land.

A window was banging to and fro. Celia shivered violently. Was someone watching her? Had they left a man behind to spy?

'Celia.' The whisper was as soft as the wind's sigh. 'Celia. Don't look round. I'm in the willow arbour.'

Celia crouched to tug a lily from its rubbery stem. She put her nose to the waxy petal. Even at this level, she could not really see under the fronds of the weeping willow, so thick as to seem an impenetrable curtain from outside when Lotte, aged eleven, had hidden there. She used to invite Celia to tea parties, and Celia had pretended to enjoy kneeling in a dusky den consuming lemonade and biscuits from doll-sized china.

She moved sideways, picking more flowers, and then sat on the grass near the tree, her legs out before her in the sun, the posy in her hand.

Lotte was cowering on the ground, her back against the tree trunk. She was wearing a brown dress and hat, which concealed her hair, but her face and hands gleamed pale in the green shade.

'Turn away,' she whispered. 'Hold the flowers to hide your lips moving.'

'Lotte, I – '

The girl's voice was old with experience of furtiveness. 'They came for Mutti and Michael. They took them away.'

'Lotte, what is happening?'

The answer was flat, uncompromising. 'Because we are Jews.'

'But – '

'And Michael has written articles and pamphlets.'

'Your mother?'

'She's his mother, and Jewish. That's more than enough. But they don't need reasons. I should have been there too. What do you think Mutti will say now? Will she be glad I stayed out with Klaus or do you think she'd have preferred me to be arrested virtuously in my bed?'

49

'Where were you when they came?'

'I was at Klaus's place. He is my lover.'

'But Lotte, you're not seventeen.'

'How old were you when Michael seduced you? I go to Klaus at night. I creep out of the back door now the servants have gone, after Mutti's in bed. She doesn't approve of him, because he's working class and a communist. I met him at a protest meeting. She said he – oh, God, Celia, she said he was dangerous! And there I was, safely with him, while she – '

Celia listened to the muffled sobs. She thought, Lotte's a child, nobody would do anything to her. She began to approach her and Lotte hissed, 'Don't come near me. They may be watching.'

'You'll be safe enough with me. I'll take you back to my place.'

'Oh, you, Celia, you don't know anything. I'm staying with Klaus anyway, we've got work to do. You don't imagine that everyone has knuckled down, do you? This is our country, not those gangsters'. We have got to fight for it. That's why Michael wouldn't emigrate, and Mutti had to stay with him even after Pappi . . . do you know what happened to Pappi, Celia?'

'I was so sorry to hear of his death.' How absurd the conventions sounded in these circumstances.

'He was murdered. They killed him and sent his ashes home in a cardboard box.'

'Lotte, that can't be – '

'You don't believe it, foreigners never do. I don't expect you would believe that Klaus's brother was tortured till he died either. But you might learn. Will you be here long?'

'I've got a job at the British Embassy.'

'Then you'll see, and if you don't that's your lookout. We don't need you. Any of you. This is our problem. You keep clear, hide your eyes, wash your hands. Why should you care what happens to us? I'm off before they come back.'

'How will you go?'

'The same way I came. I was creeping in through the garden so I'd be tucked up in bed before Mutti woke me when I heard them. I've been hiding here ever since. Silly of me. I should have left as soon as the trams started.'

'Where can I find you, Lotte? Where does Klaus live? Is he on the telephone?'

'It's obvious that you really don't understand what's happening here, Celia. One does not ask such questions, and our telephones are tapped. We have to pad them with cushions before speaking in our own houses. What would you say if someone asked you where I am, later on? But you can leave me some money if you have any. Just put it on the grass.'

'I wish there was something more I could do.' But what could Celia do, constrained as she was by her official position? She could not interfere with Germany's internal affairs; she might be declared persona non grata.

Who knows, she thought, perhaps they do have some grounds for arresting Michael. He was always a bit of a red, and anyway, nothing too dreadful can happen to him or his mother. This is a civilised European country. There's still a rule of law.

Lotte said, 'You might write to my aunt Lisbeth.'

Lisbeth Silversmith, the English version of Hanne Silber-schmidt, an *haute bourgeoise* with her substantial house in London's Bayswater and the equivalent dedication to good works and good living. Celia had been to dinner there several times during her last year of working in London. Could one imagine that secure, domineering lady being arrested at dawn, her daughter cowering like an animal at the end of the garden, her husband a handful of ashes in a cardboard box? No, it was inconceivable. England was different. Wasn't it?

'Tell Aunt Lisbeth what's happened. Say I'm all right, in case she can get in touch with my mother. I must leave now, but you had better go first,' Lotte urged.

'Lotte, I . . .'

'Go on.'

What else could she do? Celia went.

9

Celia's letter to Lisbeth Silversmith crossed with one from Mrs Roget to her daughter.

'I saw some old friends yesterday! Frau Silberschmidt and her son are staying in Bayswater with the Silversmiths. They arrived last week from Germany having had to leave behind everything they possessed. So awful. And something even more shocking – Lotte has not come with them. I hardly recognised poor Hanne. She has suddenly become an old woman and I know you will be sad to hear that Doctor Sigmund died last year. I am afraid there is very little more that I can tell you about them because your father would not let me stay for more than the briefest visit, but I shall call again next time I am in London. If the cook who came just before you left does not improve I imagine I shall have to go there to search for a new one very soon, as the register office in Norwich could only offer me a cook and house parlourmaid who wish to work together as they are sisters, but I could not give notice to Ethel who has always been very satisfactory and understands the inconvenient hours we have to keep in a doctor's household. In any case they turned out to be educated people and Jewish 'refugees' from somewhere in South Germany, so I doubt whether they would have suited our needs. I shall never forget how awkward it was when your grandmother had a lady who had escaped from Belgium as her maid in '15. Paul came home for the weekend but slept for most of it, since he is on night duty at the hospital at present. He said that he had dinner with Peter Hoyland who asked very kindly after you, and is planning to go on holiday to Germany for the shooting later in the year, so perhaps you will see him. He is such a nice young man.'

Celia smiled at the transparency of her mother's motives. It would be nice to see Peter if he turned up in Berlin, but her mother need not imagine that she would change her mind about marrying him or anyone else. Her smile grew broader at the idea of voluntarily giving up the work she was doing now in exchange for playing eternal second fiddle to a man.

She loved her job. The life she led, the people she met, the problems she confronted were exactly what she had hoped for. She felt more alive here than she had for years – since her last stay in Berlin, in fact, when Michael Silberschmidt had brought another part of her to life.

Some of the sensation of well-being was due to the air of Berlin itself. In the famous Berliner Luft one needed less sleep and had more energy than anywhere else except, she had heard, New York. The true source of happiness, however, was being free to do what she had chosen to do, and the knowledge that she was doing it well. The two reports Celia had so far written had been praised by her immediate boss. One concluded the Germans were preparing their forces and armaments for defensive purposes, not for aggression, the other was a discussion of the way in which the present government of Germany had managed to increase employment and prosperity among the working classes. Mr Lockwood had forwarded both unaltered to London.

Celia put the letter into the shagreen writing case her brother Paul had sent as a going-away present and turned the key. Frau Eberhart read anything Celia left accessible, and although the reference to the Silberschmidts was unlikely to mean anything to her perhaps it was better kept private.

How had Frau Hanne and Michael managed to reach London? Had they been arrested simply to be deported? One had heard of such things happening. Celia hoped Lotte knew her fears had been misplaced, but girls of her age tended to live melodramatically.

The weather had become very hot indeed, though still overcast. The ever-present Olympic broadcasts were part of the background to daily life and Celia no longer listened to the words, but the announcement of a British win caught her attention as she turned into the Embassy and the porter so far relaxed his dignity as to smile when he said good morning.

Celia's office was small, overlooking an air shaft and equipped with the undistinguished furniture to which her rank entitled her. Heavy net curtains ensured that the electric light stayed on all day and the leather chair was so big that if Celia leant against its back her feet did not reach the ground. The only picture was a daguerreotype of Edward VII in the uniform of an admiral of the fleet.

Her surroundings delighted Celia. When she powdered her nose she saw that her expression showed exactly the same soppy smugness she had observed in a friend who, having married straight from Cambridge, insisted on showing off the niceties of her very own drawing room. Celia had imported no personal touches. In the office next door her boss, a married man, could scatter silver-framed photographs of grinning children around while his secretary made sure he always had fresh flowers on his desk. Celia was not going to give anyone the chance to treat her as a woman rather than as an official of His Majesty's foreign service.

She rang the small brass handbell for Mrs Tozer, who would type her letters rather less quickly and accurately than Celia could have done herself, but she was careful to keep some of her own capabilities a deadly secret. Shorthand had been useful for making notes from books when she was safely hidden in an obscure corner of the University Library, but never at lectures where anyone might see. Touch typing was for private purposes only.

'Keep it under your hat or you'll be a secretary instead of having one,' a friend who had gone into publishing had warned. 'Cooking ditto. Never let anyone know that you can do anything a man can't do, and anything he can do you had better do a damn sight better than he does.'

Mrs Tozer had made no secret that she resented being asked to work for another woman and thought Celia's professional pretensions an impertinence. To Mr Lockwood she took tea in a flower-patterned service on a tray with a cloth and English chocolate digestive biscuits. Celia's came on tin, ready poured into standard issue, thick pale blue cups. Mr Lockwood's mail was presented to him for signing at the end of the day arranged like works of art in a Florentine folder. Celia had to fetch her own from the secretaries' room, where women older than herself looked her up and down and smirked.

This morning Mrs Tozer had not yet collected the visa returns which Celia needed before she could finish the note of advice she was compiling for Mr Lockwood.

But this was not the moment for a confrontation.

'Never mind,' Celia said, 'I'll go myself.' She walked past the other woman, getting a whiff of lavender on the way.

The consular department was in the Tiergartenstrasse. Celia had not been there before and was surprised to find the waiting room was completely full. Every seat was taken and many people were standing. There were men, women and even children, some staring into space, one or two with their eyes closed, a few weeping tactfully into their handkerchiefs. All eyes swivelled towards her as she looked into the room, and a man began to rise as though expecting her to call his name. Celia backed out and went up to the next floor, where she introduced herself to a cheerful cockney youth who was banging away at a large typewriter.

'What on earth is going on downstairs? Is it always like this here, so crowded?' Celia asked.

'Oh, this is nothing. When I first came they used to be down the stairs too, but now we turn them away once the waiting room is full and tell them to come back another day. The real scrum is before the office opens, early in the morning. You sometimes see them fighting to get to the front of the queue.'

'Who are they?'

'People who want entry permits.'

'So many of them?'

'Most are refused, of course.'

'But I – ' Celia checked herself. No gossiping with the office staff. 'Can I see the Consul for a moment?'

'He's on leave. Mr Leary's in charge.'

The waiting supplicants eyed her jealously as she was shown ahead of them into a room even smaller and shabbier than her own. Leary's ginger tweed jacket was tucked over the back of his chair, and his shirt sleeves were held up with expanding metal bracelets. The desk was piled high with disorganised papers and more piles surrounded him on the floor, each held down with a piece of broken tile. Some gaps in the fire surround showed where they had come from. A row of dusty cacti decorated the mantelpiece. The room was stuffy and smelt, as the waiting room had, of humanity.

Declan Leary knew what impression he would be making on

Celia Roget; she would see him as a disappointed man, shabby, seedy, beneath her attention. He rubbed hopelessly at a stain on his tie and smoothed the strands of hair across the dome of his scalp. His hair had been a startling red when he was young. He had been thin then, excitable, enthusiastic. Vibrant, Mary had called him. She was dead long since, one of the many to succumb to the influenza of 1919, and these days Declan Leary was a plodding pessimist. Most things were for the worst in the worst of all possible worlds.

He let his bulging, faded eyes rest on the girl, so self-assured, so self-disciplined. Miss Roget of the Foreign Office . . . she must be the age he was when he had abandoned personal ambition. Would she still want success when she was fifty? Was she, at twenty-three, prepared to risk being denied it?

He shuffled together the forms she required and held them across the desk.

'You're very busy,' she said.

'Snowed under. One could work twenty-four hours a day and not cope with it.'

'Isn't there some way of limiting the demand for visas? Not all the people out there are going to be granted them, presumably. You'd have thought they could see it's not worth waiting.'

'We are their last hope,' Declan Leary said.

'Isn't that a little over-dramatic? I mean, they might be a bit better off out of Germany, but a lot of the emigrants are going simply because they can make a better living elsewhere.'

'Is that what they are saying up the road?'

'There are conflicting views, naturally, but I'm inclined to agree with Mr Lockwood. He believes the economy is coming round and other things will get better when it does.'

Declan Leary stood up and went to his window. He had removed the standard issue net curtains and by craning his head could see a triangle of sky. 'Two men looked through prison bars. One saw mud and the other stars,' he said. He fumbled in his pocket for a pipe, which he began to scrape with a worn-down old penknife before going on, 'I dare say it's a question of one's point of view. Maybe you would not think it so dreadful to be unable to work in the Civil Service. If you lost your job you could find another, a clever young woman like you. And you probably wouldn't worry about being unable to marry whom you choose.

You're going to lose your job if you get married anyway.'

'I don't see the relevance,' Celia said coldly. 'What has that got to do with the people outside?'

'Only that they are seeking asylum in a country where they can work, and marry whom they choose and even, once they are citizens, vote. Here they are ostracised. It's a crime for them to have affairs with Aryans. They mayn't even speak to foreigners. These people are outside the legal, social and political fabric of their country. No wonder they want to find a new one.'

'Aren't you exaggerating rather?'

He went to the door and opened it for her. 'Thank you for coming to see me,' he said gravely. 'Perhaps when you have been in Berlin a while longer we may meet again.'

He made a note in his diary that evening about Celia Roget's visit to his office. He used the Irish language and a variant of Pitman's shorthand, learned in his youth when he started as an office boy at the *Liverpool Echo*, planning to become first an ace reporter and then a national editor. The war had changed his mind. All he wanted afterwards was a routine job that would not require initiative or energy. It was an irony that fifteen years of clerking in the Civil Service should have brought him here.

Declan Leary was an assistant in the consular department and was not likely to be present at the functions Celia found herself attending. She had not expected, in her relatively junior position, to go to so many, but this month of the Olympic Games was presumably not typical.

It was very interesting, an exciting start to the posting, but Celia found herself preoccupied by the unprofessional consideration of her clothes. If only she could wear the same evening dress night after night, as her male colleagues did. Her two new dresses from Madame Firman of Manchester Street and the three old ones from last year seemed shamingly inadequate.

She wore the flowered organza for the reception at the Portuguese Embassy. An African discus thrower put his heel on its hem and tore it, so it had to be the amber lace for the British Embassy the next evening.

Most of the members of the British team were unused to grand entertainments and showed how uneasy they felt in the company of the ambassador and his grandee guests. In the moments she could spare from trying to make the athletes feel comfortable Celia was enthralled by watching the rest of the company. Deposed royalties behaved, and were treated, as though they still reigned. Beside them were their usurpers.

'Imagine what it must have been like in Paris under the Directoire,' Mr Lockwood said. 'Do you think it's a good parallel?' He held a double first in modern history and was writing a biography of one of Napoleon's marshals in his spare time. His attitude towards his work and the country in which he was stationed was one of disillusioned patience; he had told Celia to be careful not to take sides, not to get involved, not to care too much. 'That way madness lies,' he had said.

She looked around the room trying not to let it show that she was thrilled to be in it, and impressed the scene upon her memory. It would be material for an autobiography one day. How would she then, with hindsight, describe these people? Would their names be known to history? Was the air marshal a modern Bernadotte, perhaps even with a throne awaiting him? Was Ribbentrop, just nominated as the new ambassador to London, a modern Talleyrand?

The next evening Celia was at a reception given by Goering at the Air Ministry.

Searchlights were mounted on the buildings all around, their beams illuminating a thousand guests, many of whom seemed astonished by the lavish arrangements that met their eyes as they moved into the huge gardens.

Their host sat beside his wife to greet his guests in front of a pavilion which was part of a miniature eighteenth-century village complete with inn, bakery and carpenter's shop. Out in the garden a dance floor had been laid over the lawns, three bands played and the swimming pool had been filled with lilies lit from beneath by multicoloured bulbs.

Celia was torn between admiration for the splendour and regret that she had nobody to express it to. I am, she thought, probably the only woman here who has not come as an appendage to a man. It was something to be proud of, but on her own she felt inadequate and out of place. You can't go to formal occasions on your own, her mother had protested.

'Yes I can,' Celia had insisted. I can, she told herself now, and drew reassurance from her own reflection in the decorated glass beside a shooting gallery. She was wearing the Mainbocher and would die sooner than confess it had come from a second-hand dress agency in west London. The young officers at the shooting gallery seemed to approve, at least. She watched them for a while as they competed for the prizes: cigarette cases decorated with the Nazi insignia. An English couple came and stood nearby.

'There can't have been anything as sumptuous as this since the court of the Sun King,' the woman said.

'Perhaps not since Nero.' Her husband was a Member of Parliament. They had come over for the games and were present at all the entertainments. 'Or maybe one of the Emperor Claudius's great events. I expect Goebbels and Ribb are wildly jealous.'

Celia walked on. She met nobody she knew in the polyglot crowd. Many guests were far more splendid in their national costume than the entertainers dressed as Tyrolean peasants who were dancing with loud whoops and slaps of the hand against their leather bottoms. She refused beer and pretzels from fat, jolly women going round with trays slung on straps around their necks.

The evening did not seem so splendid to her. One needs, she thought, to throw oneself into the spirit of a party, and one can't do that alone. To a solitary observer the entertainment seemed tawdry, the company boring. Celia's spirit momentarily quailed at the prospect of such events being part of her lifetime job.

'Miss Roget. C-c-come and join us if you're on your own.'

'Mr Whitchurch. Good evening, Baroness, Baron. Hullo, Duggy.'

'Jolly good show.'

Absorbed into a group, Celia saw the evening with different eyes. It was elegant, it was impressive – it was fun. Moments after words had been spoken they were forgotten. The conversation frothed and burst like the bubbles of the sweet, insubstantial champagne they drank.

Suddenly the darkness at the end of the garden was illuminated by powerful, pastel-coloured beams from more searchlights. Huge screens were drawn aside, revealing a procession of white horses, donkeys and singers in fancy dress who led the way into a full-scale Viennese funfair.

'A merry-go-round!' Julian Whitchurch emitted a hunting field view-halloo. 'Come on, I love them. B-b-bags I have the chestnut.'

They were held back while the host himself climbed on to a white horse with flaring red nostrils and green eyes. He rode round and round to the cheers of his audience.

'Luna Park,' said Duggy.

'The White Horse Inn,' said Celia.

'Carnival.'

'Tivoli.'

'We could do with some fireworks,' Julian said.

Brilliant rockets blasted punctually into the night sky.

Beckoned forward for their turn on the carousel, Marianne von Beowulf and Julian leapt on to fiery steeds. Celia climbed into a golden coach with Duggy. She said, 'I hope I won't be sick.'

'Not you, nothing so undiplomatic.'

The brilliant scene rose and fell before them. Hubertus, watching. Mr Lockwood. Round again. A group of uniformed soldiers. Mr Lockwood. Acrobats poised in impossible geometry. Marianne's skirt flew into a wineglass shape above her head. Shrieking with laughter, she pulled it down. Jugglers. Up and down. A fire eater. More officers.

The roundabout slowed. The crowd separated to make way for a party of bigwigs, the air marshal with a selection of royalties. One of the sons of the Kaiser in green uniform, the Kaiser's daughter in a marabou boa. Bows and curtseys. Celia craned her neck for a better view.

A man who had been riding on the plaster elephant stood up in its gaudy howdah. He was wearing a brocade turban with a cockade and an embroidered coat. His face was sallow, his eyes dark.

'That's for my brother!' he cried. Stretching his arm out, a gun in his hand, he pulled the trigger. But words delayed him, giving time for a young officer to make a gymnastic leap from behind to thrust the man from the wooden surface as the gun went off. Screams from the crowd masked the agonised cry of the would-be assassin and another quickly silenced gasp from a girl in a sari who was perched on a plaster giraffe.

The royalties, smiles frozen on their faces, walked on. Their host paused. He stared at the man being dragged away. 'You, I will see later,' he said, and turned to follow the others.

The girl on the giraffe kept her hand, heavy with rings and trembling, holding the light fabric of her veil over her nose and mouth. Only a small sweep of her black hair could be seen. But the eyes were unmistakable, a pale amber under straight, strongly marked brows with a dot of red on the light skin between them. It was only a few days since they had fixed their frightened gaze on Celia's own as Charlotte Silberschmidt cowered under the willow tree in her parents' garden. The hand moved so only the forefinger was over the mouth. The eyes' expression changed from horror to pleading.

Shaking, Celia sank back into the cushions of the carousel's golden coach. Duggy was no longer beside her. He was standing on the ladder by which riders mounted the giraffe. He said loudly, in English, 'My dear, come down, there's nothing you can do.'

An officer in black uniform marched up to him. 'You know the young lady?' he said in German.

'We're in the same party,' Duggy replied in the same language. 'We're with Baron von Beowulf.'

'Ah, in that case . . . ' The man saluted and moved away.

Celia, her knees weak, moved across to Duggy Dugdale. He held his hand up to help the girl descend. Together they walked across to the steps and down from the merry-go-round. Its attendant was already shouting his wares and other people, who had probably seen nothing, were queueing to have a turn.

Julian Whitchurch and Hubertus von Beowulf were watching Marianne as she swept all before her on the dodgem car circuit.

'B-bad show, what?' Julian said.

'What will happen to the man?' Celia asked.

'He'll get what he deserves,' Hubertus said. 'Cowardly filth. But what can one expect?'

'Expect?'

'He was a Jew, of course.'

Celia turned towards Duggy. The girl was no longer with him. 'Where – ?'

His hand gripped her arm, painfully tight. He said, 'There's a stall with Wiener Würstchen over there. Are you hungry?' They went slowly through the ever-thickening crowd. 'She got away,' he said softly.

'Do you know who – ?'

'Never met her in my life.'

'Why did you say she was with us?'

'Any damsel in distress will do for me.'

'But – '

'Look, there's the big dipper. Come on, Celia, I dare you. Forget about the girl. We aren't likely to see her again.'

10

Tobacco smoke swirled above the marble-topped tables and wooden chairs and settles. By the door a dark matron sat in a booth to take money and keep watch. Newspapers in several languages, attached to mahogany poles, were stacked in a rack; some were two days old.

The coffee was served in thick brown pots with horizontal handle bars protruding from their squat sides. Regular customers poured it in dribbles and drank it in sips, spinning out the time during which they might occupy a table without ordering more.

It was real coffee. The cakes were like cakes back home. The chat he could hear was in the language of his childhood.

Michael Silversmith could not bear it.

He pushed his chair back, its legs screeching on the tiled floor, and searched his pocket for a threepenny bit to leave the waitress.

She was beside him. 'You haven't drunk your coffee,' she said in German, her accent softer than his own clipped, sharp Berliner's speech.

He replied in English, 'I don't want it.'

'But it's good for you.'

He glanced at her, and then gazed. She had black hair, white skin and brilliantly blue eyes. Her uniform was like a musical comedy costume with its absurdly starched frills and cap, but the dominant impression was not of frivolity but of acute intelligence.

'I'll finish it if you keep me company,' he said.

'And get the sack?'

'Would you really?'

'I might anyway. I'm not servile enough for the boss's liking. I'm already in bad odour with her and the *bei-unsers*.'

'The what?'

'Haven't you heard them at it? *Bei uns* things were done differently. Back home, in the old country . . . You'd have thought they

63

would be as glad to have escaped from home as I am. I can't understand them,' she said. 'They sit around in this little corner of old Berlin in Britain, going on and on about how things were done over there.'

'This place could have been transported bodily from Germany,' Michael said gloomily.

'Is it your first time? I thought I hadn't seen you before.'

'They gave me the address at that refugee place in Woburn Square.'

'Me too, but that was because I said I knew how to wait at table. You aren't looking for a job here, are you?'

'Hardly.'

Three irritable syllables came from the gorgon by the door. 'Irene.'

'Yes, Frau Rosenberg, I'm coming right away,' the girl said loudly.

'What time do you get off work?' Michael asked.

'Eight thirty.'

He picked up his bill. 'I'll meet you outside.'

'Ee-ray-na.'

'She'll turn me to stone,' Irene whispered. She picked up her tray and clicked on high heels towards the glass-fronted counter where two other girls were serving rich cakes with dollops of whipped cream. The three waiters, shabby in greening evening dress, trotted anxiously between the tables and the kitchen swing door.

Michael held the street door open for an English couple, but before it had swung closed behind him they had followed him out again.

'Did you see? They were all foreigners,' the woman hissed.

'Never mind,' the man said aloud. 'There's a Corner House up the road, we can get our tea there.'

Michael understood only too well what had repelled them. It repelled him too. The tearoom exuded despondency and helplessness. Some of his fellow immigrants, even the younger ones, were like people waiting for a train, passing their time with idle chat about memories and dreams, waiting for something to come along. These sad people lived in small, interdependent circles. They were bitter and excitable and quarrelled passionately about trifles, obsessed less by the immensity of their calamity than by trivial complaints about which they made endless, futile protests.

One did not have to be like that, Michael thought angrily. Why weren't they fighting? In safety themselves, they should be trying to save others. The very least they could do was try to convince the outside world of what was happening in Germany.

The British would learn, they had to learn. They must be woken from their lazy indifference. If only there was some way of over-turning their prejudices. What would convince them that iniquity was flourishing in the country of Goethe and Beethoven, right here in Europe, almost on their own complacent doorstep? The British preferred to believe that the refugees' memories were warped and subjective, that their stories about arrests, torture, murder, were exactly that – mere scare stories. Even if such things did happen, occasionally, by chance, just once or twice, what were they supposed to do about it? One offered them proof and they said, 'You chaps don't want another war, do you?' Michael had half hoped to meet some like-minded people here today. Only half; the other half of his motive in taking the bus north to Hampstead had been unadmitted even to himself: he was lonely. Homesick.

The very word infuriated him by popping undisciplined into his mind. *Heimweh*; a sentimental, Teutonic concept. He was glad to be out of it, glad not to be in Germany. Much of his mother's extended family had settled in England in the previous century. He had been born in England when his father was studying at St Thomas's Hospital and now, mercifully, Michael was entitled to British nationality without the five years of residence required of other refugees.

The English Silversmiths and German Silberschmidts had al-ways kept in touch, even during the aberration of the last war, and first Hanne and then Michael had been warmly welcomed when they appeared on the doorstep in Hyde Park Gardens own-ing nothing but the clothes they stood up in.

Hanne Silberschmidt was still living with The Family, two words which always seemed to be in capitals when referring to Michael's English relations. Michael went there to dinner on Fri-days and had adopted their English form of the surname but would not accept their hospitality or charity for more than a few days. He was grateful to them, though. They let his mother talk about Lotte and the old days and the dreadful things that were happening and whether the house was standing empty now and whether her possessions would really be sent on and, again and again, about Lotte.

She was alive, or at least had been alive last summer. That much they knew from Celia Roget, who had written to Hanne saying that she had seen her in the distance looking quite well and beautiful. From Lotte herself there was no word. About her there were, alas, too many. For Michael, dinner with his family once a week was quite enough.

He had found lodgings in Somerstown, a district to the north of Bloomsbury of which the Silversmiths had never heard. He made enough money from giving evening classes in German and from some freelance journalism to support himself, and had gone only once to the reception centre for refugees. He had been dismayed by its atmosphere of emergency. It seemed both hopeless and insignificant. These bossy, well-meaning women and their dispirited clients were not going to change things.

Michael could imagine no purpose in his own escape, no benefit it could cause, other than this one: that he should play some part in fighting – if only there were some fighting to do. Compared with the importance of that, his own happiness or its reverse were too insignificant to consider.

It was five o'clock in the afternoon. Now the light had started to fail, the fog that had persisted all day was thickening into a proper London Particular. Michael walked slowly up the hill towards Hampstead village, stepping aside for uniformed schoolchildren and high-heeled ladies with their little dogs. By the tube station the paper boy was shouting about a football result.

How parochial these British are in spite of their empire, Michael thought. Protected by their unbridgeable Channel and their invincible smugness, they would let every Jew and liberal in Germany disappear before the news displaced a test match result.

A Marx Brothers' film was on at the Everyman. Michael bought the cheapest ticket. Apart from a few courting couples in the back row the auditorium was almost empty, and after the usherette had shown him to the front Michael moved further away from the screen. The fog had penetrated even in here, and the beam from the projector shafted through a perceptible haze.

In unrelieved melancholy he sat through the second half of *A*

66

Night at the Opera, a newsreel (royalty, sport and a horrible murder in south Wales) the advertisements (Butlin's and Player's Please), a Donald Duck cartoon and the first half of *A Night at the Opera*.

Nothing could distract him from his familiar and gloomy thoughts, but at least he had killed an afternoon and now there would be an evening with that peach of a girl. He left the cinema and felt his way from lamp post to lamp post down Rosslyn Hill. A few cars and buses were driving along, almost blind. A horse-drawn delivery float, dimly illuminated by an acetylene lamp, moved steadily and dangerously between them.

Even on foot it was not easy to see the way, and Michael only just reached the tearoom as Irene came out. She was muffled up in a long, dark coat, a cloche hat pulled down to her nose and a scarf tied over her mouth, but those glorious eyes were unmistakable.

Fog encouraged intimacy. By the time they reached Belsize Park and the beckoning lights of its tube station, Michael had discovered that Irene lived in Kilburn, had been in London for nearly a year and was alone. She had come into the country on a domestic servant's permit. For a few months she had been a maid of all work for a dentist's family in south London. 'I don't really blame them,' she said. 'We would probably have done the same at home if things had been that way round. At least I learned the language.'

'Is this job any easier?'

'Not on my feet,' she said. 'But I can call my soul my own for a few hours a day. And it gives me time to study.' Irene had saved enough to pay for a postal course and registered for an external degree in law at London University. 'It can be difficult because four nights a week I'm working late, and sometimes I get casual jobs helping out as a waitress for the caterers at big parties. But there's no hurry. It will be years before I'm qualified, even if . . .'

There was no need to finish the sentence. Michael's plans and ideas ended with the words 'even if' too, unless he was feeling unusually optimistic and then he said 'afterwards'.

'Would you go back, if things change?' he asked.

'Not after this. I wouldn't mind going to America or maybe Palestine, but never back there.'

Irene had come to England alone. Her mother was long since dead and when her father also died she left, walking across the 'green frontier' out of Germany at Aix la Chapelle. 'I couldn't wait to get away. I would have come in March 'thirty-three, the moment that man came to power, if it hadn't been for Pappi. He kept thinking it would be all right in the end.'

'What happened?'

Irene's father had been a successful lawyer in a small Bavarian town; in the war he had been an officer and won the Iron Cross. 'After the Nazis came he just carried on. Everyone knew him, it didn't seem so bad. Then one day he had an Aryan client in a simple case he was sure to win. He met the judge in the corridor. His lifelong friend. I called him Onkel Franz. He and my father had been at school together, at university, his wife and my mother had been friends and she used to send me birthday presents. Onkel Franz told him he could not win the case. Law and justice didn't count. The Jewish lawyer would not be allowed to triumph. It broke my father's heart. He took to his bed and died within weeks.'

It was another version of a familiar story.

Such things could not happen in a civilised country, the doubters would say; it was a mistake, a misunderstanding. The old man was obviously ill at the time, already dying, unbalanced. He must have got hold of the wrong end of the stick. And so on and so on, excuses and rationalisations and justifications to mask the hideous truth, because if they believed it they would have to do something about it. That was what it always came back to, in the end.

Irene's room was nowhere near a tube station. Michael's was not far from the Northern Line and the fog, he was sure, would not be so thick down there. It was not much of an argument but Irene did not need much convincing. They went back together to Michael's place, enjoying the sulphurous, choking air because they were breathing it together. Michael's landlady lived in the basement. Irene could get upstairs without being spotted and once inside, so long as they whispered and tiptoed, nobody would hear them.

It was damp, dank, dark. The gas fire had hardly lessened the chill before the meter clicked for more coins. Neither of them had any.

The narrow bed had a lumpy flock mattress, and its iron frame creaked no matter how cautiously they moved. But it was not long before they forgot that or any other caution.

11

The fog cleared in the night and it was a damp but clear light that fell through the unlined curtains on to the pair of fish-white bodies.

'I could draw your skeleton,' Michael whispered, running his lips over Irene's unpadded ribs.

'Stop, stop! You're tickling!' She buried her face in his skin to muffle her giggles.

The house was full of footsteps: down to the lavatory on the first half-landing, up again to the gas ring, shared by all the tenants, on the second floor, beating impatient time as the kettle heated up, tramping between cupboard and washstand as the other lodgers hurried to get ready for the day.

'We'll have to get you out before Mrs Heather comes up. She won't have young ladies in her rooms.'

'She would probably call me a young person. It's one down on the social scale.' They embraced luxuriously, the contact of night-warmed flesh so delicious and so different from that first coming together, chilled and unfamiliar, the evening before.

Moving cautiously, so as not to set the springs of the iron bedstead jangling, Irene rose to pull on her clothes. She grimaced at her reflection in the small, spotted square of glass propped on the mantelpiece. Below it a narrow gas fire had been fitted into the grate space, with a slot meter. On the wall above was a picture of King George and Queen Mary in coronation robes.

'You had better look out while I leave.'

Michael said, 'In this country we call it "keeping cavee".' He left the room first and peered down the stairwell, then beckoned Irene to follow. They tiptoed down the narrow stairs and out into the street. 'There's a café across the road.'

'Do they mind women coming in?'

'It's not a gentleman's club,' Michael said, laughing. He had made friends with the proprietors and took most of his meals there in the company of a changing group of regular patrons; one was a long-distance lorry driver, another a porter at Covent Garden. They treated Michael like their resident intellectual, and sometimes asked what he thought about current events.

Ray Cassidy, the café's owner, had started life in the Gorbals. He had become a corporal in the Rifle Brigade – 'But only because my mates were killed. Arras. Mons.' Give him a chance and he would list his battle honours, but now he was bald, toothless and fat, presiding like a Buddha over his urn and counter with a tea cloth tucked in behind his braces as an apron. His cockney wife and he had made a pet of Michael. They called him 'the poet' although he told them he was only a journalist. To them anyone with a pencil and notebook was a poet; anyway, Michael looked like one.

His hair was prematurely silver, as his father's and grandfather's had been by the time they were thirty, and he kept it longer and wilder than was quite respectable because in Germany men's heads were almost shaven. His clothes, too, were in the general category of 'arty'; but Irene thought he would look poetic even in Junker uniform. She approved of his wide mouth and indented lips, his thin, prominent nose, and above all his large eyes, a clear grey-green under arched, dark brows.

Jests, joshing and introductions over, Mr Cassidy brought two plates overflowing with fried food to the corner table.

'What's this, Ray? I can't – '

'On the house.'

'Your young lady looks as if she needs feeding up,' Mrs Cassidy called through the open kitchen door.

Michael was dismayed by the greasy mixture. 'Now we'll have to eat it,' he muttered.

'That,' Irene said firmly, 'presents no difficulty to me.' She plunged her fork into the egg yolk. 'I feel newly made, like a human being again. It's a long time since I did.'

Irene's reaction to the trauma of exile had been, she said, different from Michael's. 'I've hardly given Germany a thought since I came here. My mind slides away from it. I feel as though I'd been born at the frontier. I have become a person with no past or attachments.'

'And no responsibility?'

71

'What do you mean?'

'Don't you feel obliged to do something about it?'

'What is there I could do?' Irene asked.

'If only I knew.' Michael had tried so many things. 'I've spoken to everyone I have ever met in this country, written to them, waited on their doorsteps to buttonhole them ... there must be someone, somewhere, who wants to know what's going on. There must be someone who would let me help stop it. But I can't find anyone to listen to me. I've tried to get in touch with the Army, the Navy, the War Office, the Government. I've written to politicians of all colours. I have offered my services to newspapers and charities. I have even been to places where refugees meet. Thank God for that, at least. I met you! But the refugees listen and can't do anything, and the people who could do something won't listen.'

'Have you tried the communists?'

'Well, not ... '

'I suppose you might do better with your rich and influential relations.'

'They may be well-off but they aren't influential. The money comes from the shop, you know, not from the city or even industry. They don't have any more contact with powerful people than ... than I do. Oh, the name does mean my letters get answered, the clerks who brush me off do it politely, but the message wrapped up in their good manners is always the same: go away and stop bothering us.'

'I expect they think you are a spy.'

Michael stared at Irene, taken aback. It had never crossed his mind.

She said, 'I'm sure the German authorities have spies placed in Britain, not just to find military installations and that kind of thing but to check on us refugees. I daresay there are British spies in Germany too. After all, some people in this country are getting ready to fight. War must come.'

'I can't bear not doing anything!' Michael buried his face in his hands.

'Here you are, ducks, have another cup.' Mrs Cassidy's bulk loomed over Michael as she directed a stream of orange liquid into his mug.

'This breakfast is wonderful,' Irene said. She rubbed the last crust of fried bread against the last trace of egg yolk.

'What's wonderful is finding you,' Michael said.

She gazed at him, briefly solemn. 'I shall bring you luck, you'll see,' she said.

12

Celia had leave at Easter and returned to England. With her parents in Norfolk, she felt like a visitor to the house in which she had grown up. The homely decorations of childhood still filled her bedroom. The doll's house, the rocking horse, the Peter Rabbit books in their miniature cabinet, the row of dolls in national costumes that had once seemed so sophisticated a collection: they now belonged to a person she did not know and could hardly remember.

It was not possible to speak of reality in her mother's presence. With her the conversation was about neighbours, clothes, crops and servants. Celia advised taking German refugees, but Mrs Roget was adamant.

'Your father is becoming obsessed about that. Don't you start. I'm not having it. One wouldn't know who one was letting into one's house. Don't tell me they are all so innocent. I've heard stories about thieves and worse. Spies,' she added in a stagy whisper.

'Here?' Celia said, as much amused as irritated.

'Your father is so unworldly, he always thinks the best of everyone. I really don't want to discuss it any further.'

Celia's father summoned her into his consulting room, as though she were his patient, and there they sat, surrounded by the mechanisms of mercy, discussing murder.

Dr Roget had come to Germany at the New Year, meeting Celia at an inn in the Black Forest. They had gone on together to Heidelberg. 'You might prefer not to know what I'm doing here,' he had said, and took care not to tell her in so many words. But she guessed. He was meeting Jews, surreptitiously and unobserved, to take charge of their small, portable valuables, which he intended to convey out of the country on their behalf. They would not be permitted to take wealth when – if – they emigrated. Taxes, fines and confiscations were designed to send them destitute into exile.

'How do you arrange it?' Celia wanted to know.

'Let's just say that I'm not the only person at home to be dismayed by our government's supine attitude. Shall we leave it at that?'

They were standing on the promenade beside the castle, high above the town, the very picture of a father and daughter interested only in the delights of the scenery; and when a man in leather shorts and a green loden jacket came within earshot, John Roget was speaking about the harmonious view, the rust-red roofs and creamy walls of the houses, the ice-green waters of the Neckar, the dark hillsides enfolding the ancient, civilised city. Over dinner in the Europäische Hof, their conversation was in a kind of code. They discussed their Huguenot ancestors, an earlier generation of escapers from oppression, and the help that family legend said they had received from English well-wishers.

In Norfolk it was possible to speak freely.

'I'd like to know exactly what you do, how you got into contact with each other and whether I could help,' Celia began, but her father shook his head.

'Don't ask.'

'Does Mother know?'

'Your mother takes her political prejudices from dinner party chatter. She prefers to be shielded from current affairs.'

So did many of the people Celia met in England during that visit. She went to two lunch parties and a dance with her parents and did not enjoy them. An unmarried woman was pitiable by definition. 'Your turn next, dear,' said the mothers of the girls she had grown up with, and told Celia about Sheila's or Shirley's good steady husband and sweet babies.

Celia was beautifully dressed, and had turned out much better looking than anyone ever expected. 'Who would have thought it of that funny little dark creature, so skinny she used to be?' What was more, she was doing well in a career they would have been proud of for their sons. No wonder they made her feel an outsider.

Peter Hoyland was at the dance. Celia had achieved a better degree at Cambridge than Peter – or would have, if women were awarded degrees. She had come out far ahead of him in the final examinations, and then he had failed the Civil Service exams and

Celia had refused his proposal of marriage. He had good reason to resent her. Instead his welcome was the only consolation for an otherwise dismal evening.

'Friends?' he asked, holding both her hands.

'If you want to be.'

'Friends, then. Let's go down to the supper room and fill in the gaps.'

Celia had been Peter's partner at May Balls, run with him after the University beagles, kissed him – oh, she had thought at the time, such innocent English kisses in some innocent English greenhouse in a Cambridge don's garden, as she breathed in the scent of ripening tomatoes along with Peter's hot and tennis-sweaty odour. How fraternal and meaningless it seemed beside her pre-university experience of what passion should be; oh, that pink boyishness of unsophisticated youths at frolic beside the Cam!

He had settled down; at Cambridge he was already older than the other undergraduates, after beginning a career in the military and being invalided out on account of an incurable though, Peter insisted, not incapacitating injury to his knee. Now, at thirty, he had qualified as a solicitor and was about to join his brother in the family firm in Devon.

'I wear the regimental brooch,' Celia said.

'And remember my mistake? We would never have suited, you and I. Seeing you here in Norfolk I realise how much you would have disliked sharing my boring life in Devon.'

'I would, but does it show?' Celia asked.

'I was watching you when you came in. It isn't just that you are in this year's clothes. You look . . . worldly. Cosmopolitan.'

'You have never said anything I would rather hear.'

'It's true, but it wouldn't do for country life. You're better off in Berlin.'

'I am having a fascinating time there,' she said.

'I might come and see you this summer. Or perhaps you could get across to see me. I'm taking a few weeks off to sail through Europe.'

'Don't you mean round?' Celia asked.

'People are always surprised when I say that, but I'd have thought you would know about the canals. I'm taking the boat across to the Hook of Holland and then I can wiggle right through to the Black Sea.'

'On your own?'

'Yes. I know lots of chaps who'd like to come, but she's really a one-man craft. I'm planning to use her as a base for looking around, see how the regime works. Do you think it would catch on here? People seem to be talking about it an awful lot these days. In my club the other night, that chap Whitchurch was saying he had just come back.'

'I see him in Berlin sometimes.'

'He's got a girl there, I believe. Sounded very keen on the place. I'm looking forward to seeing what's going on.'

'Take my office number with you, then, in case you get into trouble.' But Celia knew that Peter was protected by British immunity. It isn't fair, she thought then, and thought it again later in the week.

She had one night in London before returning to Berlin.

'You can go to the Silversmiths for me,' Mrs Roget had said. 'I don't like refusing their invitations, but I'm hardly ever in London and it always seems so depressing there these days. Of course, nobody could be sorrier for poor Hanne than I am, but one never knows what to say. You won't feel it as I do. You are so concerned with all that.'

All that; well, if Norfolk closed its mind, Bayswater could not. Some of the men and women at the Silversmiths managed to keep up the jollity, but in corners of the three large reception rooms solemn groups of guests stood talking in low voices, waving their hands in defensive, despairing gestures.

The front drawing room, the back drawing room and the ballroom were on the first floor, connected by high-panelled doors which stood open this evening to encourage the guests to circulate. The rooms could hardly have changed since the last century, still in heavy colours, much adorned with gilt-framed pictures and fringed lampshades. In the dining room downstairs the smell of rich food lingered in the air.

Hanne Silberschmidt was sitting there in a high-armed chair near the fireplace with a screen drawn up behind her to keep off any draughts that managed to penetrate the dark green curtains. She looked chilled all the same, her hands washing against each other, round and round, her bluish lips trembling. This time she knew who Celia was. She showed no sign of remembering their last meeting near the British Embassy in Berlin and Celia did not remind her of it, but stayed nodding and murmuring sympathy as Hanne went over again and again the details of her escape – or her abandonment of her daughter.

'They promised they'd bring her, they said they would find her and bring her.' Her voice was reedy, high, infinitely pitiful.

Michael Silberschmidt had promised his aunt that he would come to the reception, wondering whether she would want him as a guest in her well-tended house full of servants if she knew where he had spent the earlier part of the day.

Journalism was going badly. There was too much competition for it or, indeed, for any other work Michael was qualified to do. In the end he took a job for which he was not qualified. Irene mentioned that Searles' was taking on part-time staff. The company supplied not only caterers and food but also extra servants. It needed men, for women were not acceptable to wait at table or at receptions in the best establishments.

Michael, though untrained, knew how he had been served in the old days. He wrote himself a couple of references, one on his aunt's own headed paper, another on some he took from the writing room at the Dorchester Hotel. With a gaiety born of desperation he impersonated a footman to the satisfaction of the company's manager. 'Your hair's too long, get it cut. At least the calves don't need padding. You'll do as long as you keep your mouth shut.'

There was little temptation to speak. Michael found that in his frogged and braided livery, with white gloves, a powdered wig, knee breeches and patent leather shoes, he was depersonalised. 'I've turned into a piece of furniture,' he told Irene.

'Me too. People don't see other people's parlourmaids or footmen. We aren't human beings. Haven't you noticed how nobody acknowledges we are there? They don't say thank you for their food or drink, they don't look at us. If you spoke they would be as surprised as if words came out of the candlestick.'

'We didn't treat the servants like that.'

'Bei uns?'

'We didn't,' he insisted. 'They had names, they were part of the family.'

'That's exactly what the slave owners used to say. Oppressors always do.'

78

Oddly enough Michael did not feel oppressed. The man who stood by a door holding a silver salver or whose arm presented sauces or vegetables from behind a guest's left shoulder was transformed in his own mind, as in the world's, from an individual into an automaton. He did the work, took the money and was as little affected by it as though he had been unconscious. On the day of the Silversmiths' party he had spent four hours at a luncheon party in Grosvenor Square, ignored by the Members of Parliament and socialites who attended it. Then he went back to Searles' in Bond Street and changed from the protective colouring of the flunkey before going home to change yet again, this time into the uniform that would re-admit him to membership of the class waited on by other anonymous people in uniform.

Michael's clothes were hand-me-downs. He had arrived in London with none, and on his second morning at the Silversmiths had gone into his bedroom to find his uncle's valet hanging suits and ties in the wardrobe. Stacks of laundered shirts and collars were already on the shelves. Ivory-backed brushes, a box of collar studs, even some monogrammed cuff links, had been arranged on the dressing table. On the washstand a safety razor with shaving brush and bowl; on a hook on the back of the door a brocade dressing gown. A cousin's name was written on the tailor's labels: Mr C.B. Silversmith.

Cecil had died in Africa three years earlier after an accident on a big game hunt. It was a noble gesture on the part of Aunt Lisbeth, Cecil's mother, to let a destitute foreigner wear the clothes she had preserved, but Michael was unable to thank her for it. Cecil's name was not to be mentioned and when, on the third day, Michael put on a shirt with a visible monogram, the valet caught him halfway down the stairs to breakfast, apologised profusely for his own mistake and begged Michael to change into unmarked linen.

They had been much of a size. Cecil's evening clothes fitted well enough to make Michael look like the English gentleman he was not. When he called at Irene's house, as arranged, her landlady greeted him with a respect she had not shown before and could be heard, before she closed the door of her front room, telling her husband that Miss Strauss's gentleman friend looked like a real toff.

But Irene had not transformed herself into a real lady to go with him. 'I'm not coming,' she said. His relations would despise her, his mother would hate her and in any case nothing would induce her to set foot inside that bastion of class privilege.

'You do every day, for Searles'.'

'I'm paid for that. Anyway, how could I go with you when you look like that and I – ? Look at me!'

Irene's only evening dress was two years old and represented a taste she, and fashion, had grown out of. Her clothes hung behind a curtain in her one-roomed lodging. The alcove was narrow but not full. She always wore either the black dress that was a waitress's uniform or a brown tweed suit, and when Michael pushed the flowered cretonne aside he was struck by the poverty of her possessions. A smell, stale but intensely sexy, had been trapped by the curtain. Almost automatically he put his hand to his white bow tie to undo it.

'Not now, for God's sake!' Irene snapped.

He was obviously not going to be able to suggest a more suitable garment. He said heartily, 'You look very nice as you are. Anyway, nobody's going to notice. There will be so many people there.'

'I don't want your mother and her capitalist friends to see me like this.'

'But it would be a chance for the two of you to meet.'

'I don't think that's such a good idea.'

'Oh come on, Irene. You'll have to sooner or later.'

'I don't see the necessity.'

It was a familiar barrier. Michael thought Irene should marry him. Irene said marriage was a bourgeois word for enslavement and they were fine as they were.

Their disagreement moved from clothes to the much more important, much less reconcilable subject of their future, together or apart. Neither said anything new, but they advanced from discussion to argument to a quarrel. In the end, very late, Michael went alone to his cousins' house.

The street was full of cars and chauffeurs and a red carpet covered the front steps. The atmosphere of sedate festivity was at once familiar from the old days and dreadfully strange now so much had changed.

Michael sought detachment. Why should a wave of nostalgia

sweep over him? He stared with determined dispassion at the furniture, the decorations, the guests, the servants, the dazzling chandeliers until he had quelled the unruly, undesirable emotion. In any case, this did not resemble his home in the least. The Berlin Silberschmidts had lived a much less social, less showy life than their Anglicised relations. At home there had never been footmen and seldom glasses of champagne on silver salvers. Coffee and cake had been the form, and lace-trimmed afternoon dress, not bare bosoms and tiaras.

The Bayswater house was ostentatious, he thought, designed to impress visitors to it with the certainty of its owners' British-ness. The furniture and fittings were the best of a kind that could be found from castle to cottage wherever the English gentleman felt at home: sober Hepplewhite and Chippendale and gilt-framed pastoral landscapes. One container full of Hanne's belongings, packed by an Aryan friend, had arrived from Berlin. The foreign furniture was in store at Whiteley's Repository.

Michael walked through the rooms, nodding at the few people he knew, until he found his cousin in the ballroom. 'Your dear mother is downstairs,' she told him. 'Do go and find her.'

He listened to scraps of conversation. Palestine, work permits, so-and-so in Rome, such-and-such settled in Buenos Aires, this committee and that committee, questions in the House. It was useless; as useless as his own thoughts.

Celia Roget was repeating to Hanne Silberschmidt her last sighting of Lotte the previous August – an edited tale: Lotte at a fancy dress party, well, in good company, leaving before Celia could speak to her.

Michael waited until he could take Celia away and question her out of his mother's earshot, but there was no more she could (or would) tell him; she had not set eyes on Lotte since.

'What about you?' she asked. 'How did you get away? I heard you had been arrested. I went to your house the same day and Fräulein von Noltke told me what had happened, as I wrote to your mother.'

'Champagne, sir?'

Michael put his empty glass on the silver tray and took a full one. He had told nobody about his escape. He had been asked not to do so, and understood that future fugitives would be in more danger if he did; in any case, he avoided the whole subject. Every refugee had his or her own story. They wanted to tell not listen – but Michael did not want to tell . . .

13

'Say nothing of your sister,' Hanne Silberschmidt whispered as he was pushed after her into the back of the black van.

'Silence!' one of the men commanded.

His mother's teeth were chattering. She clasped her hands tightly together. He stretched to put his own on hers. Neither spoke. There was nothing to say.

The van hurtled through the streets, flinging them against its windowless sides. Michael had seen the progress of such vehicles often enough in the last three years. He knew that those pedestrians who were out so early would scatter, that their faces would be expressionless, masking fear of the same fate and relief that it had come to someone else instead.

The drive had already been longer than he had expected. They were not on the way to the Gestapo headquarters.

Was it to be straight to a camp, without even the pretence of interrogation and trial?

Michael had not embraced his mother more than formally for many years. Now he edged himself closer to her and put his arms around her trembling body.

The van turned, paused, moved forward and stopped. Hanne Silberschmidt closed her eyes.

The doors opened. It was dark. An electric light was switched on. One of the men who had arrested them stood before them. He was smiling. He had unbuttoned his tunic, revealing a striped blue and white shirt. He held out his hand.

They were in a garage. It smelt of fuel.

'I'm afraid you're going to have to hurry,' the man said.

He had spoken in English.

Michael's mother slumped forward, all strength gone, and Michael and the man lifted her out of the back of the black van.

'In here,' the other man said. 'Make it snappy, old chap.'

'What . . . ?'

'No time for questions and answers, my dear fellow. Just thought we'd snatch you from under their noses, don't you know?'

There were two cars parked beside the black van. Hanne Silberschmidt was seated, almost propped, in the back of a grey Daimler.

The second officer came round the car. He had changed into a chauffeur's dark green livery. He patted the pockets. 'Tickets. Your mother's going by train. We'll put her on the ten thirty to Boulogne. It goes right through.'

Michael muttered something about a passport. 'Don't you worry, that's under control.' The young man bent forward. 'Your son will travel separately, Mrs Silberschmidt. You'll see him soon, I promise.'

'Lotte . . .' the old woman whispered.

Michael said, 'We can't go without my sister.'

'We'll find her. She can follow you to England, Mrs Silberschmidt, they won't be bothered about her. Look here, old chap, you duck round here while we open the doors.'

The Daimler backed out on to the street and was gone.

'I'm not leaving my sister behind,' Michael said.

'Where is she?'

'I'm not quite sure at the moment.'

'Can you leave it to us? I promise we'll bring her on afterwards. You'll be no use to her in a camp, and that's where you are going to be if you don't get out of the country soonest. They were coming for you this morning and will be hunting for you at this moment. And they don't give up easily.'

'I know, but . . .'

'Well then. Come on.'

Michael had replayed the conversation in his head over and over again since that day. He should never have left Lotte. He had to leave Lotte. He made the wrong choice. He had no choice.

'You really can't help her by staying,' the young man said gently.

He was pulling off the black boots and breeches, hanging them in a walnut wardrobe that stood incongruously against the garage wall. He dressed himself in grey flannel trousers with a yellow waistcoat, tweed jacket and striped cravat. He put on brightly polished brown brogues and combed his hair to fall carelessly across his forehead. He arranged a spotted handkerchief to spill from his breast pocket.

'The very image of the English gentleman, what? Come on, time for us to be on our way. Let's just see . . . ' He stared at Michael for a moment. 'Suit's all right. You need a tie, though. Here.' He handed Michael a tie striped in black and pink. 'Old Carthusian, very convincing. But I think you need a hat to hide that hair. Try this one.' Michael pulled a brown trilby over his hair and forwards to mask his profile. 'Nearly there. I know, have this.' He gave Michael a fawn-coloured waterproof trench coat. 'Drape it. Don't worry if it makes you look like a bookie's tout.'

They climbed into the second car, a small Austin. 'We came over for the Olympics. Now we are on our way to Zermatt for some climbing. Our friends have gone ahead with most of the luggage in their car and we are meeting them there. Your name is Robert Hoyland – here's your passport – and you've just qualified as a lawyer. You're having a holiday before starting work. Read the small print.'

The photograph was indistinct enough for a cursory examination. Nobody checked it carefully. Two superannuated students in a small car and speaking no German were obviously harmless. The other man said he was called Hugh. He talked about shooting, flying, the London music hall, mountain climbing in Kenya and the migratory habits of storks. When Michael asked him a more personal question he said, 'Least said soonest forgotten, what?'

Michael slept for much of the journey, waking apprehensively as they approached the border and customs post on Lake Constance, but they passed through with no trouble. 'Keep it up,' the young man warned. 'They've got a lookout this side too.' He drove through the pastoral neatness of eastern Switzerland, reaching Zurich in the late evening.

Hugh gave Michael a booklet of tickets. He was to go to Geneva and change for Paris.

'You should be in London in time for dinner on Friday.'

When Michael tried to thank him, Hugh said, 'All part of the service, don't you know?', and drove abruptly away.

Michael did reach London on the Friday. He was in time for dinner, here in this very house, which his mother had reached two days earlier. He had no idea who the men were, or how they had come to whisk them away. Hugh had said nothing more than, 'We got a warning.' After Celia's first letter, Michael ached to know what it had been and from whom. How had his rescuers known that the Gestapo would come for the Silberschmidts that day?

In Michael's mind was preserved the memory of a young, intelligent English face, of a determined frivolity, of a car registration number. Many of his enquiries in the last months had been in the unadmitted hope of meeting Hugh again. He wanted to thank him, of course, but above all he wanted to join him. Those two young men were doing what he wanted to do. Somehow he must find them; and meanwhile never mention them.

Celia was waiting for him to tell her how he had escaped. She seemed . . . damn it, she seemed protective; authoritative. How dare little Celia look as though she were about to patronise him? When the last time they met she had gazed at him with those great worshipful cow eyes and promised to love him for ever?

'Tell me,' Michael said kindly, 'about your career. Who would have thought you would become a diplomat?'

'No, you start. What are you doing yourself?'

'I am a professional pest,' he said lightly. 'I ask everyone I meet about working in some kind of resistance. They are beginning to think I am an infernal bore.'

Celia asked whether he was involved with any of the refugee organisations.

'I don't have quite the right qualifications,' he said. 'You need to be patient and motherly and winning. My friend Irene queues at obscure embassies to beg for visas to enter countries we have never heard of. Some of my Silversmith cousins turn up to look after the kids who are sent out on their own. I am afraid what I am looking for is action.'

'I thought there was some kind of organisation trying to rescue people,' Celia said.

'Did you? Is there? I wonder, by any chance, would you know how to get in touch with it?' Michael asked.

'I don't, I'm afraid,' she said, and reminded herself to write to her father. No, better use the telephone. Nothing on paper for her mother to find. She would make a trunk call tomorrow, catch him when he was at work and suggest he invited Michael for the weekend. As Dr Roget had rightly said, it was preferable, in her official position, to guess but not to know.

14

Celia was invited to the Beowulfs for the New Year, having met Hubertus and Marianne, separately and together, at several parties and functions. Hubertus seemed to combine an affection for England and the friends he had made during his year in Oxford with a passionate patriotism that rendered him touchy and easily offended by those very friends. One had to speak carefully in his presence; but then Celia was trying to make thinking before she spoke an invariable habit, alien as it was to her natural behaviour.

Celia liked Marianne rather against her own will. The girl was beautiful, frivolous, self-centred and ignorant. She was completely uninterested in current affairs or anything apart from sport and parties. In fact Marianne was exactly the sort of person of whom Celia had always felt subconsciously envious and consciously contemptuous.

The old Baronin wrote that the Honourable Julian Whitchurch would be at Heorot as well as the Lockwoods and a French diplomat called le Comte de Savary with his wife and a Mr Thaddeus Burton from New York. 'It will be an international party and we look forward to including our foreign friends in our traditional German festivities.'

Heorot was in south Saxony, a long train journey from Berlin during which Celia read a novel by Thomas Mann in German, rather slowly and breaking off every few chapters to gallop through some of the new Dorothy L. Sayers mystery which her mother had sent for Christmas. Over luncheon in the dining car she studied Baedeker's descriptions of her destination.

She was to change trains in Dresden ('The German Florence' according to Herr Baedeker) but as it was dark by the time she got there nothing could be seen of the city, nor, on the last leg of the journey, of the Erzgebirge chain of mountains which marked the frontier with Czechoslovakia.

Twentieth-century history and politics seemed to have passed Heorot by. Saxony had always been a kingdom of vast estates, and it seemed that the Beowulfs had retained much or even all of theirs. Celia was brought to Heorot's door after an hour's drive along narrow roads through fields and forests dimly picked out by the headlights. As far as she could see they passed no towns, not even a village. The silent chauffeur could have been a coachman, the Mercedes a horse-drawn carriage, the century the last or any other than this one.

The outside of the house was lit by flaring torches set in sconces on its long, low frontage. Celia saw whitish stone, three tiers of tall windows and a deep mansard roof pierced by eaved casements. Two servants in grey and green hunting costumes waited on the wide, shallow steps. The pillared entrance hall was illuminated by gas mantles and candelabra, and the old Baronin wore a black, floor-length dress with lace inserts and onyx jewellery.

Celia, tired and chilled in spite of her grandmother's remodelled furs, uncomfortable in her short skirt, felt out of place and had to stop herself from currying favour with the sketched curtsey, or *Knicks*, that an unmarried German girl would have made to her hostess.

An open door to one side of the hall showed a long suite of nearly dark rooms, their connecting doors open. At the far end of the enfilade, a hundred yards away, a man sat at a desk. Its one lamp outlined his shape, a beacon at the end of a tunnel. He rose and moved towards the hall, and Celia saw that it was Hubertus himself, wearing breeches and a jacket with velvet facings. Then Marianne came out of a room at the back of the entrance hall, a welcome sight in her knee-length, fringed silk dress with its low back and cap sleeves.

'Come in, you must be frozen!' Marianne exclaimed, putting her arm through Celia's. 'Don't keep her standing out here, Mother. It's like the grave. Let's get back to the warmth.'

The rest of the party was assembled in a high, bright room whose French doors opened into a subtly lit orangery. There was a vast porcelain stove in one corner and a gramophone in another. Julian Whitchurch was performing a lazy tango with Mrs Lockwood, but they broke off to greet Celia.

'You're just in time, we are expecting more snow,' Mr Lockwood said, shaking Celia's hand as though he had not seen her in the office the day before, and almost every other day in the past year.

'So romantic,' his wife sighed.

'Miss Roget would like to go upstairs,' the Baronin said.

'Come on, Celia, I'll show you,' her daughter said. 'We have put you in the Elisabeth Room. The Empress of Austria slept there sometime in the last century.'

'Is it the same bed?' Celia asked, looking at the high, elaborately carved furniture covered with tiny fluted pillars, flowers, faces and twining leaves.

'I should think it might be a different mattress. Here's the dressing room. No bath, I'm afraid. Hubie's trying to persuade Mamma that we need them.'

'I love hip baths,' Celia said.

'The bell's there. Ring for whatever you want.' As Marianne left the room, a maid came in and asked whether the gracious lady would like hot water now. She would, and it came in a copper ewer; the soap was Parisian, the towels Turkish, the embroidered carpet covered with faded garlands of flowers. Celia washed, changed, repainted her face and tidied her hair in the flattering candlelight.

Dinner was served in a large, apple-green room in which a servant stood behind each chair. On their account, or perhaps that of Baronin von Beowulf, conversation was painfully bland. Julian Whitchurch and Thaddeus Burton apparently knew each other well. They and Marianne met throughout the year on the sport and parties circuit: big game and big games, east coast, west coast, Scotland, Alaska, Southern Rhodesia, India. Only Julian knew India. 'Born there, actually,' he said. 'M'father was out with the Viceroy.'

'You grew up in India?' the Comtesse de Savary asked. A silly question. Naturally Julian Whitchurch had been sent back to an English nanny and English nursery before going to board at prep school and Eton.

Celia's attention wandered to the portraits on the walls. Little candle holders were attached to their frames, each one swung out so the light beamed upwards to their subjects. Stout, pink-faced men with blue eyes and raised brows stared haughtily over their embroidered brocade clothes; equally superior women displayed their husbands' wealth on bare, spacious bosoms. At the far end of the room smaller, darker pictures were crowded together in frames whose gilt was dulled with age; bland, secretive faces, as unreadable now as the mediaeval minds they masked, with symbolic motifs in age-dulled paint, proclamations of status and achievement that their contemporaries would have understood.

'Family portraits never go far enough back,' the Comte de Savary said. 'Now if there were some representation of the Beowulf of whom the Anglo-Saxons sang . . . '

'Is there a connection?'

'How not? The house is even called after Hrothgar's Hall.'

Celia desperately dredged her memory. 'Surely it was in Denmark?' she ventured.

'Bravo, mademoiselle. Can you possibly be one of the few people who has read that endless recital of dragon-slaying? I confess I have not but my secretary was determined to give me my homework.'

'I don't know anything about the poem except its name,' Celia said.

'Ah, then I am safe in pretending to knowlege that I truly have not got. My poor young secretary is a scholar manqué. He produced far more information than I thought I required.'

'About Anglo-Saxon poetry?'

'It is three thousand lines of epic verse. The subject is a monster called Grendel and a hero called Beowulf. There is much fighting and feasting in a palace called Heorot.'

'It is a tale of heroism and self-sacrifice,' the Baronin interrupted. 'The hero dies for a cause, for the good of the nation. He rids the people of the monster that preys upon it.'

'My mother takes family tradition very seriously,' Marianne said. 'We were brought up on stories of the dragon-slayer.'

'As a good example, perhaps,' de Savary said.

'An ever-present one, at any rate,' Hubertus said. The light glinted on his pale, flat hair and cast sculptural shadows on his narrow face. It also made the duelling scars more noticeable than usual, a hatchment of gleaming lines, only one of them a little puckered, across his cheeks and brow. The process had been explained to Celia. Although it was now illegal so long and supposedly honourable a tradition did not disappear as the result of a single decree.

Hubertus would have been protected by gauntlets, goggles,

body armour. Only the face was left unprotected. The sword blades, as sharp as a razor, jutted at the end of the two partici-pants' outstretched arms. The young men would stand completely still, except for those flashing wrists and hands, their reputations dependent on never flinching while the tribal emblem of gashes was carved upon their skin. Afterwards salt was rubbed into the wounds. Celia felt a sudden excitement overcome her disgust at the thought of their infliction.

The servants, in unison, removed one set of plates (fine, flowered, fluted) and replaced them with others, white with gilt rims and a crest in the middle.

'There's the dragon,' Hubertus said. Everyone looked at the china. A gilt dragon, its feet splayed, its head twisted back over its body, its mouth open wide around a lance held in a mailed hand. 'You'll find it all over the place. I used to try and count them but I kept losing track somewhere in the high hundreds.'

The Baronin said, 'When my dear husband, Hubertus's father, went to the war he took the family emblem as his guiding star.'

'And his family as his war band,' de Savary whispered, and added, 'his wider family, you understand: blood relations and natural children. There were many.'

An improper remark. Celia kept her face expressionless.

'My noble husband died bravely under his ancestor's example. Now another generation must find its own hero to rid it of its enemy. We know who has taken up the lance in Germany today.'

Mr Lockwood changed the subject. How did he do it so smooth-ly? Celia re-ran the diplomatic dialogue over in her mind. With-out seeming to interrupt, he turned the old lady's attention from heroes with lances to runners with batons in relay races, to the Olympics last year and Marianne's role in the Winter Games. The local conditions, the climate of the Heorot district and, reassur-ance at last, round to that safe subject, the weather; it looked, Mr Lockwood thought, like snow.

It did snow in the night, but not too heavily. The men went out before it was fully light. Celia, woken by barks and exclamations below her window, drew her curtains and opened the shutters to see what was going on. The shooters stood with their dogs and loaders outside the house. The servants held lanterns on out-stretched arms. Four horses stamped and jingled their harness, pulling at the braked carriage behind them. Then the party moved off briskly across the white ground towards the trees, and Celia jumped back under the plump feather quilt.

Two hours later she was woken again when the housemaid brought a breakfast of coffee served in flowery Luneberg china, with poppy-seed rolls and cherry jam; then two maids in print dresses carried in an enamel bath and a series of copper jugs full of water. One of the girls looked disconcertingly like Marianne, and Celia remembered de Savary's hint about the old Baron's morals.

Celia dressed in appropriately rustic brown tweeds and painted her face with a discretion designed to disarm the Baronin.

'I should be so interested to see your house,' she said. 'I don't think we have anything like it in England.' It was the right opening. The Baronin sent a maid to fetch her a wrap.

'I have never visited your country. My husband and I were busy within the Empire before the war, and of course afterwards things have been different. But Heorot stays always the same.'

'How old is the house?'

'Nearly a thousand years.'

The Baronin was possessive but ignorant. Interrupting every sentence with calls to her dog Spitzi, she showed Celia through rooms of varied styles. There were ceilings painted in celestial colours showing pastoral scenes within frames of shells, sheaves, garlands; there were gilded arabesques and wrought metal twirls and branches. There was highly polished marqueterie and inlay, and other, older cabinets with twisted columns and gargoyles carved on their doors. And over all lay the chilly light of the snow-covered landscape outside, where the shapes of statues emerged from their white shrouds and rooks cawed in skeletal trees.

The Baronin knew little about her possessions, except that they were something to be proud of – not on account of their beauty, though most were exquisite, but because they had been hallowed by association with the von Beowulf family.

For generations they had been soldiers and landowners, supporters of their prince, their king and at last their Emperor. Once or twice the Baronin spoke wistfully of the Kaiserszeit, the days of the Emperor, of which her own boudoir was a period piece in darkening browns and yellows, with faded Turkish rugs and beige silk draperies over mantelpiece, piano and the top of each commode and table. It was full of framed photographs, most, presumably, of her own family, but many of royalty, their signatures at an angle across skirts or spurred boots. A wreath of myrtle crowned the portrait of the old Baron, a fierce-faced martinet in his spiked helmet and high collar with a row of medals on his chest.

'How like his father your son looks,' Celia said.

'Please God he is like his father in every way.'

The ladies went out to join the shooters at lunchtime. Celia walked with Marianne and heard her say to her mother, 'Can't the men clear the snow from the paths when we are here? The place is not as well run as it used to be in Johannes's time.'

'Who is Johannes?' the Comtesse de Savary asked.

'A former employee,' the Baronin said repressively.

'He was the estate manager,' Marianne said.

'He had Hebrew blood in him,' said the Baronin. 'It was best that he went.'

'His wife made the best gingerbread.'

'Marianne, that will do!'

'I liked playing with Hansel, too,' Marianne added.

'Silence!' her mother snapped. 'The place is now managed by Holzer. Your brother is perfectly satisfied and so am I. We shall say no more.'

They met the shooters in a wooden hunting lodge which smelled deliciously of pine resin and smoke. Everyone sat at a table covered with red gingham to be served soup, venison pasties and plum cake.

No wonder Hubertus is so rigid, Celia reflected as she watched his curtness to his servants and his easy but indefinably artificial jolliness with his guests. He is the product of this confined environment. To question, to reform, even to think freely must be anathema to him. No, she corrected herself, not that, but difficult. He looked up and caught Celia's eye, holding her gaze with a pale, intense concentration. Then the Comtesse de Savary asked him something and he turned towards her. Celia saw that the Baronin was watching her intently, almost suspiciously, but she too looked away when she saw that Celia had noticed.

After lunch Marianne and Celia stayed while the other ladies returned in the pony chaises to the house. The sharp air was reviving after the heavy meal.

Marianne had her own gun. Shooting was an unusual accomplishment for any female; watching her smooth movements Celia felt a sharp pang of envy. I could do that, she thought.

Instead she stood in a hide beside Julian Whitchurch. The partridges flew in swift, sudden bursts, dashing across the light sky. Once shot, they fell like stones. It was a swift death, but Celia, who had lived in the company of sportsmen all her life, winced at the efficient slaughter.

'Not happy about b-b-b-blood sports?' Julian Whitchurch enquired in an interval between drives.

'I have no objection on principle, but for a moment it seemed . . . an unfair contest.'

'Manhunts would be fairer, eh?'

'Do they have those here too?'

Celia had met Julian several times by now. He was often with Marianne, whom he seemed to be courting, but he usually gave some sporting reason for his trip: he was here for the races, or the sailing, even once for a dog show.

Celia had despised the over-privileged, frivolous, pleasure-seeking young aristocrats she used to observe at Cambridge, as they wasted the intellectual opportunities of the University and teased or terrorised contemporaries who wanted to work. Julian Whitchurch was another of them, a playboy like Thaddeus Burton (a Yale man, he had informed her) who would inherit enough from his family's newspaper empire to have no need to work or to take life seriously.

Other women thrived in their company. To Celia, their courtesy indicated the arrogance of people born to the power not only of inherited wealth and influence, but also of the physical confidence derived from being six foot tall and naturally athletic. When they deferred to a woman, or opened the door to let her precede them, or stood up when she came into the room, they patronised her by their chivalry.

No wonder such men felt at home in the atmosphere of this 'might is right' country. They would not think about what was going on in it. Celia had learned a lot in the time she had worked in Berlin and wondered if Julian Whitchurch could say the same. Perhaps he would be shocked if he saw a work camp or a bullied

Jew or a tortured liberal, and would wade in to stop it; but out of sight out of mind, and she doubted whether he had even questioned the system his friends were supporting. To him, Germany meant snowy mountains to ski down and decent countryide to shoot in.

So she was amazed when he said, 'These b-b-birds have a better chance than human beings, poor devils. Flying out of range isn't so easy for them.'

'London is full of refugees who have managed to escape, you know,' Celia told him.

'With somebody's help,' Julian said. His usually vapid expression was momentarily grim.

'I expect you are right.'

'From people such as yourself.'

'What? What do you mean?'

'You must be in a good position to do something about it, in your job,' Julian suggested.

Was he looking for information? Had he heard something about the organisation her father was involved with?

'I really don't know what you mean,' Celia said coldly. 'I couldn't possibly consider such a thing. You must know that the question could never arise.'

The servant handed Julian the other gun and said in German, 'It begins again.' A little while later, he said, 'Good. The gentleman was very good.'

The whistle shrilled. Marianne called them over. There was coffee and schnapps. Afterwards Celia found herself beside Mr Lockwood.

'I was surprised to see you here yesterday,' he said.

'Didn't the Baronin tell you who was coming?'

'You weren't mentioned. I had no idea you knew the Beowulfs. Have you been friends for long?'

'I met them when I first came to Berlin. We have been running into each other ever since.'

'You should have told me.'

'I'm sorry. I didn't know,' Celia said.

'Perhaps not. I should have warned you that it's always worth mentioning your friendships with foreign nationals wherever you are posted, and especially if it's somewhere as tense as this country is at the moment. Hubertus von B. has some interesting contacts. Look, Miss Roget, you can just make out the Fichelberg in the distance. It's the highest peak in Saxony. I remember staying at the Sporthotel up on the top there when I came out here as a student . . . '

Hubertus had come within earshot and now stood close to them. Celia felt intensely aware of his physical presence, tall, hard, very masculine. He smelt faintly of bay rum. Close to her, but not touching, he radiated warmth. I shall remember this moment, she thought.

'You might like to go up the mountain, Miss Roget. The view is quite something.'

'The border runs along the top, doesn't it?'

'Yes. At present.' He moved across the hard snow to speak to de Savary. Lockwood said in a low voice,

'Heavily guarded. It was possible to get out that way until a year or so ago, but not any more. God knows where the poor devils try these days.'

'Mr Lockwood, can I ask you something?'

'Ask away.'

'If it were suggested that we – Embassy staff, that is – should help in some way – '

'Be careful what you're saying. You can't consider getting involved in the internal affairs of the sovereign state to which you're accredited. And, Miss Roget, a word to the wise: I should be a bit careful of some of our own compatriots, if I were you. There are some who let their friendships take them a bit far. Remember where your loyalties lie.'

'Do you mean – ?'

'No names, no pack drill.' His expressionless glance across to the next butt was information enough. Julian and Marianne were very close together, gazing into each other's eyes.

Hubertus was approaching again.

The thought sprang from nowhere into Celia's head: he's a wonderful-looking man. Out here on his own land, dressed in the style of his ancestors, in command of so much and so many, one could see that the salient characteristic of his face was authority. A powerful man. The memory of herself in bed with Michael Silberschmidt came into Celia's mind. The image of Hubertus von Beowulf, fair not dark, burly not thin, solemn not laughing, superimposed itself.

'You are cold,' Hubertus said. 'One more drive only.'

The men raised their guns. The light had changed from blue to thin grey. Darkness would soon fall. Meanwhile renewed firing echoed over the landscape.

15

Irene would one day describe this part of her life as a chronicle of despondency. Her days were filled with pitiable refugees, pitiless officials, pitifully ill-informed and incredulous outsiders who, even after five years, refused to believe what was going on over there.

Some days she spent trudging round from embassy to legation to consulate of ever-more obscure countries trying to get visas for refugees to enter them.

On other days, before going to work in the late afternoon and evening, she helped as a volunteer at Woburn House.

Today there had been a young couple with infant twins: a doctor, his psychiatrist wife, one child with a shrivelled arm. They might manage to find work as domestic servants. Meanwhile they shared an unheated attic and starved.

There had been a still stout, still glossy shopkeeper from Frankfurt unable to believe he had lost everything. He expected to awake suddenly from his nightmare.

There had been a girl of sixteen from the country near Munich. Her mother and father refused to leave their own elderly parents and had sent her away, or ahead, on her own. She would not be so difficult to place. A strong girl could always scrub floors. She stuttered and trembled so incessantly that she was literally unable to hold a tea cup to her lips.

There was a man called Hans Hahn. Like many of the refugees who turned up at Woburn House, he could not stop talking about his escape. To the staff of volunteers who worked there it was a familiar story in essence if not in detail and they listened with half an ear as they tried to find jobs, homes, missing relations and hope for the stream of displaced people who knew of no other address in this strange land.

Hans Hahn had been unable to get permits or visas to leave his own country or, for that matter, to enter any other, but he had also heard that the British had never yet deported anyone who managed to reach the island.

Part of his journey had been in a horse box. 'Show jumpers travel in luxury, they are far more valuable than we humans,' he said, baring his teeth in a desperate smile. 'And the smell was such a comfort. The horses, even their excreta, like a farmyard. I kept thinking,' he added in a lower voice to one of the men nearby, so the busy women should not hear, 'I kept thinking I could have been in a camp by then, lying in my own shit and vomit instead.'

No one wished to hear the tale. Horrors were piled upon horrors these days. Anyone would go mad who thought too much about the people arrested within yards of a border, or shot as they crossed it; of Barbara who had been drowned trying to swim Lake Constance; of Gerdt who fell to his death at the bottom of an Alpine precipice; of Benjamin whose crushed and bleeding body was found adhering to the roof of a train when it reached Holland; of Felix, discovered asphyxiated in a sail locker on a Danish fishing vessel; of Marthe, her body pierced by bayonets as she lay concealed under bales of hay.

'You're here now, safe,' Irene told him. 'You have to think about the future.' But she knew it was difficult to do so immediately. People needed time for mourning.

Hans Hahn was a neat, narrow figure of a man, medium height and weight, with blue eyes and light-coloured fine hair. He wore a crumpled dark suit with stains that showed signs of inexpert attempts to remove them. He had a black eye and sprained hand. Some Blackshirts had been waiting at Tilbury to give the new Jewish arrivals a taste of London life.

Irene made him rest the swollen hand in an enamel basin of cold water until she could ease a ring from the third finger. She said, 'I don't think anything's broken, but this finger doesn't look quite . . .'

'Don't worry, they have always been the same length. It is a family trait.'

'Oh, good. I was afraid it had been dislocated.'

With his other hand he took the towel to dab her fingers dry before kissing them. 'How can I thank you?'

'It's all part of the day's work.'

'You are English already,' he said, laughing. 'So modest!'

100

Irene sat down to make a note of his particulars. He had been a student of history, he said, originally from Chemnitz.

Hahn. Another refugee, a pharmacist from the same town, said he did not know the name. Where had the family lived?

In a street running beside the local history museum but they moved to Berlin when things got difficult – 'Ach Gott, such times to live in!' interjected the pharmacist – and there he had become involved with left-wing protest groups. What would he do now? God knows. Fight, if he could. There must be people organising resistance over here. Hans could drive a car or carry messages or operate a printing press, anything to be involved and have the chance to strike a blow for freedom.

Irene directed him to a hostel in Stoke Newington and an employment agency that specialised in placing professional people. He might get a post as a clerk. Couldn't he be a translator? Unlikely; they were a glut on the market. Or do something connected with his former work?

Irene had the address of a group of sympathetic dons. Hans might be lucky enough to be taken in at one of the universities. He was in a better position than most refugees. Some had qualifications that were never going to be any use outside Germany. What, for instance, could an elocution coach from a theatre in Darmstadt, who spoke no language but his own, do to earn his living in a foreign country? She told Hans Hahn of a lawyer who had become a rat catcher, an opera singer serving behind the counter of Fairhazel's delicatessen in Goldhurst Terrace, a publisher who sold encyclopaedias door to door. 'We have to do what we can,' Irene said.

Michael was doing better with his journalism at last and had hopes of being taken on to the staff of the *News Chronicle* or the *Manchester Guardian*. Meanwhile he carried on with the job at Searles. Only as a last resort would he accept the help his English relations kept offering. So far he had earned enough to support himself. He knew it was absurd to be so proud. If their situations were reversed, the Berlin Silberschmidts would have done all they could for dispossessed British cousins.

If their situations were reversed . . . it was a common topic of conversation amongst the refugees. Could it happen anywhere after a lost war, economic disaster and social unrest, or was there something unique in the German character that had sent them mad? Could it happen here, in England?

This evening he almost thought it could. The English guests hardly differed from their German hosts in appearance, opinion or behaviour.

It was a last-minute job for Searles, offered to Michael because, unlike the other men on their books, he was accessible on the telephone. He accepted the work although he and Irene were supposed to be going to a reception at Mrs Franklin's that evening. She turned up at Woburn House every week and invited everyone within earshot to her regular parties. So large a proportion of the guests consisted of displaced persons that the entertainments were rather cheerless but kindly meant. This time Irene could go without him.

Tonight's emergency had arisen because the son of the German ambassador was a pupil at Westminster School. There was a measles epidemic there and the boy had given the disease to half the embassy staff.

'The German Embassy?' Michael, who was buttoning the knee breeches over his white stockings, paused. 'I'm not sure . . . '

'Never done an embassy before? Don't worry. It's no different from any other posh place.' The other temporary footman was a professional. He had been a gentleman's gentleman until he married a young lady from a shop who refused to live under any snooty employer's roof. Now they had a tobacconist's in Streatham and were saving up to buy another. John Masters was going to have a chain of emporia before he was through, and working evenings helped towards his goal.

'But . . . '

'What's the matter, mate? Don't like the Huns?'

'Not much.'

'Shake. Me neither, not after what they did to my old dad at bloody Wipers. But the money's good.'

The money was good. The food they served was less so, and made worse by John Masters spitting on the plates he put in front of the German diners.

It was a big dinner party, very formal and pompous, with silver gilt plate and crystal and an army of liveried servants. In their powdered wigs, with their padded calves and constricting collars, the footmen were indistinguishable, which was just as well,

102

Michael thought, since one of the hosts, a member of the diplomatic staff, was a familiar face from Michael's days as a Berlin socialite: Hubertus von Beowulf.

But nobody ever looked at servants. Michael served Hubertus with a drink before the meal, standing within six inches of him. Holding himself with the rigidity of the parade ground, Michael could have been a block of wood rather than a man.

When they were not placing plates and food before the guests with their anonymous white-gloved hands, the footmen waited against the wall of the dining room. The meal was prolonged as course followed course, and Michael had plenty of time to identify and overhear some of the guests, who included a Member of Parliament and his wife, the Marquess and Marchioness of Londonderry, a newspaper proprietor, several Germans who were in England for Wimbledon and Ascot along with others whose purpose and status Michael could not tell.

The Germans were by definition Nazis. Michael stood at attention meditating murder, at once castigating himself for not daring to commit it and telling himself that it would solve nothing if he did.

A jab in the ribs from John Masters's elbow returned him to reality. He served sorbets to glutted diners, poured a sweet Mosel wine.

Poison . . . a stab from one of the carving knives . . . a bash on the head with one of the huge candlesticks . . .

An ice pudding. Frosted grapes.

The host spoke English to his guests with a perfect American accent. His wife stumbled over the language. She wore a high-necked, dull beige dress and looked homely beside the other women whose expanses of skin and impressive jewellery were dazzling.

When the ladies went upstairs, a tall man in the dress uniform of an Uhlan regiment moved to sit beside Hubertus. They spoke in German, discussing a shoot in Canada: wild geese, their habits, their predictability. The growth in skiing – some polite compliments on the prowess of Hubertus's sister. The morale of the army, much better than it had been, the soldiers' eagerness to show Europe what they could do. Wiping out the memory of defeat. The image of Germany abroad, the unfair criticism, the comforting support. The damaging publicity from exiled Germans. Who, where, why . . .

Hubertus mentioned the British readiness to believe the worst of Germany. Propaganda, misinformation, the flood of refugees reciting baseless horror stories.

The Uhlan would be worried about subversion. What were the exiles planning, what contacts still existed within the Fatherland?

'That is indeed a matter of great concern.' Hubertus poured port and passed the decanter clockwise as he had learned in Oxford years before.

'Not that the people who come here could do much. The dregs of the earth,' the Uhlan added.

Hubertus said that he had set a rat trap.

'A very wise precaution. What form does it take?'

'An . . . ' Hubertus hesitated over the word. 'An observer. A person who should have the opportunity to hear what is going on. A distant cousin of my own, as it happens.'

'A Jew?'

'Certainly not.' An angry flush, a hand to the sword hilt.

'I do beg your pardon.'

'A brave man who can pass as one. A little Jewish blood to be sure – on the other side of the family, of course.'

'Of course.'

'Just so we know what they plan. If they have a plan.'

16

Half a century later Celia Roget would say that she began to live on the first day of 1938. Her previous existence no longer seemed to be her own. It was as remote, as alien as the story of a book she had once read or a film she had seen.

Pre- and post-Hubertus.

And during Hubertus: a time of obsession. Never before had Celia lost control of her feelings. She had not believed it was possible; not, at least, for her.

The emotional intensity of those months remained indelibly in her memory. In a way, it was the first thing that Celia Roget really remembered. The girl who had grown up in Norfolk, been educated, trained, passed exams and won competitions, was an intellectual construct. The woman who quivered and thrilled to Hubertus von Beowulf – that was the recreated Celia, a human being with unoriginal reactions who could be touched by, be warm towards objects to which she had previously been indifferent: babies, little animals, an unworthy man. Celia hated to remember it, going hot with embarrassment even years later. She had been ashamed of herself at the time.

Back in Berlin after the short winter holiday, Hubertus had invited her to dinner. They went to the Hotel Adlon. He wore uniform and behaved with impeccable correctness. They ordered and ate, sipped Rhine wine, spoke of impersonal issues, behaved as a diplomat and a dignitary should. Hubertus did not touch her. When he made the hand-kissing gesture on meeting his lips did not brush her skin, but his fingers burned under hers and at moments throughout the meal she rubbed her thumb against the still-tingling spot on her palm.

He invited her to dinner again, and to a reception at his house, and then to ride with him. He sent her flowers, raising her stock with Frau Eberhart, who naturally checked on the sender's name and was much impressed by the titled, crested card.

He touched her. Like teenagers, they sat in his car and embraced. There was plenty of contemporary slang for what they did. They went in for heavy petting. They necked.

Celia had known lovesick girls. At boarding school they had pined in the most innocent possible fashion for the attention of their elders. The fashion was to 'be cracked' on a prefect, dogging her footsteps, offering to carry her books, fetching her bars of chocolate from the tuck shop. Celia had admired a tall, deep-bosomed girl called Sheila who was the captain of the netball team. But she did not want to be loved by Sheila, she wanted to be like her, and knew even then that she never would be.

Later on, no junior had a crush on Celia. It was for the other prefects that a row of little girls waited outside the common room. Celia made them obey the school rules. She had no compunction about administering the few punishments available to prefects and sending malefactors to teachers for other more severe ones.

'They don't like me because I keep them in order,' she told her sloppy, popular friend Pamela. Pamela wanted to be a nurse. She cared about people. She wanted them to be fond of her. 'That's the difference between us,' Celia said. But when she got to Cambridge she too wanted people to like her – men, not the other dreary girls at her college – and men did like her. She became a scalp collector.

'They are more than welcome to love me from afar,' she wrote to Pamela, who was insincerely fending off the medical students at St Thomas's.

Celia did not meet any men at Cambridge whom she wanted and who did not want her. In fact she wanted none of them and assumed herself to be immune from the malady that demented so many of her contemporaries, male and female. She had been inoculated by Michael Silberschmidt. He had turned her into an adult, past the stage of dreams.

What an illusion! Now Celia found herself subjugated. The condition was her admission ticket to the human race. For the first time she understood the words she had learned during that chilly, academic, thorough education, the poetry, the music, the impulse that had launched a thousand ships or lit the fires of Actium. She hummed a sad German song called *Sehnsucht*: yearning. She yearned, not in love, as she knew even then. Not for a person she could ever love, but for an object of desire. Celia wanted to make love to Hubertus. She wanted him to want to make love to her.

Their affair progressed from its first introductory movement to a more passionate second phase. But, in the language of the time, sexual intercourse did not take place. Why? There, and then, one would not have needed to ask the question. This was no longer the louche and licentious Berlin of the Weimar Republic. In any case, Celia was never so overwhelmed by passion as to loosen the bonds of caution.

Looking back later, she had to remind herself how scared she was of pregnancy. How disastrous it would have been and how difficult it was to avoid when the only contraceptives were a Dutch cap or a French letter, neither readily available and both unreliable. Caution was second nature.

So Hubertus and Celia held back from 'going all the way'. She found herself repeating words she had once derided, trite rhymes and combinations of words. Now she understood why love went with dove, moon with June and soon.

She doodled calculations on her blotter, cancelling out the letters in her and her beloved's names and was dismayed to find how few matched. She assigned numbers to the letters' places in the alphabet and added and subtracted until they were reduced to a single digit; and then could not remember which were supposed to be lucky. Once she even wrote Celia von Beowulf on the pink, soggy paper. But immediately she tore it from its holder and then into little fragments which she burned, one by one, in an ashtray.

The stormy third movement: Celia still ached for Hubertus and at the same time hated herself. She hated him.

I hate and I love, she thought. I want to embrace but wish to kill. During those months, as the winter turned to spring, as Hubertus and Celia carried on but did not consummate their relationship, and then as spring turned to summer and they kept their predetermined assignations at irregular hours of the day or night, Celia realised that it was she who wanted him, who needed him. Their intimacy was purely physical. He did not want her as wife or as friend or perhaps even as his mistress. Why did he carry on with her? How did he put on so good a show of wishing to?

107

Celia could not help knowing the answer to those questions. Perhaps they were right, those die-hards who said women would be dangerous in the professions. I am vulnerable because I am a woman. As an intelligent person I realise what is happening and know what I should do. As a lover I am deaf to my own persuasion.

Grimly, repeatedly, and without any doubt that she was right, Celia told herself that she was useful to Hubertus and his masters. He had been told to keep her on a string.

Grimly, repeatedly, and knowing how wrong she was, she ached for his touch. It was a physical aberration, an illness in which Celia's body betrayed her into an irresistible passion that her mind and soul rejected. The essential, intellectual person who was Celia Roget could not desire anything of a man who would use her to further the aims of a regime that was beyond redemption.

There was no pretending that he did not know what he was doing. He believed in his cause and made no secret of the fact. He was a member of the Party, close to its ruling echelon.

Celia and Hubertus did not meet very often. There were dinners, with feet stroking and twining under the table. There was the theatre, when the touch of hand and knee distracted all attention from the stage. They went to parties and behaved as though they were mere acquaintances, to play tennis where their games suffered for – not love; it was never love. For obsession.

Sometimes Celia went to the big house beside the Tiergarten, where the old Baroness presided over the tea tray and Marianne pranced past with her tennis racket swinging, like the heroine of a musical comedy, or trailed by the ambiguous Julian Whitchurch.

Having met him several times, Celia still felt she knew him no better than at first sight. Because he stammered, nothing he said seemed to have any spontaneity, as though he used the speech impediment as a brake on saying what he thought . . . if he thought. So far Celia had not detected any signs of intelligence. He masked any ideas – and perhaps he had none – behind an exaggerated courtesy. The code of manners he used made its object seem less of a person. Celia's conclusion was that he was the sort of man who was uncomfortable with clever women. No wonder he preferred Marianne. Like his German friends, he probably disapproved of females who had escaped from the kitchen, the nursery and the church.

Celia tried to avoid going to Hubertus's home and having to talk to his family or guests. What she wanted from him had to be provided in privacy. And by now she accepted that it was she who wanted and he who provided.

Every time they parted Celia told herself it was for ever. She would deny herself to him ... next time. But again she welcomed him, deferred to him, accepted the little he offered to keep her happy. She surrendered herself to him – in part. Only in part.

Celia was later to look back on her own degradation with incredulity. 'Perhaps he cast a spell on me. But at least I learned something from it.'

It was a useful lesson – that such emotional mastery was a force as powerful as any in the world. If she had not been unusually strong and well-armed against it even she, even Celia Roget, would have been turned from agent into instrument. 'How could I do it? I laid myself open to him as submissively as any Hitler *Mädchen* to her master.' She could never answer the question, either at the time or later. All she knew was that for a time she was in subjection quite as surely as if Hubertus had fixed a slave collar round her neck.

At the end of May Hubertus was posted to the London Embassy under von Ribbentrop. At their last meeting before his departure, Hubertus and Celia went to his house. Marianne was away.

Their self-control gave way. 'After the longest foreplay in history, the shortest consummation,' Celia was to say years later when emotion was blunted. 'And the most disappointing. And embarrassing. A disaster.'

It was a one-off. 'Once I had had him, I didn't want him. Five minutes' pleasure, one month's pain – the pain of worrying whether I was pregnant. Such fear ... my period was late. I planned suicide. But it came; and unlike the poor Queen of Spain, I don't have to end my rhyme, "One month's leisure, then at it again". It was over.'

Hubertus said he would write, and did: stilted little letters about the weather and the theatre, but Celia did not reply. She had nothing to say. Words were not what she had ever wanted from Hubertus, and now, thank God, she did not want anything. It was over and nobody had noticed; she supposed.

'The top of the morning to you, Miss Roget,' Declan Leary said over her shoulder one morning. He had come up behind her as she walked towards the Embassy, silent on his rubber-soled, two-tone shoes. Still, or again, he wore the hairy tweed in which she had first seen him, in this very place two years before. He had become quite bald but for a thin edging of fading ginger hair, and either that or a great increase in lines and wrinkles made him seem an old man.

'Good morning, Mr Leary. Lovely day, isn't it?'

'The weather's fine, sure.'

'Are you going on holiday soon?'

'I have had a week this year.'

'Somewhere nice?' Celia asked politely.

'I went motoring in Thuringia and Saxony, looked at Dresden and the mountains. I believe you know the area yourself.'

'I've been there once, but how do you know?'

'A little bird told me that you stayed with the Baron von Beo-wulf.'

'Do you know him?'

'Know? Hardly. I would think he and I would have very little in common.'

Curious, Celia thought, that this small, undistinguished figure could look momentarily so dignified, so judgemental. She felt her cheeks reddening under his gaze. She changed the subject. 'You must be keeping busy,' she said.

'Isn't that the truth?'

'You ought to take things easier, have another break.'

'Miss Roget.' He stopped on the pavement at the foot of the Embassy steps. Celia placed her white-gloved hand on the balustrade, but waited to hear his murmured words. 'You tell me to take things easy while men like me or women like you are hunted through the country like animals. You may choose to turn a blind eye to what is going on here but I cannot.'

'But what can I do about it? In my position . . .'

'You,' he said with bitter emphasis, 'can evidently do nothing. That is your choice.'

The porter had opened the door. Celia moved towards it. 'You make everything sound so easy,' she said. 'You don't understand.'

'Understand? Oh yes, I understand. Good day, Miss Roget.' He turned and stumped away, a square, ugly, unimpressive man.

At the time Celia felt irritated and even indignant. She ignored him, going on with her work, listing evidence of expansionism, anti-Semitism and militarism; drawing deductions, making assumptions, suggesting, recommending, proposing. She was scrupulously careful to remain unemotional, sending in pages of acute analysis, essays that would have earned her another first-class degree, for the eyes of men not so different from those who had taught and examined her; she knew what would please them, she knew how to make them approve of her, even though she knew also, as she composed her lucid prose, that the only good it would ever do was to Celia's own career.

In July she went home to England for ten days. At Wimbledon's centre court she saw Hubertus with a blonde and blue-eyed beauty. 'That's one of the Mitford sisters,' her mother said, raising her lorgnette to stare.

After the game they met on the way out. Hubertus kissed Celia's hand, lingering over it. 'Can we meet while you are here?' he said. Celia replied that she had to go back to Norfolk and introduced him to her mother. For the remaining days of Celia's stay, Mrs Roget spoke frequently of the Baron's good looks and charm. Her enthusiasm contributed to the waning of Celia's, and she returned to Germany like somebody recovered from a long illness. It was over.

August in Berlin was hot and heavy. Celia felt imprisoned by the oppressive atmosphere and sent in an application to go on a course to learn Roumanian and Hungarian. 'I'm betting that for the next few years the plum jobs will be in Eastern Europe,' she wrote to her family.

September kept Celia and everybody else at the Berlin Embassy so busy that she had mercifully little time for thinking of anything except the political crisis, which concerned the Sudeten Czechs. The resolution of the problem, described by the British Prime Minister as 'peace in our time', was very soon seen to be temporary. It became known simply by one word, 'Munich'.

In October Ambassador Ribbentrop was recalled to Berlin and Hubertus von Beowulf came back at the same time. Celia saw

111

him in the distance at a reception in the Brazilian Embassy, her last formal function before going to England for six months.

She knew every inch of the man, every fold and scar. She could still feel his skin's plastic roughness under her fingers. But no reminder of lust trickled through her body. Instead she was disgusted by the thought of touching him. I'm cured, she exulted silently.

Thaddeus Burton was in Berlin on his way between Perthshire and Poland (grouse and wild boar, he said, enthusing about the sport). But he was a good dancer and Celia agreed to go with him to the latest nightclub. The band was not bad but the cabaret, a much-discussed new attraction for the season, was bland and boring. It was, of course, subject to strict censorship, quite apart from the inevitable retribution faced by its artists if they were so careless as to make spontaneous comments displeasing to the authorities. Thaddeus spoke wistfully of the nightspots he remembered in the Berlin of a few years before. The energy, the colour, the wit, the fun.

'The world is a duller place,' he said solemnly. 'Better but duller.' He drank steadily, and each time they returned to the dance floor his steps were less precise, his guidance weaker.

The club was full. Its clientele was decorous, most of the men wearing some kind of uniform, the women with high necklines and unmade-up faces. Many of them were familiar. This was a fashionable place to come. Hubertus arrived with a small party. His table was in the gallery and he stood and looked down at the dance floor and the tables below. Thaddeus waved at him.

'Shall we join the Beowulfs?' he said. 'Haven't seen the old boy for months.'

'Why not? I'll be with you in a moment.' Celia went to the ladies' room. She looked with distaste at her own reflection. She was out of love with herself, too.

Another woman was leaving her silver fox furs with the attendant. She came to stand beside Celia at the looking glass, leaning forward to scrutinise herself. A bottle blonde with cropped hair. Too much make-up. A gold lamé dress stretched over a tiny, boyish figure. Celia half watched as the girl redrew the bow of her scarlet lips. The eyes were startling with that light hair: amber, with the brows plucked into an thin arch. She wore a strong, musky scent. A high-class tart, Celia concluded, applying her own restrained powder and lipstick.

There were two other women washing their hands. Neither used cosmetics and both looked disapprovingly at those who did before leaving the room. Alone with Celia, the girl said, 'You don't recognise me.'

Celia caught her breath as the other girl said, 'Carla Schmidt. That's my name.'

Charlotte. Little Lotte.

Two more women pushed the door open and went into lavatory cubicles. Celia said, 'It's been such a long time.'

'Summer 'thirty-six. I remember it well.'

'What . . . how . . . ? I mean, where do you live now?'

'I have an apartment in town. It's convenient for entertaining my friends.'

Her meaning was very plain.

'I live well,' she said. Her gaze met Celia's in the mirror, uninterested, indifferent. She picked up her bag, a small, metal envelope. She drew out a large note and threw it into the saucer of coins. Together they left the room and walked along the corridor towards the noise.

'Have you heard anything from –' Celia began.

'I have completely lost touch with everyone from the old days.'

'Perhaps I could tell Michael, or Hanne.'

'Please don't interfere. I have made my own life.'

Berlin was full of young women who lived on their wits and their charms. So many who had lost their families in the war or after it, so many whose families had thrown them out.

Did Lotte blame her mother and brother for abandoning her? Was she in disguise, still dedicated to undermining the regime, or had she become what she seemed, a good-time girl, a prostitute? Celia had no right to speculate. What, she thought painfully, did I ever do to help her? She remembered her previous glimpse of the Silberschmidts' cherished daughter, in trouble and in terror. I let her go then. I didn't help when she needed it. I can't criticise now.

'Carla, there you are!' It was Duggy Dugdale. Did he realise that this was same the girl whom, two years before, he had saved from arrest? How well did he know her? Was he one of her clients?

'Darling!' Her voice was husky and inviting.

'And Celia! What luck. Come and join us.'

'I'm with a friend, I'm afraid.'

'Tadd? He's at our table already. Rather the worse for wear, as a matter of fact.' The two women preceded the Englishman up the stairs. The band was playing a languorous, dreamy tune to which the couples on the dance floor swayed cheek to cheek.

Thaddeus, flushed and sweating, had loosened his white tie. He tried to rise as the women approached but collapsed back on to his chair. Julian Whitchurch and Hubertus von Beowulf stood up.

Carla seemed to know Julian already. Duggy introduced the other people at the table. Baronin von Beowulf. Fräulein Etzdorf – a mousy looking girl in too-bright a blue who giggled every time she opened her mouth. The Baron von Beowulf.

Hubertus looked at Carla. She looked at him. Their eyes, topaz and aquamarine, met and held. Carla's glistening lips parted, her cheeks seemed to flush under the triangle of rouge. There was a moment, an appreciable moment, of silence. Then Hubertus turned to pull back a chair for Carla, to pour her wine, to offer her a cigarette and his lighter. It trembled in his hand. She leaned towards him, eyes still on his, as she sucked in the flame.

The Etzdorf girl said something meaningless about the band. Marianne pointed out a friend who had just come on to the dance floor. Julian Whitchurch and Duggy Dugdale exchanged bland glances. Celia departed quite soon, leaving someone else to get the drunken Yankee home. Neither Hubertus nor Carla had yet spoken. But they had not stopped looking at each other.

Celia wrote to tell Frau Silberschmidt that she had caught sight of Lotte in a crowd. Lotte had not heard Celia calling and had disappeared into the underground railway. But there was no need to worry about her. She looked very well and quite happy. And nobody, Celia did not add, would ever take her for a Jew.

17

After Munich even the phlegmatic British realised that war would come.

At last.

Michael knew his name would be on the black list of those whom the victorious Nazis would remove. Nobody doubted the list's existence. Everybody also assumed that another list was being compiled, of those people who would not oppose the conquerors; or would welcome, help and support them. A white list for the lily-livered? A red list for the bloodthirsty?

Michael had ceased to care that there might be a spy amongst the German refugees.

'Whatever could he find out?' Irene had asked.

Nothing. There was nothing to discover or betray. Nothing that was not or should not be public knowledge.

'Lots of fine talk, but no action . . . except for your friends.'

Michael had laid his hand across Irene's lips. 'Ssh. Don't mention them. Don't even say that much.'

To be naturalised, Irene would have to live in England for five years. Michael predicted that life wouldn't be comfortable for enemy aliens. As his wife, Irene would immediately be entitled to British citizenship. He wanted to get married.

Irene said, 'I would if I could but I can't.' She was married already. She had been seventeen years old. He was eighteen. He had been fighting his true nature, but it was not long before he admitted defeat and went to live with his new boyfriend. Irene's mother had just died. She moved back home to take care of her father, started at the university and put Gerhard out of her mind.

Irene was pregnant.

'You're as good as divorced. Let's get married anyway,' Michael said.

Bigamy was a crime. 'I might be deported.'

'Who would know?'

'I daren't risk it.' But she agreed to change her name by deedpoll and they told Michael's family they had married quietly in private. All the same, Irene was counting the days until the date she could really become an Englishwoman: 13 September 1940.

Irene's daughter, illegitimate though nobody but her parents knew it, was born in February.

'It's a bad time to have a baby,' Irene said.

Michael put his finger to the soft new cheek. 'Has there ever been a time when parents had no fear for their children's future?'

Celia Roget's father had put Michael in touch with a group of young men. Michael immediately recognised Peter Hoyland who had been one of the men disguised as a Nazi officer that day in Berlin.

They arranged to meet at London Zoo. 'Sorry we couldn't get together before. I'm only just back myself,' Peter Hoyland said. It was high summer and the smell of the animals, and the shrieks and murmurs from the crowds, made an incongruous background to the story he told Michael.

'I was supposed to be making the journey from the Channel to the Black Sea by water. Along the Rhine, Ludwig's canal, the Danube. It can be done. A chap called Minshall managed it ten years ago.'

'What for?'

'The sporting young Englishman having his strenuous fun, you know – but really so as to be there with a mobile base we could use as a hideout. I'd inserted the neatest secret compartment, about the size of a small man's coffin, but it didn't work. The Boche has got too suspicious. I managed to keep one chap under cover until we could get him out of the country, but it was no good otherwise. They hauled me in twice on suspicion of spying and then the boat was impounded at Dusseldorf. I gave up and toddled along home.'

The group was loose knit. Michael was not told who all its members were.

'Just some chaps who thought they could help a bit, don't you know? It seemed rather a lark at first. Now, of course, it's something else,' Peter Hoyland said.

'You've got to let me help.'

'What can you do?'

'I can drive, I can speak German, I can fight – there's nothing I won't do.'

'Except set foot in Germany. You couldn't do that.'

'I'd be protected by my passport. I have a British one of my own.'

'Is your naturalisation through already?'

'There was no need. I was born in London when my parents were staying with the English relations. It means I have always been entitled to dual nationality. I ought to be safe enough.'

'Don't you believe it,' Peter Hoyland said grimly. 'I can tell you one thing for certain, old man: it wasn't His Britannic Majesty's jolly old preamble in my passport that got me out, it was my own undoubted innocence. They didn't have anything on me. You see, I hadn't been spying. That wasn't what I was there for.'

He was adamant, as, subsequently, were his friends. The only trip Michael was permitted to make abroad was to Switzerland. The group sometimes used a house in Basle, separated from the fast-flowing Rhine by a narrow towpath.

An elderly Scottish aunt of one of Peter Hoyland's friends was writing a book about the wild flowers of Switzerland and had lived there since before the war. Her home became an informal reception centre for people who had been smuggled through the woods or up the river on freight-carrying barges.

Michael had been asked to go and confirm the identity of a left-wing journalist.

'Old Grizel's a bit worried that he isn't what he seems. There's always a chance they will put a ferret down the hole to flush us out,' Peter Hoyland had explained. 'She can't put a finger on it but something doesn't ring quite true.'

The man was indeed what he claimed. Michael remembered him well, a gadfly writer who had preferred a clever phrase to caution once too often. His time in a camp had altered him, and no wonder. Such an experience changed everyone who survived it. But Michael was certain he would not lead the enemy back to his rescuers, and he did not.

It was arranged for the refugee to settle in France. On the way

117

there by train, alone in his sleeping compartment, he cut his throat with a razor blade and was found dead in the morning.

Since that journey, Michael had chafed at his uselessness. All he could do was collect information, pick up hints, ask questions and pass on information about people who had no hope of visas and the constant fear of arrest.

The other men did the real work. One was Sir Douglas Dugdale, a baronet who wrote about international sporting events for society magazines. Michael remembered him from Oxford. Another was Hugh Wintle, who had driven Michael through Germany back in 1936. He worked in the City, but seemed to need to make regular personal checks on recommended German investments.

Michael was never told who the remaining members of the group were nor which man was its leader. He made guesses but did not tell even Irene what they were. 'If it's who I think it is, better not to say.'

She tried to tease it out of him. 'Anthony Eden,' she said. 'Leslie Howard. No – it has to be someone who goes to Germany and has the confidence of the Nazis. It's the Duke of Windsor!'

'It's no joke,' Michael said. 'Whoever it is, he's a very brave man.'

Irene was to spend the usual three weeks in the nursing home after Anne's birth. For the first two she would not be permitted to put foot to the ground. Parturient women were at risk of haemorrhage, prolapse and even death if they disobeyed.

On the second evening of her confinement, Hugh Wintle came to the flat in Gray's Inn Road where Michael and Irene now lived.

'I wouldn't ask you,' he said. 'The trouble is there simply isn't anyone else.'

'I keep telling you I want to go into Germany myself,' Michael said. 'The sooner the better. I'd like to be back before Irene leaves hospital.'

He was to travel on a passport borrowed from a school friend of Peter Hoyland. 'Not your brother's, this time?'

'No, it's been in and out of the country too often. This one is a chap called Oliver Watson's. He's so blond, your hair will do, but you'll have to wear glasses, and put pads in your cheeks. Luckily Watson was sporting a showy sort of moustache when the passport photograph was taken. Thank the good Lord for spirit gum.

The mouth is always the hardest detail to disguise. Watson was in the Fatherland for the long vac. last year. That's when he'll have done his courting.'

Michael was to get married. The paperwork had been completed and arrangements made at the British consulate in Munich. His new 'wife' would acquire Oliver Watson's nationality and his right to leave Germany and enter England.

'She's been involved in an underground protest group, and now her friends have been picked up. They'd have got her too if she hadn't been away, and her identity won't be a secret for long.' There was no need to spell it out. After a pause for gruesome thought, Peter went on, 'She's hiding in Nürnberg. We got a message to her saying where to meet you. She'll be carrying a violin and a bunch of white flowers. You must be carrying your hat and a copy of the *Morning Post*. You'll be wearing a British Warm greatcoat and a white flower in your buttonhole.'

'Oliver Watson' travelled via Calais. He saw two people he knew on the ferry. Lisbeth Silversmith was escorting her younger daughter Heather to a finishing school in Paris, and one of the men in the queue at Dover was Hans Hahn.

It was impossible to avoid him. Now a research fellow at King's College, Cambridge, Hahn had rapidly learned excellent English and the two men, both superficially Anglicised, spoke in that language. Hahn congratulated Michael on the birth of his daughter. 'I paid Irene a quick visit on the way through London this morning. She didn't tell me you were travelling abroad. Going far?'

'I have to see someone in Geneva,' Michael said.

'Ah yes, your journalism. I read you religiously.'

Irene liked Hans Hahn. What did women see in the man? Small, narrow-shouldered, insignificant, dapper, he seemed . . . what was the word? Sly? Crafty?

'You're jealous,' Irene had told him, laughing. 'You left out what he really is. Sexy.'

'Sexy?' Michael had exclaimed.

'It's something to do with the way he looks at one. He's absorbed, attentive, as though the woman he's concentrating on were the only person in the world who mattered. It makes him irresistible.'

'I can't see it myself,' Michael grumbled.

119

'Well, you wouldn't, would you?' She held her arms open to him above her jutting belly. 'Don't worry, he's not my type.'

Now Michael looked down at the smaller man and said, 'What about you?'

'I have some family affairs to see to. Just a quick trip.'

'Not so easy for you to travel, is it?' Michael was ashamed of himself as soon as the words left his lips. Pure chance had given Michael the inestimable prize of a British passport and it ill became him to have remarked on the difficulties faced by those, amongst whom he might so easily be numbered, who had to travel on temporary papers. He said hastily, 'Look, come and have a drink. I want to hear about Cambridge. How do you compare the university systems? I might be doing an article about it for the *Manchester Guardian*. Let me pick your brains.'

The two men were separated at Calais when the English Michael Silversmith passed more quickly through immigration control than a stateless Hans Hahn. He boarded the train and sat making notes. He needed to see his thoughts on paper to reach conclusions.

Confidence, arrogance, assurance, he scribbled, looking for the word to express his own attitude as he was waved past by the official who saw his blue and gold passport. As a British subject he felt humbly grateful, but also in some way innately superior in the same way that a pedigree dog was superior to a mongrel, a king to a commoner.

He observed his own pride because he remembered his shame. During those three years in Berlin after the Nazis came to power and before Michael escaped, he, even he, had almost learned to believe the Nazi libel. On every street corner, every day, the new edition of *Der Sturmer* was displayed in a glass case for passers-by to read its ravings about the Jewish enemy within. From every loudspeaker insults were bellowed forth. Had he begun to be persuaded, too, to believe that he was indeed inferior? Surely not. Certainly not. But subconsciously, imperceptibly . . . yes, he had to admit to having felt it, just as he had felt, this evening, superior on account of his new nationality.

One must confront such thoughts to defeat them, he reminded himself. Bunching his doodled notes into an envelope, he left the train to post them and his own passport back to London and waved to Hahn, now trotting to the other platform where the train for Paris waited. It would arrive tomorrow in forbidden Berlin.

'Oliver Watson' emerged the next day into a chilly mist and the familiar smell of garlic, smoke, sausage and the sickly emanation of sewage. Michael Silberschmidt was assailed by nostalgia and nervousness. He had been to Nurnberg once before, on holiday at the age of seventeen with his father. They had taken a cruise up the Rhine.

He remembered a happy week: Viennese waltzes played by a string trio; trout chosen as they swam in a tank and served within ten minutes; reading Thomas Mann's newly published *The Magic Mountain*; visiting Cologne cathedral; tasting wine at vineyards that ran to the water's edge. Another passenger had fed him on ripe peaches, peeled, pricked all over with a fork and placed in a glass of champagne. A man had a heart attack and Dr Silberschmidt left the chess board to tend him. In Nürnberg father and son had strolled into the old town and ordered Steinhagers at a beer cellar.

Oliver Watson had never been there before. He crossed the rebuilt bridge towards the cathedral staring around like a sightseer, stepping off the pavement to let the plump ladies pass, dodging under dangling wursts and Alpenstocks and past the protruding menus outside every beer hall. The houses in this ancient part of town were built of varicoloured bricks laid at angles like children's blocks. At first-floor level they protruded over the street, a hand clasp away from their neighbours.

The rendezvous was to be outside a cake shop next to the most famous of the beer cellars, the ancient Drei Hasen. Michael was early. He intended to have a drink first while he read his paper.

When these streets were built, the widest load to use them was a donkey with laden panniers. Now the gleaming black metal of a Party official's car filled the whole space outside the Drei Hasen. Passers-by and patrons edged between it and the walls. The chauffeur sat stiffly at the wheel, his glance darting from person to person.

Michael went inside. The beer cellar's atmosphere had changed since smoking was forbidden by government decree, but the centuries-old roof beams were still black and under them the long tables were arranged in parallel lines, close together and now almost fully occupied. All the customers were men, most wearing leather shorts or uniform and singing in short, patriotic, slightly drunken bursts. At the far end of the room three Party officials sat alone at a table big enough for thirty. On each wall hung a large portrait of the Führer.

Michael found a misshapen three-legged stool at a small table in a corner by the window. He said, 'A beer, please.'

'*Ein Viertel stark dunkel für den Herr.*'

'Sorry, I don't speak German.'

The beer was black and served in tiny glasses on a battered pewter tray. The waiter lifted the glass from the tray and stood frozen in mid-movement. The Party officials were leaving. The other customers clattered to their feet. The leading officer stuck his arm out. '*Heil Hitler!*' A passionate chorus repeated the words. Three pairs of polished boots marched in unison across the stone floor. A heel struck a spark from the stones.

Michael stayed seated. The waiter slammed the glass down in front of him, splashing half its contents on to the table. He did not wipe it up, but muttered '*Engländer!*' as though it were an imprecation.

Michael watched through a small fault in the thick, bottle glass of the window as the three men, moving like marionettes, took their places. They sat stick-straight and stared forwards under the deep peaks of their hats.

As the large car drew away the street came back to life, like a warren after the stoat has gone. Shoppers and shopkeepers resumed their business. A street sweeper pushed his broom over the cobble stones. A girl carrying a violin case and a white bouquet wrapped in tissue paper passed the window, walking slowly. She paused, strolled up and down, stood waiting. She wore a dark coat and a small close-fitting hat under which very fair hair curled over her ears. She was tall and thin, and moved with an athletic grace that was both attractive and familiar.

I know her, Michael thought. I have seen her before.

It was time for him to go out and meet her. The newspaper, three days old, was on the table before him, the white flower in his buttonhole, the train to Munich due to leave in less than an hour. He paused, racking his brains. Had she been part of those groups of voluble, left-wing students with whom he used to spend long, smoky, drunken or drugged evenings in the old

Berlin? But she looked too young for that. A school friend of Lotte's?

The painful, useless thought of his sister, and the recognition of the girl collided in his mind. Not Berlin, but Oxford.

Eights Week. Picnics, punts, college dances, champagne on ancient lawns beside brilliantly coloured and sweet-scented flower beds; girls in dresses that floated in the light breeze; dawn over the dreaming spires.

She was Marianne von Beowulf, the sister of Beowulf of Balliol. Michael had danced with her at the Christ Church Ball.

It was past time for their meeting. The girl was looking at her wristwatch, tapping her foot, smelling her flowers, looking up and down the street. Even if she stared into the window of the Drei Hasen, she would not be able to identify faces behind that mottled glass. Michael beckoned the waiter and said, 'Another beer, please. *Bitte.*'

The sister of Hubertus von Beowulf could not possibly be a left-wing opponent of the regime, on the run and in fear of her life.

She was bait. She was there to trap him.

She was still waiting when Michael came out of the beer cellar, his steps artistically unsteady, twenty minutes later. His light hair was concealed under a brown trilby; his coat still hung on a hook in the lavatory and he had flushed the white carnation away and left his newspaper on the table. He turned into the street away from the girl, who could see only his back. Walking quickly, he reached the railway station just in time to jump on to the Munich train. By midnight he was in the Oberer Reinweg in Basle, knocking on Grizel Dugdale's front door.

18

The Berlin to which Celia Roget came back in the summer of 1939 felt completely different from the city she had known. Her return had been delayed because when the language course was nearly over she went down with glandular fever and was forced to spend several weeks with her parents in Norfolk.

She was passing through on her way to a new posting in Bucharest. On crossing the border into Germany, she immediately sensed impending catastrophe. There were more hate-filled posters than ever, papers with two-inch headlines, raucous loudspeakers broadcasting abuse of the Jews all day long, and of a new enemy, the Poles. Mobilisation had started and the streets were full of even more uniformed men, flags, bunting and patriotic advertisements.

Frau Eberhart greeted Celia with a kind of sniffy triumph: now you'll see what we Germans are made of.

The Embassy resounded to war talk. Work there seemed to consist largely of making preparations to stop work. Even those officials who had been dedicated to maintaining their professional aloofness allowed themselves to become patriotic and partisan. A few, Lockwood included, still spoke of averting disaster. He could not believe that the British government would be so foolish as to plunge into war again for the sake of some Slavs and a few Jews. But most of the diplomatic staff behaved as though they were living on borrowed time.

Some of Celia's acquaintances were no longer there. Mrs Tozer's husband, a representative for Cook's Tours, had reached retirement age and the couple were now living in Folkestone. Mrs Tozer's place had been taken by a pretty, bossy young woman who had formerly worked for the cultural attaché. She seemed to have time to gossip.

Did Celia know that Mr Lockwood's wife had gone back home again, pregnant for the fourth time? They were hoping for a son at last. Had Celia heard that Mr Jones of Chancery had been caught by the First Secretary *in flagrante delicto* with his typist and been posted to Ulan Bator in disgrace? Did she know that the man from the Consulate always called our oldest inhabitant, having been stationed in Berlin since Methuselah – 'Do you mean Declan Leary?' Celia interrupted, and the other girl paused briefly in her flow of talk to agree; well, Mr Leary had been found out. He had issued ever so many passports and visas that he shouldn't have done, and the worst part was that he destroyed his records so nobody could catch up on the illicit immigrants at home and send them back. 'Hundreds, they said, if not thousands. Wasn't that awful?' Of course he had got the sack at once; instant dismissal, without even time to clear his desk. A sympathetic clerk had sent his pots of cacti after him.

Celia's former desk and office were occupied by a pale, fleshy man called Cyril Clumber Robinson who made no secret of hate at first sight.

Celia had been a bit of a one, ha ha. Gone in for a bit of fratting, he had heard. Fraternisation with the natives, ha ha. That was what came of letting women into the office. He could have told them it would never work.

Celia had some engagements over the next week, but not enough to fill her days. She spent some time walking round Berlin. She paid farewell visits to her favourite museums but did not go into the once-magnificent department stores, N. Israel and Wertheim, which had been expropriated and renamed. Later she sat for the last time at tables on the pavements outside familiar cafés, and was often recognised as English.

She sensed hostility. Elbows jabbed into her ribs, heavy shoes stamped on her toes, doors swung back into her face. A man in brown uniform, with shiny boots and a pillbox hat, blocked her way across a road until she gave money for the Winter Help campaign. Groups of men in other uniforms marched, singing, along roads applauded by passers-by. 'That's what you're up against,' an onlooker told her gleefully.

At the zoo a keeper gestured Celia to go away. 'I was only looking at the pelicans,' she protested.

'You have no right. They will have to be destroyed when you attack us. Go on, get out of here. English!'

In the Grünewald the scent of pine trees was overwhelming. The great wood looked peaceful and summery, a vast pleasure park for the city's inhabitants; but here, Celia knew, hunted Jews and dissidents had hidden day and night.

Celia walked along a soft-surfaced path towards the wooden hut where the Silberschmidts used to have picnics in happier days. Michael's grandfather had built it with his own hands, taking delight in his artisan's skill. It stood in a clearing he had made himself near a small, muddy, reed-fringed pond where the sun fell only in the morning.

The family loved it for its snugness, its woody smell, for the fun, the freedom of their days there when rules were left behind.

The hut was still standing, its cheerful red-checked curtains drawn across inside each shuttered window. In this law-abiding country property was safe, even when its owners were not.

It was impossible to see into the tiny room, in which Celia remembered no furniture other than a pine table and four upright chairs with heart shapes carved into their backs. Celia went up the three steps to the porch that ran the length of the structure. On its railing they used to hang their wet costumes after bathing in the pond on the far side of the clearing. Someone else had hung a towel here today, a small white piece of cloth like a baby's napkin.

This was where Frau Silberschmidt would play at being a pioneering mother, producing food from great hampers. She used to enjoy the simple life so long as it lasted only a very short time.

Even in this little playhouse of a home, she had been surrounded by *Gemütlichkeit* and the security of tradition. Here her husband had taken his first steps, here both Michael and Lotte had done so, barefooted on the soft grass; here, she used to predict, her grandchildren would do the same. 'That's what my mother says when we go to the seaside,' Celia had said. That was what mothers said.

Was this a hiding place now for hunted fugitives? A rustle in the bushes to one side. Was that a face peering at her? Should she speak, tell them not to worry, promise that she presented no threat? No; keep quiet, keep clear, keep out. I can't help. It's nothing to do with me.

She walked on to another clearing, another pond, on which the sun shone at this time of day and sat down on a tree trunk seat beside a bank of palest pink wild roses. Several people sat or walked or lay sunbathing nearby. Two small naked children played in the rushes at the water's edge. It was an Arcadian scene, but Celia thought how glad she would be to get away from Germany. It had been poisoned. Hubertus would be the enemy soon. Good.

She promised herself there would be no emotional involvement in Bucharest. It was a place without memories or associations for her. She would keep her distance. The post was a step up, but again, of course, Celia would have to fight for her rights. That was a life sentence.

'Celia!'

It was as though three years had been a dream. Suddenly Celia was back at the Silberschmidts' house, the young Charlotte hissing from her concealment under a willow tree. A dream?

No: it was Charlotte Silberschmidt herself. She had bare legs and a cretonne summer frock. Her hair was dark at the roots, her fingernails unpainted.

'Carla?' Celia said, hesitating. 'Lotte?'

Tears spouted from Charlotte's tawny, red-rimmed eyes. She stepped forward and knelt to fling her arms around Celia, pressing her wet face into her neck, her body heaving with deep sobs. Awkwardly Celia patted her back and murmured, 'Don't cry.' Then she said, 'There, there.' And soon, 'I told your family we met last autumn. I saw Michael in London. He's married, did you know? They had a daughter. You're an aunt.'

After a while Charlotte pulled back and sat on the fallen tree beside Celia. She took a handkerchief from her pocket and mopped her face.

'Sorry about that. I don't usually. It was because seeing you reminded me,' Charlotte said.

'You don't look very well,' Celia said.

'I'm all right now. I was ill for a while after – ' The thin hand gestured towards a pram.

'You've had a baby?' Celia exclaimed.

Speaking very softly, Charlotte told Celia what had been happening to her during the last few months.

Hubertus von Beowulf had been violently attracted to her. 'You were there, Celia. You must have noticed. You had a personal interest, didn't you?'

Celia blushed violently and turned her head away. There was

a smell of woodsmoke, a faint blue curl rising behind the trees. She said, 'You seemed to like him yourself, I thought.'

'Yeah, convincing, wasn't it? I may be a tart but I can act. I'm not like you, Celia, bowled over by a handsome face. I knew exactly what I was doing. That meeting had been arranged.'

'You mean Dug – '

'No names.'

'Sorry. But why did you want to meet Hu . . . him?'

'To get close to his friends. I thought he'd take me with him to see . . . people.' She edged closer to Celia and whispered, 'I always carried a knife.'

'What for?'

'To kill *him*.' In English she hissed the two words, 'The Leader.' Then reverting to German, she went on, 'I pretended to worship him. You should have heard me! I slobbered over the right hand that had touched *his* precious flesh, I ranted about my ambition to see *him* in the flesh. Hubertus believed me, too. It should have worked. He kept promising to arrange it. Sometimes true worshippers had the honour, and then I could have got close enough to – '

'But what would have happened to you?' Celia exclaimed. 'The danger!'

'I didn't care. It would have been worth everything.'

Celia took the thin, clammy hand in hers. 'I'm glad you never got the chance. It makes my blood run cold to think of it. In any case, assassination would not have been the solution.'

'You think not?' Lotte said. 'I don't agree. But there is no point in considering it now. It's finished. When my "friend" found out who I was he turned me out of the apartment. I don't know who told him. Was it you?'

'I haven't spoken to Hubertus since that time at the nightclub.'

'Someone wrote to him, just before the baby. Of course, he assumed it was his, a *Mischling*, a Jewish baby for the Aryan Junker. He said I was filthy and disgusting and I'd defiled his blood, and anyway screwing a Jew is a criminal offence.'

'But Lotte, whose is it then? If you were living with him?'

'What a question to ask a whore!' Lotte said derisively.

Celia could not conceal her horror. 'Do you mean you don't know yourself?'

Lotte got up and walked over to the pram to lift the swaddled bundle in her arms, momentarily pressing the small cheek against her own. 'Here,' she said.

Celia reluctantly accepted the warm, damp creature. 'I didn't know they were so small,' she said. The lolling head was about the size of a small grapefruit.

'You've never held one before? You have to support the head,' Lotte said. The eyelids were closed. There was a tiny, snub nose, a well-shaped, full-lipped mouth, hands the length of one of Celia's finger joints.

'How sweet it smells,' Celia murmured.

Lotte smiled, her lips closed; a secret, knowing, archaic smile. 'Somebody's having a fire. Dangerous, when it's so dry. I'd better pick up my jacket. I left it over there.' She moved across the glade. The shaft of sunlight fell on to her head. From this distance she looks like the young girl I remember, Celia thought. She turned her attention back to Lotte's child. Perhaps one could identify the features: the tiny ears, the straight, strong eyebrows . . .

A shout interrupted Celia's musings. Four uniformed officers surrounded Lotte. The other people who had come to enjoy the summer afternoon in the greenwood retreated, eyes averted, gathering their children close, picking up their rugs and clothes from the grass, escaping from contamination, from danger, from the fear of being involved.

The fire, wherever it was, had caught hold. Celia could hear it crackling. Other, more distant shouts could be heard in the distance.

Celia sat paralysed, clutching the baby. It began to wail, a slight, high-pitched sound.

One man from the small crowd of bystanders came forward. He seemed to be asking a question. His outstretched hand was knocked away by the leather-gloved fist of one of Lotte's captors, who snapped some words Celia could not catch. Another officer drew his revolver from the waist holster and gazed fiercely around the clearing. He saw Celia staring.

'What do you think you're looking at?' he shouted. 'Mind your own business. Keep your baby quiet.'

Celia half stood, glancing desperately around. What should she do? The clearing was empty now, except for the four men and the girl. In the trees to the side a few fleeing onlookers had paused to look back. Among them was a face Celia knew: Julian

Whitchurch. He panted and sweated like a man who had been running but stood still, grim-faced, watching as the men took Charlotte away.

She went with them without argument or struggle. She did not look back.

Celia was left holding the baby.

At the end of August Michael Silversmith received a message about his sister Charlotte.

It was an appeal for rescue which got through to the refugee centre at Woburn House. The message mentioned 'The picnic spot', a reference Charlotte's brother would presumably understand.

Hans Hahn had been on duty when it arrived. He was away for two days after that, and on his return told everyone concerned that he had sincerely advised Michael not to take any action. There was no certainty that the message really came from Charlotte Silberschmidt. Like Chinese whispers, it had been passed on by so many carriers that it was almost certainly garbled. In any case the time gap between her cry for help and any possibility of answering it meant she would no longer be in the same place.

Michael told Irene but not Hanne. He left London on the evening of 30 August. He had decided to enter and leave Germany from Switzerland and he went to lunch the next day with Grizel Dugdale in Basle, leaving her house in the early afternoon.

Irene never heard from him again.

On 1 September the German Army invaded Poland.

On 2 September the Honourable Julian and Mrs Whitchurch arrived unannounced at his ancestral home with their daughter of three weeks. They had married at the British Embassy in Berlin and been travelling in Europe on a prolonged honeymoon. Their child was born prematurely while they were still abroad.

The Viscount Blanchminster was pleased that at least one of his children had at last decided to settle down. His elder son and heir seemed to prefer horses to women; his daughter was a flibbertigibbet. He had no children by his second wife. It was time there was another generation, though a pity the first one was a girl. Better luck next time, he said.

Julian's nanny, who still lived at Blanchminster, was delighted to have a new generation to care for and took charge of the baby with instant efficiency.

War was declared on 3 September.

PART III
WAR
and
POSTWAR

19

18 January 1991: To find myself on this date writing about a war of long ago today seems a curious and dreadful irony. It is the second day of what history may call the Iraqi War or perhaps the Jihad or even the last crusade. By the time I have finished this book we may know. I dread reading these words with hindsight.

For this is the day on which reports say gas-filled missiles have landed on Tel Aviv and Haifa.

In the small hours of the morning my friend Rachel rings to tell me. Horrified tears spout from my eyes. To gas the Jews . . . it is fifty years since the juxtaposition of those monosyllables acquired their dread meaning.

I return to bed and lie still in the darkness, ashamed of my immunity.

What must the nights have been like for my mother, alone in blitzed London, thinking of her friends and family, defenceless against their enemies?

She had sent me away.

Michael had disappeared. Irene was penniless. She had good cause for post-natal depression, now she was alone with a new baby. Both mother and child were in a bad way when Aunt Lisbeth Silversmith came to call in the third week of September.

Irene and Anne were whisked off to shelter in Wiltshire. A Silversmith daughter, Hazel Montagu, whose husband was in the Army, had gone to live there with her sons aged five and four and their nurse. During the phoney war it seemed safe enough.

Then the Germans moved westwards through Europe. Holland, Belgium, France . . .

The trickle of British children being evacuated across the Atlantic grew to a flood. Jack Montagu's aunt lived in New London, Connecticut, and invited his family to stay for the duration.

Hazel Montagu, the nurse, the two boys and the baby girl set off together in May 1940.

Do not pity me. I remember nothing about it, or about the years I spent in America or about the journey home.

Pity my mother.

Two weeks later Irene was arrested as an enemy alien; she was not yet naturalised, and living in sin with Michael had not conferred his rights of citizenship upon her. She was taken to an internment camp in the Isle of Man.

Irene spoke lightly of the experience afterwards, saying that her time there was as good as two terms at university. Many of the internees were academics, scholars, professional people, musicians and artists and if only to save themselves from going mad with boredom they taught, performed and argued. Irene became interested in the archaeology of the area at classes given by an internee from Germany called Bersu, and began to read philosophy after hearing Steinhauser lecture. Hans Hahn gave seminars on European history – the rise and (please God) fall of tyrants. Irene was taught to do gros point embroidery by a former naval surgeon. And sooner than some, if not as early as others, she was released and returned to London, where she eventually got a job organising the cleaning and maintenance of government offices.

What was her daily life like? Was she racked with anguish and longing for Michael or for Anne? Was she afraid?

Perhaps she found lovers.

I do not know. I do not wish to know.

In later years she occasionally mentioned rationing or power cuts or air raids. During one my grandmother Hanne Silberschmidt died from a heart attack. But Irene never talked about emotions, her own or mine.

She must have written to me. My hosts must have written to her. No letters have survived. Nothing is left from those years except a few black-and-white photographs: Anne as a toddler with a beaming smile, Anne aged three holding a doll, Anne at five carrying a school satchel, Anne wistful, missing – what? Her home, her mother, the parents she cannot remember?

And suddenly a whiff of recollection: a man with a camera –

'Smile for the birdie and I'll give you a Hershey bar' and then, 'Sit here, honey, look as though you are longing for something . . . maybe you're waiting for a train. That ole train's been a long time a-coming. Look, thataway, up the line . . . Some day my train will come,' he sings. I want him to think I'm a good girl. I want approval, Auntie Mamie's approval, Aunt Hazel's, Nanny's; Bob's and James's. I stare into the distance.

Aunt Hazel took Bob and James back to school in England before the end of the war. Anne was left at Auntie Mamie's as long as the Montagus' nanny was willing to stay there too, but in 1945 she got a job with a show-business family and moved to California and Anne – I – was sent home in a party of other child evacuees. The journey was by sea to Lisbon, then by flying boat to somewhere in southern England and on to London by train.

I remember that. The harsh fabric of the seats against the back of my bare legs. The floor thick with cigarette stubs and torn paper. The stale smell of British bodies – no deodorants then, and soap on coupons; the competing stink of sulphur from the steam engine. I brushed my doll Babette's golden curls and arranged her new pink clothes so she should look her best. Babette had a little trunk of her very own. Auntie Mamie had given it to me as a leaving present.

I was to wait in the compartment, they said, until my mummy came to find me. I was very much afraid she would not recognise me.

Irene recognised Anne. My mother recognised me.

'Awful, you looked,' she told me later. 'Long, matted ringlets, lots of fake jewellery, a sickly pink dress covered with frills and furbelows. The very first thing I did was take you to the hair-dresser.'

My hair was cut short, my fancy dresses exchanged for grey flannel divided skirts and sensible hand-knitted jerseys. The jewellery disappeared, ear studs and all. The holes in my ears took longer to close up than my American accent to disappear, for I acquired protective colouring very fast, learning not to mention candy, Coke, chewing gum or even bananas.

Irene had started a domestic agency, supplying cleaners, servants and mothers' helpers. It was a difficult time. The first postwar winter was the coldest within living memory. There were power cuts, gas cuts, a coal shortage. Food rationing was more severe than it had been during the war itself.

In the immediate aftermath the news from Europe was so appalling that there were days when Irene could not bring herself to read it. She made sure I did not see the pictures in the papers or, once I had caught up with English children and could read, that I did not read them. Years later I wondered why Irene had been and remained so reticent. 'I didn't want another generation's life to be poisoned as my own was,' she said.

It took a long time before Irene learnt the fate of her friends and relations. Names trickled through gradually; names of those who had perished in concentration camps; names of those who had simply disappeared; sightings of a few – tragically few – who seemed to have survived.

Of Michael there was no news at all. Anything was possible. In one of the transports from the East, in some benighted hospital, in an obscure corner of liberated Europe, there might be Michael or at least some word of him.

His name was added to the Red Cross lists, broadcast on its Search Service. 'Cristoph and Hildegarde Schmidt, twins aged ten, blond, wearing matching red jumpers, last seen on February the first nineteen forty-five waiting to cross the bridge at Dirschau . . . Ilse Hoffman, seven, dark-haired, blue woollen cap and gloves, last seen in a crowd outside the railway station in Stettin . . . Michael Silberschmidt, last heard of September the third nineteen thirty-nine.'

Somebody, somewhere must know what had happened to him after he said goodbye to Grizel Dugdale and travelled with his borrowed papers and his dyed hair from Switzerland into the Third Reich.

Irene had contacts in the Control Commission. Hans Hahn was one.

It was not until many years later that those who had taken part in the administration of Germany after its defeat began to publish their memoirs of the experience.

After Hans Hahn was released from internment in the Isle of Man he joined the Alien Pioneer Corps, its 'gravedigger's badge' showing a crossed spade and pickaxe to signify the wearer's noncombatant role. He was posted to Berlin as a member of the Control Commission in 1945 and kept a diary in which he recorded his schizophrenic state of mind on returning to the country where he had grown up and from which he had been forced to escape. He had to try to reconcile pity and loathing, revenge and hope.

Hans inevitably met German acquaintances of pre-war days, though his own home was now in the Russian zone. His family had not survived. 'I was an Englishman,' he explained later. 'I wanted to dissociate myself from the enemy. But even I soon learned to go beyond the strict regulations. Nobody took any notice of the orders that prohibited fraternisation and the sharing of the allies' food.' He wrote that it was taken for granted among the British that humanity must temper the strict application of regulations.

'It was their habit of automatic obedience that had brought the Germans to their present state. No wonder many independent-minded allied personnel acted as we thought best, so long as we could get away with it. Soon I was taking the chance to pull strings or cut corners to help with a prisoner's swift rehabilitation or release. I am not ashamed to confess that I gave help to former friends. I was not alone in doing so. Perhaps we shall even now be called to account, but I did and do not have any qualms about my behaviour. We should have been no better than our enemies if we had behaved otherwise.'

By the middle of 1946, Hans was a first lieutenant. As in London before the war and even in the internment camp, he made friends easily and it was, as it later proved, a fruitful period in the young historian's career. He made useful contacts, among them Julian Whitchurch who introduced Hans to some American friends. They later invited him to teach at Harvard.

On a weekend break in Heidelberg, which was the headquarters for the American zone, Hahn met Thaddeus Burton; many years later he became a benefactor to Hans Hahn's Cambridge college. Burton, described by Hahn as a 'pre-war playboy', had served on Eisenhower's staff and was now beginning to take an interest in his family's newspaper empire. He had arranged for Celia Blanchminster to go to Germany with a commission to write 'colour pieces' about the state of the defeated nation. It was her first journalistic assignment, and her first article appeared below her by-line in Burton's *Biweekly Magazine*.

Social life in ruined Berlin, full as it was of conquered and conquerors of many nationalities, she described as village-like with its gossip and parties and interlocking circles of acquaintances. Everyone knew what everyone else was up to.

Hans Hahn's work was cheerless. He dealt with human wrecks trickling westwards, unrecognisable and many of them incurable.

Rumours abounded. Hitler had appeared, or Bormann. A grave had been found of the one, a witness had come forward to testify to the fate of the other. Officials would be summoned to reception centres: take a look at this man, we need a second opinion. Is he good or bad, victim or villain? Lies, incomprehension and misery made the possibilities endless; people had to be checked against lists of those wanted by the Army, by the legal system, by sorrowing families. Lost children, lost parents, lost siblings, and among them men (nearly always men) whose chief aim was to remain unfound. Tattoos, name tags, claims and denials. Changed identities, lost identities, escapes and retrievals. It was a chaotic time.

'A rumour reached me that Michael was on a transport from the East, but it was nothing more. He was not there,' Hans wrote to Irene.

Hans would make enquiries. So would Jack Montagu, now a brigadier.

But apparently there was nothing to know. Michael seemed to have vanished off the face of the earth.

Meanwhile other women's husbands were coming back from the war. Irene found herself alone with a daughter who was a stranger. She had little experience of children and was not sure what to expect of her own. Anne distracted her. Anne made demands that Irene did not know how to meet. It was no life for a child alone with her mother in a two-roomed flat, in which Irene slept on the living room couch. Anne must go to boarding school.

The Abbess of Whitby's Academy was recommended by the Silversmiths, who also offered to help with the school fees. I started there in the autumn of 1946.

Irene's agency specialised in matching servantless English employers with desperate German domestics. The fashion for employing young women 'au pair' had not yet started. The Germans who were granted visas to work in English homes came as maids and were glad to have the chance.

But it was not through Irene's agency that Marianne Beowulf came to England.

She had reached Berlin a few months after the end of the war, having walked from the East with a group of other displaced persons. Hunger, destitution and the experience of rape melted class barriers. The small group of fugitives included women of all kinds and, until some died on the road, of all ages. When they got to Berlin they joined other women in clearing rubble with their bare hands or queueing for pitiful provisions.

Marianne was recognised by a member of the occupying army. 'God knows how he knew it was me,' she said much later, laughing at the memory. 'I didn't look a bit like the pampered girl he'd last seen before the war. Filthy, emaciated, cold, hungry – well, it was the same for everyone. I wasn't any different. Devastation created democracy.'

Le Comte de Savary had picked her out of a gang of women passing cobble stones along a human chain. Marianne did not want to leave the other women. She had made no attempt, on reaching Berlin, to find her old friends or gain any privileges. The von Beowulfs' large house had disappeared into a crater in the ground. Marianne lived with other refugees in a boarded-up and half-roofless shack. She did not mind. The circumstances seemed appropriate, here at the end of her world.

She told de Savary to leave her be, but he persuaded her to come to his house. She put as much of the meal as she could in her pocket for the other women.

'I was groping my way out of a fog,' she wrote later. 'I lacked proper education, I didn't have the language or the frame of reference to be sure what I was thinking myself, let alone to put it into words. But the experience of the war had opened my eyes. You couldn't live through that time without realising how false everything had been before. And I wanted to know why. I needed some explanation, some reason, some way of understanding what had happened to the world. I told de Savary that if I lived I intended to spend the rest of my life trying to explain it.'

He pulled strings to help her start at the university, where she chose to study history, and in the autumn of 1946 was one of half a dozen Germans given the chance to spend a year at the University of London.

Marianne arrived with one small bag that contained all her belongings. Her hair, once so fair, was white. She had lost some teeth from untreated decay. Two had been knocked out when she was raped by some Russian soldiers; the same episode had left her with a permanent weakness of the hip joint and she walked with a slight limp. She would not ski again and her Olympic medals were irretrievably lost in the Russian-occupied zone. They and other family treasures had been interred in the pets' cemetery at Heorot, alongside the body of the old Baronin which lay in that unconsecrated ground with her dog Spitz and other victims of the Russian advance.

I happened to be at home when Marianne called. Irene said I was old enough to look after myself during school holidays, but I was not allowed to go out alone or turn on the gas stove. I was not supposed to answer the door either, but did.

'Mummy will be back any minute. Would you like to come in and wait for her?'

'I had better come back later,' the visitor said, her English fluent but strongly accented.

'No, it's all right, really.'

Irene's flat was in a pre-war mansion block on Camden Hill. Furniture and the necessary materials for repair were in short supply, as was skilled labour. There was still a three-inch-wide crack up the chimney breast, dating from the flying bombs, and the porridge-coloured wallpaper was peeling off the walls. The parquet-patterned linoleum was cracked in places, its hessian backing easy to trip over. But the furniture was good. It had belonged to my grandmother. There was a massive cupboard, carved with faces and flowers and porticoes and pillars, and another with its designs inlaid into the wood. The tea service lived in it, delicate porcelain cups and bowls too good to touch. We used Utility plates and mugs made out of thick white china, which chipped easily.

I asked Marianne if she would like some tea.

'That is very kind, thank you. Shall I help you make it?'

I put the kettle on and Marianne found the tea pot which had not been washed up since breakfast. She began to spoon the cold, sodden mess of leaves out.

'What are you doing?' I asked.

'Taking them out to dry.'

'We always throw those away.'

'Throw them away? But they can be used again.'

'Mummy never does.'

A trivial exchange. I have always remembered it. The reuse of old tea leaves became a symbol in my mind of poverty, certainly, but also of a kind of shame – the shame I would feel one day reading Oxfam advertisements in the Sunday papers at the same time as serving my family with a lavish breakfast, the shame of delivering perfectly warm and wearable clothes to a charity shop, the shame of swishing past a bus queue at the wheel of a car, the shame that comes from romanticising a war of my childhood while men and women the same age as my own children are killing and dying in desert sands.

Irene came home while Marianne was drinking the tea. The warmth had brought a faint colour to her cheeks which drained away as the front door slammed and Irene called,

'Anne, I'm back.' She came into the kitchen. 'Hullo. Are you looking for a job? This is the wrong address. You should have come to the office.'

'Not a job.' Marianne stood up. She did not put her hand out. Irene might not wish to shake it when she heard her name. 'I wanted to speak to you. I have something to tell you. I am . . . my name is Marianne Beowulf.'

Irene went as pale as her visitor. She felt for the chair and sank down.

'Mummy, is something wrong? Mummy?'

'No. No, Anne, it's all right. But I would like to speak to Miss . . . to this lady on my own. It's private. Please stay in here, darling, in the kitchen, while we go next door. It's nearly time for Children's Hour anyway.'

Irene switched the wireless on, and as soon as she had left the room and shut the door I turned it down a little and pressed my

143

ear to the keyhole. But the grown-ups were talking German. Once my mother shouted angrily, as she did when I had been naughty. Once she cried out, '*Ach, nein!*', which meant 'Oh no!' Otherwise I could not understand a word.

Irene wrote an account of their confrontation to her only surviving relation.

Marianne had come to tell her that Michael had been betrayed.

Irene knew already. He had entered Germany to save his sister and been captured. That much was obvious.

'That is not what I meant,' Marianne said. She would not sit down and, once Irene had entered the flat, would not have any more tea. She felt as though she were polluting Irene's home. She should have kept away. 'I am sorry to be here, sorry someone of my name should intrude upon you. My brother – '

'I know about your brother,' Irene said coldly. 'The war criminal.'

'Yes.' Marianne bowed her head.

'Is he dead?'

'I think he was killed on the Eastern Front in the last days. They say so, at least.'

'But?'

'But I met someone who thought she had seen him in Berlin afterwards. A prisoner, she said. But I made enquiries and the authorities say there is no record. They are most efficient, and in any case if he . . . if they . . . you know he would be put on trial.'

'I hope so.'

'I hope,' Marianne whispered, 'I hope he is dead.'

'I daresay you do, Fräulein, but quite frankly I don't give a damn. I don't want to think about him or have this conversation at all. Is that why you came here, to tell me that?'

'No. Only that he was responsible for your husband's capture. I can't ask you to forgive him. Or me, for that matter, though I had no part in it. I was yachting in the Adriatic when he . . . when war broke out. But there had been an earlier attempt to arrest him.'

'When you were the decoy.'

'Yes. If only I had understood then – but you don't want to hear that.'

'I certainly don't,' Irene said.

'But I must tell you: the other time they didn't need me. He was followed from Switzerland. They knew he was coming.'

'Oh, no!'

'I am so sorry. That is what I came to say. I don't know who it was, but someone on this side sent a message. Michael was betrayed.'

20

Irene never knew the names of all Michael's fellow conspirators, but she had met some of them before he disappeared and when she was interned they went to some trouble to ensure her release. The authorities received guarantees of her innocence and good character from Dr Roget in Norfolk and another from Sir Douglas Dugdale. As a result, she was allowed to leave the Isle of Man before other detainees who were not lucky enough to have any influential English friends.

Not many of Irene's were left by the end of the war. The only one alive, as far as she knew, was Duggy Dugdale.

Dr Roget took his sailing boat to Dunkirk in 1940. When it capsized he was drowned along with the soldiers he had taken off the beach. Peter Hoyland died at sea, too, in the North Atlantic convoys. Hugh Wintle had been sent to Malaya and perished in a Japanese prisoner-of-war camp.

They were names from the past and the past was best forgotten. Irene was one of those who argued against holding the Nuremberg Trials. She believed that no judicial sentence and punishment could match what the war criminals had done.

Was there any point in thinking about vengeance for one man when nothing could avenge millions? And even if there were, how would she ever know who had betrayed Michael?

'I wasn't there,' Marianne had said. 'That time it was nothing to do with me, thank the Lord. But I should have tried to find out where they sent him. So many things I should have done, so much I should have known, so much I would have done differently.'

Irene was not sure whether Marianne meant that if things had been different Germany might have won the war or that it would never have caused it in the first place. But Irene did not care what Marianne thought. She hoped never to see her or hear her name again.

That same spring, Julian Whitchurch came home. His elder brother, Cassian Whitchurch, had been killed at El Alamein. Shortly afterwards their father had a stroke and he died eighteen months later.

Julian, having joined his father's regiment on the day the war broke out, almost immediately became an Intelligence officer. He was wounded in 1942. It was painful and embarrassing but not what had, in the previous war, been called a 'Blighty One'; not, that is, bad enough to warrant his being sent home. By 1945 he was stationed in Berlin as part of the Army of Occupation until he went down with infective hepatitis and was invalided back to England.

Julian was no longer a younger son without prospects. He was the Viscount Blanchminster. He owned a house in Pall Mall, a shooting lodge in Wester Ross and a two large estates of slums, one in south London and one in Bristol; and, of course, Blanchminster itself.

It was – it still is – a substantial and uncompromising block of honey-coloured stone with stucco pillars. These days it seems imposing, even beautiful, standing on its Somerset hilltop with a vista of smooth lawns and ancient trees fading into well-farmed fields and a hazy, prosperous distance.

After the war, with the pleasure grounds ploughed up for arable, the flower beds full of vegetables and the iron railings removed for scrap, everything was shabby. The woodwork needed painting, but there was no paint. The roof needed repair, but there were no craftsmen left on the estate. The home farm was worked by land girls. There were no gamekeepers in the woods, no servants in the house. The convalescent soldiers who had lived there were gone but their iron bedsteads remained. The walls had been used as pinboards and dartboards. Many bore graffiti, a few quite artistic but some indecent. An incomplete attempt to paint those out had been made before the hospital staff finally departed.

Perdita and Nanny lived in the old servants' hall by day. At night they shared the night nursery, which was just up the back stairs. Nanny used to complain that the soldiers had stolen the use of the day nursery and painted rude things on the walls, so when they went away she locked its door to make sure Perdita would not look in there.

Mrs Dunscombe from the village came in to help do the cooking and cleaning.

Mr Hatchard from the farm sent someone to stoke the kitchen range every morning and evening. Sometimes it was one of the land girls, but occasionally one of the men called Eyeties came. They were prisoners of war. Nanny shouted at them very loudly so as to make sure they could understand what she wanted them to do. Once one of them brought Perdita a stick of barley sugar, but Nanny said never take sweets from strangers and made her give it back.

On weekday mornings Miss Faber bicycled up from the village to give Perdita her lessons. Her father had been the last vicar but one. She lived in a thatched cottage with lots of cats.

On Sundays Mr Hatchard stopped by to drive Nanny and Perdita to church. Every week, regular as clockwork, he lifted Perdita into his car and said you'd have thought his Lordship would have given some proper instructions about the young lady, and every week Nanny said in her comfortable voice that she was sure his Lordship knew what he was doing.

His Lordship was Perdita's papa. There were pictures of him all over the place. There weren't any pictures of Mummy. Nanny never said anything about her and somehow Perdita knew she mustn't ask.

Now she was a big girl, Perdita could play by herself after luncheon while Nanny had a bit of a lie-down. Sometimes she ventured into the front of the house, where most of the rooms were empty and she could slide across their wooden floors. Sometimes she went up to the attic, in which the furniture that was not in the outhouses was stored. One wardrobe held a lot of lovely clothes. They smelled delicious. They were beautiful colours, soft and glowing, and made of smooth material that was nice to stroke. Some had feathers sewn on to them, or long trains. There were blouses with pretty lace down the front and stiff collars which stood up on their own. Up on a high shelf that Perdita could not reach, even if she climbed on a chair, were rows and rows of hats, with great curling feathers around them and big shiny pins. There was a drawer full of gloves which reached to Perdita's armpits, with hundreds of tiny pearl buttons, and bags on chains with beads sewn on to them in swirling patterns, and stiff, pink Liberty bodices which did up with laces instead of hooks and eyes, much prettier than Perdita's own. They were a funny shape that stuck out in front, with little satin bows and lace frills on them.

One of the cupboards had a big mirror on its door, and Perdita liked to pretend that the girl with lovely clothes she saw in it was somebody else. She practised curtseying to her, and smiled and waved and winked. She used to think it would be nice if the other girl looked different from Perdita, who had boring brown hair and eyes. Nanny said it was a long time since there had been a brown-eyed baby in this family.

Perdita was sure Nanny would be cross if she knew about the lovely clothes but she said all those stairs were too much for her poor old legs and never came to the attic if she didn't have to, so Perdita could safely play dressing up until the clock in the old stables struck three. Then Nanny would heave herself out of the armchair, saying, 'This won't do, will it?', and Perdita would put her own clothes on again and at quarter past three they would meet by the kitchen door and go out for a walk.

The clothes Perdita wore for every day lived in the night nursery cupboards, which were dull and painted and smelled of soap. There was no mirror in there, but someone had drawn lines on the wall and written names and dates to show how the children who used to live here were growing. The writing went too high for Perdita to see. The line for her sixth birthday was below one which said April, aged five, and Julian and Cassian, aged four. 'Always been a tall family until you came along,' Nanny said. Some of the names were very faint: Alfred, Millicent, Marguerite. Alfred was his old Lordship. Nanny said Perdita must remember her grandpapa, surely, but she didn't.

There were clothes for children in the cupboards, some so tiny that Perdita was allowed to dress her doll in them. Nanny liked Perdita to look nice and held up the smocked dresses and coats with velvet collars against her to see whether she had grown into them yet. But new shoes came from a shop. Once a month, on market day, Mr Hatchard gave them a lift into Taunton and they went to the pictures and bought things like new boots and knitting wool. Once the Hatchards' son Leonard was there too and he said he would come up to the house and show Perdita how to play cricket, but afterwards Nanny said he was a rough boy and it wouldn't be suitable, and one of these days they must see about finding some nice little friends for Perdita of her own class.

'I could go to school,' Perdita said. 'Leonard goes to school. There would be lots of nice friends there.' But Nanny said that would depend on his Lordship. It wasn't up to her to make changes without him saying so, and anyway Perdita was coming on very well with Miss Faber and could read like a grown-up already, as well as knowing about the Great Painters of the World from the book her Ladyship had sent Perdita for Christmas.

Her Ladyship was really called Grandmamma but the time she came to see them, after the poor sick soldiers had gone, she was so upset at the state of the house and gardens that she went away the same day. Not long afterwards, someone called Aunt April came to visit. She arrived in a big motor car, sitting in the back with a man who was a Yank. The driver had black skin and big black eyes and he called Nanny Ma'am very politely, but Nanny didn't want him to come in all the same and she told Aunt April she ought to know better.

Aunt April talked the whole time. She was pretty. Her lips were bright red and sticky and her fingernails were dark red and very long. She said everything was unbelievable and Julian must do something about it and then she made Nanny give her the key so she could look into the day nursery and Perdita heard her and the Yank giggling, and Perdita looked through the keyhole and they were having a rough and tumble on the floor, which was what Mrs Hatchard called it when her children started rolling around and fighting and she said boys will be boys. And then Aunt April and the Yank came out, and she gave Perdita a kiss which left a red mark on her cheek and the Yank gave her something called a candy bar and they drove away.

The next thing that happened was that a man in uniform came walking up the drive. Perdita and Nanny were out. They had picked some early bluebells, although Nanny said they never lasted in water, and Perdita had found a poor little dead fieldmouse on the path and wanted to bury it. She was just beginning to say 'Please Nanny, oh please do let me,' when Nanny gave a funny sort of gasp and her face went a quite unusual colour and then she gave Perdita a push and said,

'It's his Lordship, back from the war at long last. Run along and meet him.'

Julian had not given a thought to Perdita. He had left her with his old nanny at Blanchminster in 1939 rather as he might have deposited an inconvenient puppy in the care of the gamekeeper. Plenty of room, plenty of women around to keep an eye on her for the time being . . .

Then he had been away and busy and ill and Blanchminster seemed remote and unreal.

When his father died Julian had written formal condolences to his stepmother, who had gone to stay with cousins in Kenya at the outbreak of war. If she had answered he had not received her letter. After the end of the war in Europe the lawyers had written saying she was back in England, living in the London house. He had replied that she should be invited to stay on there as Julian did not intend to use it himself. The lawyers had also asked him where to get in touch with Lady Blanchminster, and it took him a moment to realise whom they meant.

Perdita saw a tall man with yellowish skin and a big nose. He had thin, fair hair and a loose suit. He was shivering in the spring wind.

At the pictures last week in Taunton a daddy had come home from the war on the newsreel. He had hugged his son and his daughter and his wife all together with his arms and cried real tears, and the lady sitting beside Perdita in the one and ninepennies had snuffled noisily and taken a long time to find her hanky and wipe her eyes.

Papa did not smile. He didn't spread his arms widely for Perdita and Nanny to run into.

Perdita stared at the man and then shuffled her feet back towards Nanny, and pushed herself against Nanny's side. She whispered, 'He very looks cross.'

He was cross, too, especially when they went inside the house and he saw where Perdita and Nanny lived and realised they were alone there. He said he didn't believe it, how could an old woman and a child live on their own in a place like this and what had happened to everybody? And did Nanny realise there should have been at least a dozen people under this roof every night when he went away, not including family?

'How did things get into this state?' he demanded, and Nanny said that he didn't understand what it had been like during the war and he said, 'But didn't my father make any arrangements?', and Nanny said, 'You know what his Lordship was like, Mr Julian. He wouldn't countenance interference.'

And then Papa said, 'Couldn't my stepmother have done something about it? Or April?', and Nanny said her Ladyship had been too far away in Kenya, it wasn't her fault, and everything had been all right until Mr Cassian was killed. Papa said he knew that, did Nanny think he was a fool?, and she said she had done the best she could and what did he expect? She was an old woman now, and she sniffed loudly and Perdita looked at the angry stranger and wished she could make him stop it, but then he stamped out of the house and she saw him through the window going across the stableyard and along the back drive and hoped Mr Hatchard would make everything all right.

When he was out of sight, Perdita said to Nanny, 'I don't think he's very nice,' and Nanny slapped her three times on her legs with a wet towel and sent her to bed.

Irene Silversmith came to Blanchminster about a month after Julian's return. By then a married couple, experienced servants called Billings, had arrived. Two women from the village came every day to scrub. A few rooms had been repossessed, the furniture brought in from outhouses, the curtains down from the attic.

Having taken the morning train from Paddington, Irene arrived shortly before one o'clock. She was shown into a small room to the right of the front door which had been old Lady Blanchminster's boudoir and had become matron's office, so the flowered wallpaper, pink rosebuds on a grey background, had faded patches and the marks of drawing pins but no actual graffiti or defacement.

'His Lordship telephoned. He said you would be here for luncheon, madam,' Mrs Billings said.

'I didn't bring my rations. I really don't need anything,' Irene protested, and Mrs Billings said,

'I'm only following his Lordship's instructions.'

The mahogany table was laid for one, with lace mats, silver and crystal.

'Couldn't Perdita come and keep me company?'

'Miss Perdita is having her lie-down after her lunch.'

In spite of the May sunshine outside, there was a chill in the house and Irene wished she had worn something more substantial than her linen suit with the new hemline. She had dressed carefully for the outing, never having been to so grand a house before. She was more nervous of the servants' judgement of her than Julian's or Perdita's, and hoped she would not drop any bricks when she spoke to them.

Mrs Billings sounded noisily on the bare floor as she brought brussels sprouts, boiled carrots, boiled potatoes and a wobbling pink offering, in the form of an animal, on a large salver. 'Rabbit shape, madam.'

Left alone to eat, Irene was wondering whether she dared to take her book from her bag when she heard somebody else arriving. She stood up to look through the window but the pillars of the great portico blocked her view.

She was sitting at the table again when the door opened to admit two women. The pre-war smells of Chanel Number 5 and Je Reviens wafted before them. Both wore beautiful clothes, with nylons (Irene was wearing lisle stockings) and hats which should have been silly but were enviable instead.

The first woman to come into the room stopped in the doorway, her mouth and eyes open in vivid surprise. 'Hullo! I didn't know Julian had already – sorry! I'm April.' She came forward with her hand outstretched. 'This is Lois Grey.'

'How do you do? My name is Irene Silversmith.'

'Nobody told me you were here. Typical Julian, I must say, or I'd have rung up. But now we're here, do you mind if we join you? I'm starving. There's enough left for two little ones, isn't there?'

'I'll see what I can do, miss,' Mrs Billings said, picking up the rabbit shape.

'Thank you so much. How awfully sweet and kind.' April Whitchurch flashed a white smile at the housekeeper. 'And a drinkie too? Ginny gin, nice stiff martinis – what a drive! The traffic! And we had a puncture. Do go on with your luncheon, don't mind us.' She chose a tipped cigarette from a silver case on which initials were picked out in diamonds, fitted it into a tortoiseshell holder, lit it and took a luxurious puff. 'Funny to see the boudoir like this. My stepmamma would have a thousand fits.'

Mrs Billings came in with a tray of crockery and cutlery and began to set two more places at the table. Her husband followed with a silver salver holding two cocktail glasses.

'Cheers,' Lois Grey said.

'Cheers. Aah . . . that's better. So, where's my brother?'

'As far as I know he's in London.'

April took out her compact and looked carefully at her face. 'What a brute he is to leave you alone here already. Don't you mind?'

'I think there's a misunderstanding, Miss Whitchurch – '

'For heaven's sake, call me April. Everyone does.'

'I'm not staying here. I've just come down for the day from London to see Perdita.'

'What a deeply peculiar thing to do, for heaven's sake. Why?'

'For her mother's sake,' Irene said.

'Celia? No! How really fascinating. Do you know you're the very first person I've ever met who – I say, do tell me about her. Would you believe I've never even set eyes on her? That's Julian's wife, Lois. They got married just before the war and then he went off to his regiment and she went off to do some terribly important war work and before I'd even had a chance to see them they had both disappeared for the duration. Where is Celia, do you know?'

'I am afraid I have no idea.' Irene was relieved to be interrupted by Mrs Billings with the rabbit shape, which had been compressed into a soufflé dish and decorated with some large sprays of parsley to hide the cracks. After the housekeeper had left the room again, April said,

'Actually I shouldn't be at all surprised if it was all over. Those hasty war marriages . . . Lois knows.'

'Do I not,' Lois muttered.

'She got married in a hurry in 'thirty-nine, too,' April explained to Irene, who nodded politely. 'The trouble the poor girl's having untying the knot you simply wouldn't believe! But it might be easier for Celia.'

'Why? Is your brother a naughty boy?' Lois asked, showing the first sign of animation.

'On the contrary, actually. It's too sad as a matter of fact. You know he was wounded? Well, it was in the most embarrassingly intimate and inconvenient place. You can imagine that married life mightn't appeal to Celia any more though I suppose she might stick it out if she's really keen on the title. Some girls do, as we know.' April gave her friend a significant wink, and went on almost without drawing breath, 'What sort of person is she, anyway? All I know is that she's brilliantly clever, a real blue-stocking. Too off-putting.'

'She sounds utterly terrifying,' Lois murmured.

'You could have knocked us all down with a feather when Julian came home with a wife and baby, and I don't wonder she lay low in a way. They had to be very careful not to go into dates, my stepmamma said, and it must have been frightfully difficult. Her father's a lawyer or a doctor or something too, too respect-able, and you know how people like that care what other people think. She was probably shy of meeting us. I wouldn't be sur-prised – anyway, it was a real turn up for the book. We thought Julian was going to make an honest woman of that German girl he went round with for so long. Marianne Beowulf. You know, Lois, you must have met her skiing, the blonde bombshell. I never could stand her myself. She was always stooging along behind that incredibly glamorous brother of hers. I say, what a mercy Ju didn't marry into their family. Come to think of it, it would have been excruciatingly embarrassing. Someone was tell-ing me at dinner last week he's on the list of most wanted war criminals. What a narrow escape!'

'I thought he was dead,' Irene said quietly.

'Nobody ever saw his body, that's what I was told. He's prob-ably in South America by now. I wonder what happened to Marianne . . . I say, this food is disgusting. Ring the bell, Lois, it's there on the wall behind you – or, no, I don't suppose it still works.' April pushed her chair back and went to the door to shout, 'Hullo? Anyone there? Oh, there you are. What's this? Oh, jelly. I think I'd just like some coffee, if you would be so very sweet and kind.'

Footsteps pattered on bare floorboards overhead and came downstairs. April said, 'And who's this? Perdita! Hullo. Remem-ber me? I'm your Aunt April. She doesn't look much like Julian, does she? Is she like her mother?'

At that first sight Irene was taken aback by the likeness to her own daughter Anne, but as soon as she looked more carefully she realised the two girls were similar only in being small for their age and having dark hair. Anne had inherited Irene's blue eyes and high white forehead. Perdita's eyes were caramel brown, with very dark, thick brows and lashes and a wide, low forehead from which her plaited hair was cruelly scraped back. She was wearing a smocked dress made of flowered viyella, with tiny buttons down the back and a white collar of the kind that the little Princesses had worn when Irene first visited England.

'Hullo, Perdita. I'm Mrs Silversmith.'

Perdita came forward, shook hands and bobbed a curtsey.

April was talking to the child – indeed, April was apparently a person who was always talking to someone. Irene studied Perdita with almost painful interest. If she was Lotte's daughter she was Michael's niece, Anne's cousin, Hanne's granddaughter. Ever since Julian had come to tell her of the child's existence, and how she had come to be at Blanchminster, Irene had been thinking about her with as much dismay as interest.

When the Gestapo took Lotte away, Julian came upon Celia Roget sitting in the Grünewald, the baby in her arms.

'What am I supposed to do with it?' Celia had wailed, holding the wet and screaming infant away from herself. Julian took the baby in strong, gentling hands as he would hold a small animal. He told Celia to look in the pram, where she found a bottle of milk and a couple of clean squares of muslin and towelling. He held the bottle to the baby's lips. He had done the same for orphaned lambs as a boy. Then he undid the wet and stinking napkin, carefully so as to check the method of attaching the clean one.

'It's a girl,' Celia said.

The immediate practical problem solved, the greater one remained. What was Celia to do with the infant? Take her to an orphanage, or a children's home? – in Germany, in 1939? Impossible.

Celia became almost hysterical. 'I don't like babies. The last thing in the world I can cope with is a baby. I'm a Civil Servant and I'm on my way to a new posting. What's to become of – I don't even know what it's called.'

'She'll have to be got out of the country somehow,' Julian said.

'The Red Cross transports? The Quakers?'

'They can't take a child without papers. Where would they be – if there are any?'

Celia guessed Lotte had been hiding in the picnic hut. Someone had set fire to it and everything had been destroyed.

'What's going to happen?' Celia howled. 'Who is to take her?'

'You don't think you – ?'

'I? Take a baby – alone? As though it were my own? It's completely impossible, out of the question. What would people think? What about my career?'

Obviously the unmarried Celia Roget could not allow herself to be seen leaving Germany or entering England with a newborn baby. The fact that she had been out of circulation during the last few months, at home in Norfolk, would make everyone all the readier to believe the worst.

The worst was easily defined. It was an illegitimate baby.

As Julian spoke of the quandary Celia faced, Irene, seven years later, understood it immediately. It would have been the end of everything for Celia; even a whisper that she was a fallen woman would destroy her hopes of success in any profession, including, probably, marriage.

Flailing around to escape the trap, Celia thought of the stratagems other desperate women had used over the centuries; she could take the baby to an orphanage, leave it on the steps of a hospital.

'You might as well expose it on the hillside as the ancient Spartans did,' Julian told her. 'It would come to the same thing. But then it isn't really your responsibility. *You* don't owe anything to Carla Schmidt.'

But Celia did owe something to Charlotte Silberschmidt and to her family; not simply the debt of past friendship but another more complicated debt. For three years Celia had been immune from the storms that had swept the country in which she was living. Born lucky, she owed something to those who were born victims.

'I can't take it alone,' she whispered painfully. 'An unmarried woman. I just can't. I couldn't do it.'

A married woman could.

If Celia married she automatically and immediately lost her job. Spinsterhood was a condition of her employment.

No matter how brief, convenient and unconsummated, a marriage would disqualify her for ever from the ambition of her life. But at least she would be alive.

When Julian told Irene the story his narrative telescoped the next few days: the acquisition of a special licence of marriage, the ceremony at the Embassy, the registration of birth at the Consulate.

'We called her Perdita,' Julian Whitchurch said. 'The lost one.'

The journey, the arrival – a nightmare, relieved in the telling only by the knowledge of what much worse nightmares were about to supersede it.

'Why is this the first I have heard of it?' Irene asked, seven years on.

'You and Michael were to be told at once, of course, and his mother – '

'Only Michael had disappeared and I'd gone off my head.'

'I had heard you were ill and his mother was prostrate with grief. So we waited. The baby was in good hands at Blanchminster. It never occured to me that it would be for so long. I suppose I expected Lotte to reclaim her sooner or later.'

Unlike Michael, of whom nothing had been heard, Lotte's fate was known. She had survived for three years and perished at Auschwitz.

There were no identifiably Silversmith features on that wan little face. Perdita was as much like Julian Whitchurch as she was like Michael – which was convenient, Irene thought.

Lotte had been a prostitute. She might well have slept with Julian. The child could be his. That could explain why he had accepted the obligation. But Lotte had been the mistress of Hubertus von Beowulf.

Irene had never set eyes on him, though now she had met Marianne. Perdita did not look remotely like her. Of course, that meant nothing but Irene suddenly could not bear to think who could be the father of this child. Even if, or even though Michael's sister had been her mother, Irene felt no attraction or affection for his niece; instead, she was repelled.

An antique nurse came into the room. Irene said how do you do and goodbye in the same sentence. The nurse called her madam. April had already forgotten Irene's name.

Perdita waved from the steps as the taxi bumped down the drive and Irene began to compose a letter to Julian Blanchminster in her head.

Irene's own situation: small flat, full-time job, other responsibilities.

Perdita obviously happy and well cared for. Country air. A good start in life.

Perhaps somewhat isolated; getting a bit much for retired nurse and governess. Venture to suggest a boarding school; recommend the one at which own daughter now doing very well. Only too willing to help with arrangements.

But her meaning should be absolutely clear: the child must remain what she was in the eyes of the world and indeed according to all legal documents. She was the Honourable Perdita Whitchurch, daughter of Viscount Blanchminster. There was no altering that.

21

In February 1947 a woman called Gertrude Schilling arrived in Linz, in southern Austria. She had walked from somewhere near Kursk, across the Soviet Union and through parts of Poland and Czechoslovakia. She was carrying a boy of about eighteen months. The child was thin but essentially healthy. Gertrude Schilling had lost two fingers and four toes from frostbite, all her teeth and much of her hair. The doctor at the reception centre reported that she had a badly prolapsed uterus, chronically infected tonsils and a lump in one breast that was probably malignant. She and her baby were settled in a refugee camp along with thousands of others with similar stories of suffering and endurance to tell. Many of them passed their time doing so.

Gertrude Schilling had been born and brought up in Berlin. She did not know exactly what had happened to her after she was arrested in 1944, because her knowledge of geography was not enough for the names of her various prisons to mean anything. But she remembered faces, and during her interrogation by allied intelligence officers mentioned some names that appeared on lists of the wanted and the long-lost.

At a camp, the last camp, in the last days Gertrude Schilling had seen a man who called himself Michael Silberschmidt.

What made her remember this? Because she knew a man of that name, her parents' neighbour when she was a privileged child of the middle classes. This man said he came from the same place and the same family but he did not look like the same man.

But then she did not look like the same woman either. People were changed by what happened to them. All the same, she had been sure that nobody could change so much.

Hans Hahn came to Linz from Berlin that spring when he was on leave. He wanted to ask Gertrude Schilling more about the man known as Michael Silberschmidt.

He went to visit Gertrude Schilling in hospital where she had undergone an operation. He asked her whether Michael had known who had betrayed him, but her mind was wandering after the anaesthetic. The doctors told Hans Hahn that she could not survive very long. In fact, he wrote to Irene, she never recovered her wits enough to answer his question before she died.

'How did you know Michael had been betrayed?' Irene asked Hans Hahn, when he was on home leave. 'I was only told myself very recently.'

'It was obvious, surely,' he said.

'Perhaps you had better speak to Marianne Beowulf about it.'

'I thought she was dead.'

'I didn't know you knew her. She's reading history at University College. You could go and see her. Say I sent you if you like.'

Irene had made up her mind that her daughter Anne was to be two hundred per cent British.

The Abbess of Whitby's Academy and Cheltenham Ladies' College did the trick. I acquired an accent exactly like the Queen's and a set of smug, insular prejudices that prevented me from ever feeling, as my own children were to feel a generation on, like a European.

Irene had been naturalised too, and not only in name. Just as an exotic plant or animal species soon grows at home in the country to which it has been introduced, Irene had become more English than the English in everything except the accent she never managed to lose.

Too Anglicised to be demonstrative, Irene and I lived together during the school holidays more like flat mates than mother and daughter. But I felt a great responsibility for my mother. I'm all she's got, I would think emotionally. What if I died? She'd be lost without me.

Yet I was away for three quarters of every year, during which times I assumed my mother was alone and longing for my return.

I? A stranger; a girl who is less part of the person I am now than any of the characters I have created for my novels. Invented memories or edited memories?

Or were they edited perceptions?

What was it that the child refused to see and the adult to remember?

A man's voice on the telephone. 'Can I speak to your mother?' Irene's voice, hushed, secretive: not in front of the child.

The sponge bag on a hook high on the bathroom door; under the dirty clothes basket a small rubber dome, slick with flakes of talcum powder. An appliance with a rubber bulb on an inexplicable tube.

'Anne, what are you doing? How dare you! Give me that this instant . . . No I won't, mind your own business.'

No explanation for what hindsight could identify: a diaphragm, a douche.

Callers. Strangers.

'Anne, I'm ashamed of you, so inhospitable. Can't you be friendly to my visitors?'

'But I don't like that man. Why do you need him here? We get on fine without anyone else, don't we? Don't we, Mummy?'

'Who rang up, Mummy?'

'Just a friend.'

'You don't need them. Not when I'm here to keep you company.'

We moved from the flat to a small house in a side road off Kensington Church Street. It had one room on each of its four floors, providing separate bedrooms for Irene and me, and a tiny paved yard at the back with room for one deck chair and a bay tree in a pot. The underground railway line ran immediately below. The house regularly shuddered at the passing of an Inner Circle train.

School holidays were quiet, uneventful, dull. Such social life as Irene had must have been saved for when I was away at school.

None of my friends lived in London. In those days, before the consumer boom, the constant entertainment that my own children would one day find in 'going shopping' did not exist. There was not much to buy. Available goods were useful rather than interesting. No records. Irene did not acquire a radiogram until the middle of the 1950s. No books, except at birthdays and Christmas, carefully chosen to make the best use of book tokens.

No clothes; even when rationing ended they remained a serious matter, chosen to last, and girls wore what was, or might as well have been, school uniform until they leaped straight into fashions that would have suited their grandmothers. Every sixteen-year-old hoped to look at least thirty.

Sometimes I went to the office with Irene and pecked away at a huge, high typewriter or tidied the stationery cupboard. On Saturday mornings there was a special children's film show at the Kensington Odeon. I went often to Kensington Public Library, where I could so seldom find books I had not read that I took out again books I had not particularly enjoyed first time round. Much of my time was spent writing long, derivative stories unintentionally and unconsciously based on a favourite author of the moment. There were imitation John Buchans, Angela Brazils, Arthur Ransomes and Rider Haggards (*She* made a great impression, possibly because the chief character was so unusual in being a powerful commanding female).

I filled dozens of exercise books with naive and embarrassingly uninhibited self-revelation. When I reread these juvenile outpourings as an adult they came as a surprise. Was that what I once was?

On to Nancy Mitford and Evelyn Waugh, Angela Thirkell and Anne Bridge.

My fantasies moved away from unexplored tracts of jungle or missing treasure. Someday my prince will come. The King of the Belgians was still unmarried; or what about the Duke of Kent? I practised curtseying in front of long mirrors, but never discovered the trick of it. My adolescence was extraordinarily unsexual. Segregated from boys in an all-female home and school, they were a subject of speculation as abstract as that about royalty. I knew, theoretically, what happened between men and women, but never applied the idea to myself. Not so much innocent as ignorant, I represented the type of female child who would only a decade later be as extinct as a dodo, one who wanted to seem old, who cared about class and who did not think about sex.

I became a snob, poring over the forms of address in *Whitaker's Almanac*, working out which peers' eldest sons would be the right age for me to marry and learning the rules spelled out or implied in my fictional authorities.

'Mummy, please don't say mirror, it's looking glass. Don't call it a toilet, say loo.'

Irene, still accustomed to making mistakes of pronunciation (did a tow path rhyme with cow or low?) was obedient. It was she who had wanted me to be properly assimilated into English society. Once, I remember, she rebelled.

'Kindly remember that I don't approve of class distinctions. I was a member of the Communist Party in my youth.' Communist was a dirty and dangerous word. In the United States, the Macarthy witch hunt was in full cry. I begged her not to repeat it in front of anyone who mattered.

Adolescence: best forgotten. A source of embarrassment.

Let us ask instead, what was Irene doing during the thirteen-week school terms? Was she occupied full time with the agency, which by the early Fifties had expanded to deal with secretarial as well as domestic services? Whom did she see? Why did she hang those unrecognised contraceptives on the bathroom door?

In 1964 I had to go through Irene's address book to see who should be informed of her death. I recognised hardly any of the names.

Some that I knew were unexpected. Why did my mother keep the telephone numbers of Viscount Blanchminster, one in Somerset, one in Scotland, two in London? Old engagement diaries revealed they had met about three times a year. Dinner, Julian B., Rules, 7.30; Cocktails, Claridges, Julian; Julian here, Sunday lunch.

Other names meant nothing to me until years later. The engagement diaries are long lost, but the address book survives. Anne – I – saved up to buy the dark blue leather book from Smythson's after reading in an authoritative but otherwise forgotten novel that it was where the Right People acquired their stationery. It was Irene's Christmas present.

With a shiver of nostalgia at the sight of Irene's handwriting, I now read the names of Duggy Dugdale and Hans Hahn and realise that Irene stayed in touch with Michael's pre-war friends. She cannot have suspected any of them of betraying him.

22

When Perdita went to boarding school, Nanny retired to a cottage in her native Devonshire. It was thought inconvenient for Perdita to go home for every half term and school holiday. Once or twice she went to visit Nanny or to stay with a school friend. Occasionally she was invited for nerve-racking, best-behaviour visits to Grandmamma in Pall Mall. She stayed on sometimes at the Abbess of Whitby's, where one of the boarding houses was kept open all the year round for girls whose families were abroad or broken up.

Julian saw little of Perdita even when they coincided at Blanchminster. Not yet being 'out', she did not join him for dinner. They met over breakfast. He would make some jokes, which the adolescent Perdita found either puerile or incomprehensible, and ask if there was anything she needed. It did not occur to her to say 'Yes, your attention and company.'

Perdita found Blanchminster lonely and unfamiliar. The Hatchards had moved away and the home farm was taken over by a younger couple who had no children. In the big house there was now a proper staff but their very politeness was unhomely. Nobody ever told Perdita 'not to' any more. The housekeeper, Mrs Billings, was supposed to be in charge, but she let Perdita do as she liked.

Sometimes Mrs Billings said, 'Why don't you get some fresh air, pick some flowers or climb a tree or something?' That was what children did in books. Perdita had read the Arthur Ransome series and all the E. Nesbits until they were almost in tatters. But girls in books always had brothers or sisters or other companions. In *The Secret Garden* there was a heroine who lived in a big house with only servants for company, like Perdita, but even she made friends with Dickon and then found Colin and made him better. Blanchminster had neither a boy nor a secret walled garden, and its master remained cold and distant.

Perdita mooched around. Played old records again and again:

The White Horse Inn, *The Threepenny Opera*, a scratched version of *The Flight of the Bumble Bee*. In Coronation Year a television set was installed in the servants' hall. Perdita was invited to watch most evenings. During the day there was nothing to see except the test card. Sometimes Perdita sat and stared at the girl it showed, and wondered whether she had anyone to play with and whether she was as smug as she looked or whether she too was bored, staring for ever into an abstract, monochrome emptiness.

One unique Easter, when Perdita was fourteen, Aunt April brought a house party to stay at Blanchminster. The guests arrived in long, low cars. They played the latest songs from musicals on the gramophone and talked all the time.

A man called Euan took Perdita for a drive in his open-topped Jaguar XK 120 and kissed her carelessly on the corner of her mouth when he left. She found his photograph in Jennifer's Diary and stuck it on the inside cover of her own pocket diary. Another taught her to play canasta. The girls laughed a lot and teased Perdita. She watched them with great concentration, studying to be like them one day.

April said Perdita was a funny little thing. 'I must take you to my hairdresser. We'll arrange for you to come to London. You can go to a show with Euan and we'll give you a nice time.' But Perdita knew it would never really happen. April did not like Perdita much. Perdita had overheard her conversations.

'If only she wasn't such a plain and lumpen object,' April had said. 'Let's hope she'll improve before she comes out, so dull and shy and spotty. I'm afraid she's what my mamma would have called an antidote.'

'She'll have other charms, won't she? I mean, it's not as though your brother looks likely to get married again. Who is the heir?'

'The entail was broken years ago. Perdita will scoop pretty well everything. Poor Julian, he'd probably have liked to try for a son, but not a hope after the war. So you're quite right, of course. Perdita should do well, spotty or not.'

'She says she doesn't see her father very often,' one of the visitors added.

'Oh, I know, he's away the whole time. All that hush-hush stuff. But even if he was in the country, you really couldn't blame him for not being able to cope. It might have been different with a son, but a daughter – it's a bit much to expect. After all, I hardly

166

remember Papa addressing so much as a word to me until I came out.'

'Where's her mother then?'

'You must have heard of Celia Blanchminster.'

'No! I had no idea. She's quite something. You do mean the woman who does those war reports?'

'The very same. She did something terribly heroic during the war, parachuted into France with code names and disguises and cells – that stuff – and then she carried straight on to writing about other people's wars. She's on the staff of an American magazine.'

'I know, I've read her.'

'Well then. Anyway she never comes back to England. She probably only would if we had another war of our own to report on.'

'Some mother to live up to, I must say. Are she and your brother divorced?'

'No. Why? Are you interested in him? I shouldn't think he's very good husband material . . . not for anyone who wants a family.'

'Doesn't Perdita go and see her mother?'

'Not that I know of. Ask her yourself, why don't you?'

'It might be a bit unkind . . .'

Everybody thought it might be a bit unkind to mention her mother to Perdita. The year she was fifteen and spent the school summer holidays at a children's camp in Switzerland, where she was supposed to speak French and play tennis and actually spent most of the time in bed with measles, Perdita discovered it was far easier to pretend her mother was dead. After that she always did.

Perdita left the Abbess of Whitby's Academy at the end of the summer term before her sixteenth birthday. She went to a finishing school in Montreux, at which Aunt April had been herself before the war. After that she spent six months as a paying guest with a comtesse in Paris and another three with a contessa in Florence and then came back to England to begin her real life.

Irene Silversmith and her mother had both been only children. Irene's father had one much younger brother whom they saw seldom during Irene's youth. He left Germany even before Hitler came to power. Max Strauss was a mining engineer. After a career spent in Africa, South America and the Far East he settled in Tel

Aviv in 1939. He had never married. Irene's father made jokes about dusky maidens, half-caste children and little bastards, but Max arrived in Palestine alone.

Apart from her daughter, Max Strauss was Irene's only living relative. They had last met in 1934 and, as far as I knew, their only communication consisted of a greetings card from Irene on 1 January and one in return from Max at the Jewish New Year in September.

After my mother's death I informed my great uncle, who wrote a short, formal letter of condolence in bad English, and we then continued the annual exchange of greetings.

1990: I scribble on the bottom of the card that I am trying to find out more about my parents. I do not suppose Uncle Max can tell me much. In reply, I receive a small package of letters. The covering note is typed.

'Dear Anne Medlicott,

I read your letter to Max because he cannot see to do so any more. He told me to send you the enclosed letters and says he would have done so long before if he had not always heard from your mother that you were not interested.

Your uncle is quite well and sends you his best wishes. And may I just say how much I always enjoy your books?'

From Yael Yadin.

There are seventeen letters, one for each year between the end of the war and Irene's death. I block out the proper names that might mean anything to outsiders, and have them translated by a student at London University. Reduced to dot-matrix type on computer paper, much of the correspondence is banal: polite good wishes for Onkel Max's health, assurances that Anne was doing well at school. But sometimes Irene had written more personally. 'I am telling you this because there isn't anyone else I can say it to. No need for you to reply.'

As far as I know, he didn't. Irene sent her story into silence.

May 1946: The visit from Julian Blanchminster. The news that Michael's sister had had a child and the child had survived and was living in Somerset.

168

June: meeting Perdita.

'I have to write this to you, Onkel Max. I must tell someone what it felt like to see this child, Michael's niece – whose daughter, though? Perhaps I ought to take her on. But I can't.'

1947: Rumours that Michael had been seen alive at the end of the war. But Irene was sure he was dead.

1948:

'The child has a fleeting look of Michael. I have pored over Hanne's old photos of Lotte, not in colour, of course. I can't say that I see a resemblance. Anne does not like her. I cannot have her here.'

1949: Another visit from Julian Blanchminster.

'He comes here because there is nobody else to whom he can speak openly about his daughter, as he calls her. Michael's niece, Anne's cousin, the poor child. He is painfully embarrassed by her, has no idea how to behave with a girl of her age, especially one who is so unlike what he expects little girls to be. Perdita is frightened of horses, seems unable to learn to swim, takes no interest in natural history. 'When I was a boy the nursery was full of animals,' he says. He gave Perdita a puppy for Christmas but it makes her sneeze.'

1950:

'You ask whether I might marry again. Well, for one thing it would mean admitting that Michael and I lived in sin! I would rather Anne never knew. But that aside, I can't do it to her. She is consumed with jealousy about me, more like a husband than a daughter. She makes her resentment of any male friends so obvious that I only invite them here when she is away at school. But I don't really mind. I don't need a legal husband . . .'

Who was it Anne – I – resented?
A flash of memory: a man at dinner, with a foreign accent,

reaching out for my mother's hand. There are lace table mats, even, unusually, wine. He asks about school. What are my ambitions, my aims? How dare he? I hate him. But he does not come again. We don't need him. Mummy and Anne are fine on their own.

1951:

'I thought I should arrange for Anne and Perdita to meet again, even if we don't tell them they are related. I have discussed it with Julian and he thinks she is better off as the legitimate daughter of an English peer than if she (and, inevitably, the rest of the world) knew the truth about her birth. She is motherless either way. Celia never gets in touch, and at least as things are she has a status that still seems worth having – and, though Julian didn't mention it, is likely to inherit lots of money since he has not remarried. In fact, I believe that he and Celia never got legally divorced. I heard he is impotent (the result of a war wound) so probably he hasn't got any incentive.

So I had Perdita for the day and took the two girls to the Festival of Britain. It wasn't a success. They did not take to each other – Anne kept asking me why we had to be lumbered with Perdita and she was dreadfully shy and awkward and just muttered yes or no whatever I said to her. I took them to the Dome of Discovery and the Emmet Railway and gave them sweets and fish and chips in a café followed by a ride on a river boat. Then I offered them a go on the dodgem cars and all Perdita would say about everything was 'very nice', however far from the truth that was. She was sick on the big dipper.'

Yes, I remember now. Candy floss in the open air, in public. One did not eat in the street. It was an immutable rule. Irene bought the soft, bright pink mounds of spun sugar and handed one to me and one to Perdita. Eating out there in the open as we walked along felt like an act of rebellion. Perdita had neither the courage to eat nor to reject it. She carried her candy floss awkwardly until Irene realised she did not want it and threw it into one of the specially designed Festival of Britain litter baskets.

Another snapshot of memory: a ladies' room, Perdita crying. There are a few spots of blood on her knickers.

I said, 'You've started. I'll go and get Mummy.'

A fierce, desperate grip on my arm. 'Don't, don't! You're not to! Please don't say anything. I don't want you to.'

'All right, keep your hair on. I won't if you don't want me to.'

'It's so awful!'

'But everyone does. Women, I mean.'

'Yes, but not so young. It's common to start so young. It's disgusting!'

For the rest of the day Perdita walked with her legs as close together as possible, counting the minutes until the outing was over. I dropped behind with my mother and whispered, 'Perdita's started you know what, but she won't let me tell you.'

Irene said, 'I suppose somebody must have told the child the facts of life.'

'She's a real nuisance. I don't know why we had to bring her with us. She isn't even enjoying herself.'

'Perhaps it wasn't a good idea. We won't do it again.'

'It was a mistake to take the two girls out together [Irene wrote]. The trouble is I feel a sort of responsibility for Perdita. She has every material thing in the world, but there doesn't seem to be anyone who really cares for her. Unfortunately I don't either.'

All the same, Irene tried again. I was sent to visit Perdita at Blanchminster and came back no fonder of Perdita ('She's terribly wet, Mummy') but overcome by the magnificence of her home.

'I should never have let Anne go into that sort of world. I should have guessed she would find the whole thing dangerously attractive. She came home very supercilious about our middle-class existence and embarked on a programme of reform. I am not allowed to use the raffia table mats any more and she says I must call the shelf above the electric fire a chimney piece in future, and have our note paper (now to be called writing paper) engraved.

I also rather regret letting her meet the kind of people who were staying at Blanchminster. The last thing I want is for her to be dazzled by Bright Young Things or, for that matter, Rich Old Things. This country has been good to me and I am eternally grateful that my Anne is British and secure here, but there is still a privileged class battening on the labour of others and I wouldn't like Anne to be corrupted by her contact with it. You know that my ambition for Anne is complete assimilation – but not into the raffish, irresponsible set for whom tumbrils and guillotines may still be waiting.'

An undated letter. More about Julian.

'If only I could be sure what I think about him. Superficially not unattractive, stiff but with the exaggerated good manners that men of his type have – not that I know many. He leaps to his feet every time I come in or out of the room, and opens doors and picks up things from the floor as though I were incapable. It makes it fun for me to go out with him, quite apart from the fact that he takes me to restaurants in which my other friends might be able to afford little more than a glass of water. But he is not forthcoming, perhaps because of his stammer. He avoids sensible discussion with facetious jokes and every time I see him I can't help wondering about the truth of what happened with Lotte. All those months he spent with the Beowulfs. He was courting Marianne, who was his cousin. His grandmother was a von Beowulf. A Whitchurch went to Berlin when Queen Victoria's daughter married a Prussian prince and found his own bride there. Julian doesn't seem to have been at all interested in politics before the war. He was what the English call a playboy, interested in nothing but having a good time and playing games, but it isn't possible that he was unaware of what was going on and I find it hard to believe he really had no idea. Of course, if he knew and took no notice that is bad; if he was a supporter that is worse. He had an affair with Lotte, too, although she had also been von Beowulf's mistress. I can't work out the dates and of course can't ask him, but he seems to accept that the baby is his own. If anything, she looks a little like Hanne Silberschmidt.

Only one thing is certain – he has not the faintest idea how he should treat the girl. I have the impression that he avoids her as far as he possibly can.'

The summer Perdita Whitchurch came out I still had to get through two more terms at school. There would be A levels in the summer and Oxford and Cambridge entrances before Christmas.

I would try for both, taking their separate scholarship exams in the hope of being interviewed and offered a place at one of them. Some girls were offered places at both. The staff at Cheltenham said the competition for entry to one of the women's colleges (five at Oxford, two at Cambridge) was the fiercest their pupils would ever have to face in their lives.

I sat in the prefects' room, in uniform, and read gossip column items about the lives of rich and titled debutantes.

In those days, the girls' schools which specialised in academic education were not much patronised by the aristocracy. It was the middle classes who believed in educating women. My friends were the daughters of doctors, lawyers and university professors. None of them would do the Season. They all pretended they wouldn't have been seen dead at a coming-out ball, that a debutante was the last thing on earth they would want to be. I was careful not to let on that I would have loved to.

None of us actually resented the existence of the social season. Young people of that period were often supercilious. We sneered and mocked and envied, but anger had not been invented. We did not expect to change things.

My school friends and I were still treated as children. We had to wear the tunics and ties, the hats, the two pairs of stockinette knickers (green outside, white next to the skin) and flat shoes that were the universal school uniform for girls. Cosmetics were forbidden. We were not allowed to go out alone. To be caught, however innocently, in the company of a boy was a go-to-the-headmistress offence.

I read about Perdita's doings, cutting out photographs of her from the *Tatler* and poring over the guest list for her coming-out ball. Because I had once known Perdita, it seemed less fantastic and inaccessible. One could read about the social life of princesses and dukes' daughters with the same interest that Hollywood film stars provoked, but it was not fair that somebody one knew should be having so much fun while I was still immured with a whole lot of females. I was painfully, inadmissably jealous.

Oxford or Cambridge was to be my escape route. One girl to seven men for three whole years. There I would surely find Mr Right. Better still, Lord Right, whose wife would take her place, by right (I enjoyed puns at that age), in hierarchical English society as though she had been born in it.

When she returned to stay in Pall Mall with Grandmamma, Perdita got ready for the Season. She met other debutantes at girls' lunch and tea parties, bought dresses, hats, gloves and what Grandmamma called bust bodices. She learned to curtsey at Miss Vacani's Dancing School in Knightsbridge, hooking her right knee into the crook of the left, sinking down and rising in desperate balance. 'Keep your faces up, girls. The Queen doesn't want to see the top of your hats.'

Then Perdita was presented to the Queen at Buckingham Palace. She went to Ascot, Henley and Wimbledon, a great many lunch, tea, drinks and dinner parties, as well as other girls' dances and Queen Charlotte's Ball. Grandmamma gave a ball for four hundred people, many of whom were 'grown-ups'. Perdita wore a bright green dress made by Norman Hartnell.

Papa was back from 'abroad' and in London at the time. Perdita spent the evening half dreading, half hoping that he would dance with her. But the party divided into the grown-ups in the ball-room, which had been extended out over the garden for the purpose, and the drawing room which was decorated to look like a nightclub, where the debs and their young men could have a good time smooching or dancing cheek to cheek.

Perdita did not have a good time but it was many years before she could admit that to herself. At the age of seventeen she believed what she had been taught, which was that the acme of female joy was to wear expensive clothes at an elegant dance and be proposed to by an eligible young man.

Niall Ross was not titled nor enormously rich, but he was extremely handsome, a little older than most of the other chaps who came to dances and Papa approved of him. He had done his national service in the Coldstream Guards and always walked around London in officers' out-of-hours uniform of a bowler hat, a coat with velvet collar and an umbrella that was never unfurled. He knew where he was going, in all senses: which restaurant or shop, which play or film, what job and future.

His future was to be the managing director of Blanchminster's Bank with, as his wife, the chairman's daughter. Although not active in the bank himself, Blanchminster was still the majority shareholder and figurehead.

Her future was to fall in love, marry and be a good wife, mother and hostess. It was expected, predicted – even, in those days before women's liberation, ordained.

I was summoned to interviews at both Somerville College, Oxford, and Newnham College, Cambridge, in the first week of December. Irene bought me an interview suit for the purpose, a brown tweed jacket and skirt, at Debenham and Freebody.

Somerville was cold and scary. The candidates for places stayed two nights. I was allotted a room usually occupied by a pony enthusiast. All the pictures were of people in jodhpurs on horseback. The small bookcase held copies of *Horse and Hound* and Ruff's *Guide to the Turf*, with one or two textbooks on biology in amongst them. I slept badly and made a mess of my interviews.

'I don't think this is the place for you, Miss Silversmith,' one of the history dons said.

Several other girls from Cheltenham were in Oxford for interviews. With two of them I went on to Cambridge, changing trains at Bletchley where there was an hour to wait for the connection. Sally and Carolyn went off for a walk. I huddled by a coal fire in the waiting room with my history notes. Instead of studying them I sank into a stupor of anguish about my future. I had never been so desperate in my life – and never would be again.

There were other universities, of course – girls who wanted to do medicine went to London, less ambitious ones went to Trinity College, Dublin, or to St Andrews – but at that time everywhere else was second best. The offer of a place at one of the women's colleges was the ultimate prize and I wanted it more than anything else in the world.

A man came into the waiting room. I did not look up until he said, 'I know you, young lady.'

He was a slight, smooth man with glasses and thinning hair. He wore very formal clothes, striped trousers and a short black jacket with a dark coat and bowler hat, but in spite of his correctly clubland appearance he spoke with a strong accent and looked indefinably un-English.

'Aren't you the Silberschmidt daughter?'

'I am Anne Silversmith.'

'And I am Professor Hahn. You have grown since I last saw you.'

'Have I?'

'You look quite like your father the last time I saw him with his hair dyed black.'

'I don't remember him,' I said indifferently.

'What are you doing here?' Professor Hahn asked.

'I'm waiting for the Cambridge train.'

'And I for the Oxford one. I am going to lecture the undergraduates on the origins of fascism.' He began to speak about the Weimar Republic, the First World War, the German Empire, Bismarck, the Unification of Germany, Prussia and the post-Napoleonic organisation of Europe, rehearsing his arguments for that evening's performance. With the surface of my mind I resented him. How dare he come in and interrupt my thoughts, treat me as though I were a public meeting, assume an acquaintance that I had forgotten? But I must have taken in his words. The next day I repeated some of them, having already forgotten their source, to the history tutor of Newnham and perhaps on their account was awarded an exhibition. It was the greatest triumph of my life.

On the evening before the wedding, Papa came to dinner in Pall Mall. Niall was not there; he had gone out to a party with the chaps. April had been expected but rang up to chuck at the last minute. After the main course Grandmamma was called to the telephone. They could hear her booming voice in the hall. 'Can you hear me? Are you there?'

Julian sat at the foot of the table at right angles to Perdita. He had refused the delicious soufflé and was preparing an apple, letting slivers of peel fall over his fingers on to the plate. He offered a piece of apple to Perdita. She held out her hand for it and he paused. Then he put the piece of fruit down and took Perdita's hand in his own, spreading hers out on his palm. She had long fingers with oblong nails, painted scarlet, the two middle fingers level in length. On one she flaunted a large solitaire diamond.

'Elegant hands. Last time I looked the nails were bitten,' Julian said.

We must have gone hand in hand when I was little, she thought, but could not remember it. His dry, warm touch was unfamiliar. After a moment he let go of Perdita's fingers and gave her the piece of apple. She glanced at him furtively. For years she had thought of him looking as he had all that time ago when he came

176

back to Blanchminster after the war. She had not noticed him changing, but now realised that he did not resemble her internal image. His hair, a light, muddy sort of colour, was thin and very smooth, and his nose still jutted like a parrot's beak. Now the skin she thought of as yellow was pink with mauve patches over the nose and cheekbones and the eyes, which must also have been jaundiced, were a very pale blue with deep crinkles in the skin around them.

Julian said, 'I rather think I've done a b-b-bad job as a father.'

In the hall Grandmamma was shouting, 'I can't hear you. Speak up!'

'Oh no, not at all,' Perdita replied, much embarrassed.

'I have never been quite sure, you see, what to say to you.'

'I know lots of people whose fathers don't understand about girls, Papa. It's perfectly all right.'

'Operator!' Grandmamma shouted. 'I have been cut off.'

'About your mother,' Julian said. 'And now you're getting married tomorrow it's time that – '

'I'm trying to talk to someone in Kenya, operator.'

'I don't mind. I never think about her, honestly,' Perdita said.

'The trouble is you're still so young. Though your mother wasn't much older when – '

Much to Perdita's relief, Grandmamma came back into the room. 'I told the girl I was trying to have a conversation and she cut me off. So inefficient. I shall speak to the Postmaster General.'

Papa did not like Grandmamma. It was one of the things that was never said but never needed saying. It was just a fact. Grandmamma spoke as though she and her stepson were the greatest of friends but Perdita had always known it was not true.

Suddenly the thought came to her that she would never have to do this again: never sit, straining to think of something to say, at a dinner table with her grandmother or her father, alone, inadequate, a disappointment; never have to do what Grandmamma said again, never torment herself with worrying what her father would think. She need never wonder again whether he would take any notice of her.

Perdita Whitchurch married Niall Ross in October 1956.

It was my first term at Cambridge, and for students that

177

autumn was memorable not only because it marked their release from the restraints and restrictions of childhood, but because it brought their first political awareness. The British sent forces to Suez. The Russians sent tanks into Hungary. The world was in turmoil.

But Perdita was not interested in politics. She had been too busy planning her trousseau and the colour of her bridesmaids' dresses and whether the flowers in St Margaret's Westminster should be yellow or pink. After the wedding she would concentrate on decorating the pretty house in Chelsea that her father had bought as a wedding present.

Even when the list of wedding guests was being made out, Celia was not mentioned. Perdita sent an invitation to her, care of the magazine for which she wrote. There was no reply.

23

The past is a foreign country.

Memory itself is just a picture book.

Other writers have expressed this perception.

Some can recall everything that happened to them, having noted it all in diaries; dialogue, description, their feelings, their reactions, all the fleeting impressions of life are preserved, freeze-framed.

Others simply remember. Christabel Bielenberg, who wrote an autobiographical account of her experiences as the English wife of a German anti-Nazi, living in Germany throughout the war, told an interviewer, 'I remember exactly everything I have ever heard, everything that has ever happened to me.'

I don't. Perdita didn't.

Vignettes.

Flashbacks.

Perdita's wedding, huge and fashionable, a blur of unfamiliar faces. She moved down and up the aisle, through the throng, out to the car which took her and Niall away, in a kind of stupor. An animated, well-drilled doll fulfilled the expectations of Society.

Perdita's honeymoon on Capri. A disappointment. She had lost her virginity in Italy to a young man who called himself a marquess. That had been a disappointment too. 'I'm sorry to hurt you. It gets better,' Niall said. But he hadn't and it didn't.

Crumpets. Fullers White Walnut Cake. Panelled rooms in Trinity, with open fires and toasting forks. Gerry Medlicott. He was older than the others, a barrister, back in Cambridge once a week to supervise undergraduates. Melted butter and honey dripped down his chin. I felt an unfamiliar, shocking impulse to lick it off.

Housewifery. Cooking classes at a brides' course in South Kensington with other ex-debs. A Constance Spry Flower Arranging course. Swatches of fabric from Peter Jones. Learning to keep the charwoman sweet. Calls to the grocer and greengrocer and butcher and fishmonger, and three-course meals by candlelight when Niall came home from the office.

Dinner parties. Weekend parties in the country.

Anne and Gerry's wedding. A village church in Yorkshire, the Medlicott family farm, the Medlicotts' tactfully disguised disappointment. Not quite the alliance they had hoped for. Anne was lucky to catch their eligible son.

They were polite to Irene. Too polite.

Adam. Another disappointment. Perdita waited for the predicted rush of maternal love on first holding her son and waited in vain. Eventually she loved him for himself, a stout, funny little boy, very observant and conservative. He did not like things to change.

I wanted stability, too. I knew how to run a home and bring up children, how to manage without a man. Gerry came home to sleep. Barristers had to chose between career and family and they needed wives who would be able to manage without them, who would not make a fuss. I never made a fuss.

Perdita's first affair: a French banker, in London for six months to work with Blanchminster's on some West African deal.

The next, not so much an affair as a two-night stand with one of Niall's friends whose wife was in Queen Charlotte's having her third. 'Twins this time. How will I ever pay four lots of school fees?' he moaned as he pulled off his socks.

An actor. Another banker. The man who came to install the first fully automatic washing machine. It was the Post Pill Paradise.

Irene thought my brain was stagnating. 'Why don't you do another degree?'

'The children. The house . . . '

'Do you remember my friend Professor Hahn?'

'I met him once, I think.'

'Oh, Anne, I know you used not to like him when you were little, but you're grown up now. He thinks you should take an external degree at London University. Or you could get some professional qualification. What are you going to do all day when the children are at school?'

'Gerry wouldn't want a wife who went out to work.'

Niall holds up a blackened finger-tip.

'This place is a mess. What do Ingrid and Mrs Tabb do all day? Surely you could keep the house tidy now Adam's away at school? What's wrong? I can tell there's something wrong.'

He asked but he didn't care. All he cared about was keeping up appearances. She could sleep with every tradesman in London, so long as Mr and the Honourable Mrs Niall Ross maintained their public image.

'You need something to do. Why don't you take up pottery, or weaving or something? Alec's wife goes to Italian classes. You could learn a language.'

He had no sympathy with her. What was she making such a fuss about?

'You have got everything any woman could want. Your whole life is a holiday. A lovely house, a child, a char, an au pair, no money worries, a good husband. What on earth is the matter with you?'

No time for external degrees or professional qualifications now. Flora, Christopher, Jonathon. Once we had moved to Essex Gerry was working too hard to get home every night. He took a one-roomed flat near the Temple. Barristers have to work so hard, in court all day, writing opinions at night. I didn't mind. I always understood.

Scotland in September.

Niall's mother with her red face and ostentatiously non-judgemental air. She wore tartan skirts, just below the knee by day, full length every evening. It was the Ross tartan, with twin sets chosen to match and strings of mean little pearls. Niall's father, in very hairy tweed, slightly larger than lifesize. Gardening, stalking, shooting. The silence, the empty pages of the engagement diary. Time to fill. It was like the old days at Blanchminster.

'It's nothing serious, darling, honestly. Nothing for you to worry about. Just a small operation. My friend Hans Hahn is going to take me in.'

'Well, you won't need me then,' I said, offended.

Swinging London. A singer. A hairdresser.

The gossip columns began to hint.

Niall could not admit he knew. He told a long story of a myth-ical friend. 'The moral of that story is don't break the eleventh commandment. Never – are you listening, Perdy? – never be found out.'

'Don't bring the children. I wouldn't want them to remember me like this.'

'But it will grow again, surely? You'll be all right soon.'

'Yes, soon.'

A painter.

They met at a party in Fulham, both of them half stoned. Niall had refused to come. He couldn't risk it. One smoked pot, of course, but carefully. His was kept in the secret drawer of the Queen Anne bureau.

Phelim Carmody.

She had never come with a man before, only with a machine. No woman remains non-orgasmic with a vibrator, Masters and Johnson wrote, and Perdita had bought one and tried it and it was true. Better late than never. And now Phelim. First that and then painting. My benefactor.

Perdita had never thought of painting, not since the days at the Abbess of Whitby's when at the weekly art lesson the girls were told to draw bowls of apples or empty wine bottles with a flower in them, and she had never been able to get anything on the paper that looked remotely like the subject.

'Here. You have a go.'

'I don't know how,' Perdita said.

'You don't have to know how.'

A bare white canvas. A row of extruded mounds of oil paint, glistening and brilliant.

She tentatively dipped the point of a brush into the red.

'Not like that.' A great dollop of colour, a slash of it on the canvas. 'Like this.' Some yellow. 'And this.'

'Let me try.'

'That's the way.'

Better late than never. Afternoon classes at the Slade. Then morning life class, and evenings. The top floor, with its skylight and a great window looking out over the river, cleared of furniture and used as a studio.

'But it's my bedroom!'

Adam must move downstairs. He was hardly ever at home anyway, what with school and staying with friends and visiting Niall's family in Scotland.

'Mummy's new hobby matters more to her than I do.'

'You're driving the boy away. Can't you see your first duty is to your family? You're turning into a monomaniac.'

My first book. How pleased Irene would have been. I dedicated it to her memory.

Not quite what Gerry expected, not necessarily the right image for the wife of a rising junior at the Bar. 'You mustn't put me in it. Or anyone we know. It wouldn't help my career.'

Safer to write about an intellectual pursuit in another era. Keep emotions out of it. Gerry was not a great one for emotions.

I was invited to talk to the wives of the American Bar Association members meeting in London about writing mystery stories, invited to the boys' school to describe the career of a novelist. Success. Respectable, repeatable, inoffensive success.

Perdita was obsessed by painting. The colour, the form, the light.

'I have to make up for wasting so much time. If only I hadn't left it so late!'

Adam's Speech Day, sports day, school play.

Niall's dinners, parties, weekends with potential clients. 'It's your duty as my wife. You've got to come with me.'

Adam at Eton. Inquisitive, critical, impatient, money-grubbing. 'Who owns the shares, Mum? Are they in your name or Father's? Has he got your power of attorney? Have you made a will?'

A new thought. A new weapon.

Niall stopped demanding and insisting. He could have the money so long as he left her alone to paint.

Juan Luis Carreras. He had skipped bail in New York and his picture appeared in papers all over the world. The paparazzi caught up with him on a yacht in the Mediterranean, with Perdita on his lap. He wore two gold chains with three large medallions. She was naked.

Niall would put up with anything except being found out. He moved into a penthouse flat in Curzon Street. He turned up at the private view of Perdita's first exhibition and looked strange, remote, an outsider.

'Meet a piece of my past,' she said to the gallery owner.

Every picture was sold within the first week.

PART IV
1991

24

' "Writing means laying oneself bare: even the cleanest writer bares himself. If you do not like to bare yourself, be satisfied with your present job." This is a quotation from Primo Levi. Think about it. Love from Mark.'

I scrumple the note into a ball and look around for a litter basket. There is none; a spate of IRA bomb scares has caused the removal of rubbish bins as well as the closure of the left-luggage depot at Victoria Station. I put the paper into my pocket, but in the train to Gatwick take it out again and smooth it flat. Was Primo Levi right? Is Mark Bissenden right?

After thirty years of life with a lawyer I am not surprised by the law's delays. Lord Blanchminster's libel writ has not been followed by immediate action, which is a relief since I am not yet in a good position to defend it. But Mark Bissenden calls to say that the Cavalier Press is very interested. Can I let him have a synopsis?

How can I provide a synopsis when I don't know what happens next?

What, Mark asks, has happened so far?

I print out a copy of my narrative. Two weeks later Mark returns it to me. 'A new departure,' he remarks, in a tone that combines congratulation and uncertainty. 'It's very different from anything you've done before.'

'That's the general idea,' I say.

'But I don't quite see where the plot is going.'

Nor do I. It is, after all, not in my own control.

'And you could do,' he says, 'with a bit more sex.'

'Sex?' I exclaim, and immediately regret the tone of my voice.

'I just thought, as you are branching out into a new line, perhaps the time has come for being a bit more explicit. Less discreet.'

'It's true I have never gone in for the obligatory bedroom

scenes,' I say defensively. 'But then I've not gone into the details of other incidents of daily life either. I can never see why one bodily function is discussed to the exclusion of all others. If every heave and moan on a bed has to be spelt out, why not the grunts and groans in the lavatory too?'

'That's different.'

'Why?'

'Obviously, because of the feelings involved. I thought we agreed, Anne, you have got to stop steering clear of emotion.'

'OK then, but whose? I can't write about what Michael and Irene did in bed. I don't know anything about it for a start, and I don't want to speculate. It's taboo. And Celia's still alive. I can't start guessing about her sex life.'

'Your mother can't have been celibate all her life after your father disappeared.'

'Maybe not, but so what? I don't know anything about that either.'

'You can't be a good writer and keep all your privacies,' Mark says gently. 'It isn't just a matter of not telling. You haven't been thinking, visualising, using your imagination either, Anne. You've never peeked behind the curtain. If you're going to write what is in you, there's no place for reticence and good manners or even the parent-child taboo.'

'Or the child-parent one?' I say a little bitterly. But I do not want to talk about Flora. I add hastily, 'It's irrelevant.'

Mark looks at me with a kind of pity. He says, 'What about Hubertus and Lotte – and Julian, for that matter?'

'Guesswork.'

'Imagination, you mean. You are a novelist, remember.'

'Yes, but this book is based on factual research. Nobody has said anything about it, or at least no more than the fact that what judges used to call sexual intercourse took place. Not how, not with anatomical details. People don't – or didn't. I know my children share blow-by-blow accounts with all and sundry, but I've never discussed my sex life with anyone and I'd be very surprised if other people started telling me about theirs.' I stare at Mark across the table.

We are having lunch at the Savoy this time, from which I have deduced that he expects this book to make a good deal more money than its predecessors. I am daring him to remind me of the sexual gymnastics in which he and I had once partnered each other. Even they, more varied than any I had experienced at the time (and, yes, I have experienced: this is not a virgin's reticence, I assure you) bore shockingly little resemblance to the inventive gyrations detailed in contemporary fiction. At literary functions I look at the authors who describe them and wonder whether their respectable facades hide satyrs or whether they simply re-cycle second-hand pornography. I could write it, too, I think, but not under my name, not under the name of Gerry Medlicott's wife, Flora, Jonathon and Christopher's mother.

'It would be completely out of place in this book,' I say.

Mark's only reaction is a raised eyebrow. He says, 'Even so, you could try to get Celia to open up a bit more.'

'Don't forget all I've had to go on so far is the manuscript she sent me last autumn. But I'm going to see her next week.'

There is a discreet bustle as a pair of politicians are shepherded to a discreet table, a louder noise as an actress follows them with three men in tow and takes her place in the middle of the room. Mark drags his attention back to me and asks whether I think it is wise to fly at the moment.

At this stage of the conflict in the Gulf travelling for fun has virtually ceased and the tourism industry is in trouble, but Corfu should be safe enough. 'I wouldn't have dared when the children were younger, but it doesn't matter now.'

'Well, good luck. And I think you should speak to Marianne Beowulf too.'

'You're probably right, though I've never been able to face going to Germany before.'

'Why's that?'

'To be completely honest, I think I am afraid. Those huge, Aryan men, the idea of what they might have done . . . perhaps it's race memory. Another reason is that subconsciously I've always been ashamed of the German connection. I wanted to be British. I wanted to belong here. One of the children's friends said perfect-ly innocently that he'd heard I was German and I nearly hit him. But maybe it's just that I'm getting older, or perhaps it's because society is so much more open in this country than it was when I was growing up. There doesn't seem to be the same need to conform.'

'I should have thought there was a lot to be proud of, being part

189

of that great cosmopolitan clan, the Silversmiths, Silberschmidts. Like being a Rothschild.'

'I am proud of that now. If I were beginning my career today I'd use the name instead of hiding behind Gerry's good English one. The family history really is remarkable. It's in a book that came out a few years ago when the London firm had its centenary. But when I was young everything was different. You wouldn't know, Mark. A white Anglo-Saxon Protestant male takes it so for granted. You never had to worry about being an outsider, but my chief ambition was to merge into the background.'

'You weren't an outsider except in your own head,' he says gently and I retort,

'That remark could only have been made by a Wasp born into the establishment.'

Mark's family has been in Shropshire since the Middle Ages. He is descended from colonial administrators and members of government. He had the grace to go slightly red, and said briskly,

'Well, my view is that you need to have a look at the Beowulfs' place,' he suggests. 'Near Dresden, wasn't it? A lot of people are going back. One of my authors has a contract to do a book about staking his claim to the family estate somewhere in East Germany, because now it's been reunified the old titles to land can be reasserted.'

'After so long?'

'There's a deadline. They have to get their papers in by the middle of this year, but if they do it will be given back. This bloke is an architectural historian. He's going to restore the place and his book will be about before, now and after. It should do quite nicely.'

I say I will think about going to Germany when I come back from seeing Celia Blanchminster.

Mark says, 'Good, so let me know what happens. Meanwhile I'll keep the Cavalier Press on hold.'

I find Primo Levi's book in the airport bookstall. It is called *Other Peoples' Trades*, and the observations it contains, wise in themselves, carry added force from their readers' knowledge that this man was himself a Jew, and a survivor of Auschwitz.

He gives advice to an aspiring writer. 'After ninety years of psychoanalysis and successful or failed attempts to pour the unconscious directly on to the page, I have an acute need for clarity and rationality ... Do not be afraid of doing an injustice to your *id* by gagging it, there is no danger; the "tenant on the floor below" will find a way to show up in any case because writing means laying oneself bare.'

25

My imagination carries a pair of contrasting pictures: one is of the young Celia Roget, small, chic, ambitious. The other shows the elderly Viscountess Blanchminster, a redoubtable, intimidating figure whose lifetime achievements have made her at once famous and feared.

Her voice on the telephone was clear and very English. She wrote to me in black ink and the neat lettering of a one-time classical scholar. The notes she sent me, and from which I have spent the last weeks reconstructing her story, are clear, informative, chilly. The unemotional stance from which I have written about Celia's pre-war experiences is not entirely the result of my own inhibitions, whatever Mark Bissenden may infer. Embroidery on the plain material Celia gave me could result in my having yet another legal action on my hands.

The flight to Corfu is delayed. Although the Gulf War has ended suddenly and victoriously, airport security is still rigid. It is after midnight when we land. Clouds obscure the stars and my first scent of Greece is of airline fuel, but I have always been thrilled by arriving in a strange place.

Now I gaze eagerly from the taxi windows as we swing off towards the hotel. The driver asks in good English how long I am to stay and whether I am meeting friends, and I am reminded that this is the first time I have gone abroad alone since spending six months in Florence between school and Cambridge.

I feel a sudden grief at the thought of the fears and homesickness that must have assailed my mother when she came to England. No wonder she was not good at holding my hand. Hers had not been held.

As soon as my small bag has been carried into my room, I rush to ring home. Gerry sounds surprised. 'Is everything all right? Are you all right on your own?' There are voices in the background. He must be watching television.

'Yes, everything is fine,' I say.

'Well, goodnight then,' he says, still puzzled. 'Have fun.'

During the inevitable delays and difficulties of hiring a car and changing currency (which involves some epic queueing) I am unexpectedly aware that I am not more anxious than usual on such occasions, on account of being unprotected, but much less. Is the usual tension about delays, ineptitude or other people's obstructiveness due to nervousness about Gerry's re- action to them? Will he be impatient, is he being driven mad, did he ever want to come for our annual ten-day trip abroad? Will he be silent with me at meals when other people are watch- ing?

Alone, I watch the indifferent Corfiotes dealing leisurely with my requests, and don't mind a bit. Nor do I worry about map- reading, tracking down the best restaurant for lunch, working out the most appropriate programme for the next few days. I have no Game Plan. Gerry is keen on Game Plans. I have no escort. I do not need an escort.

As a teenager, alone in Italy, I wore layers of frilly petticoats and a tight girdle in the hottest weather, not for the sake of modesty or fashion or even keeping my stockings up but because it foiled the bottom pinchers. Now, once more alone in a Mediter- ranean country, my flesh would be readily accessible. I am wear- ing thin silk trousers with a loose shirt. Nobody touches or even notices. Yes, Gerry, I am perfectly all right on my own; and on my way to visit Celia Roget, whose life has consisted of facing far more genuine dangers than any social embarrassment, I am ashamed that the question was ever asked.

The turning to Celia's home is off the coast road. A stony, dusty lane leads to a square villa on a spur of glittering rock. The house is made of blocks of light coral and ivory-coloured stone. Its garden overflows with bougainvillea and plumbago, roses, pas- sion flowers and numerous other plants I can't put names to. Lush growth covers the undeveloped slopes around it. I recognise ilex, arbutus, olives, cypresses, orange trees. The sea is enamel- smooth and hyacinth-blue and the bleached, bare bulk of Albania across the water gives perspective to the view.

I knock on the door and wait. Pink geraniums spill from bright blue tubs. A huge yellow butterfly settles on a creamy rose. Three geckoes cling motionless to the dry wall. Five white doves sit in a row outside their cote. The air is scented with aromatic plants, birds sing loudly, a soft breeze rustles the leaves on the trees. A white yacht with russet sails edges into view from the south. A very long way away a dog is barking.

This is like every northerner's wintertime dream of halcyon days. Shaking myself from a trance of delight I walk around the corner of the house, along a flagged path and into another burgeoning garden. At the far end is a vine-covered pergola and under it is a table laid with a blue and white checked cloth, a bunch of daisies in a painted jug, a pottery mug, a red enamel coffee pot.

'All it needs is some violins and a voice-over about vermouth,' someone says in my ear. I drop my bag, scattering its contents, and spin round. A man is standing at my shoulder. He is tall and dark, unshaven though not bearded, with dark glasses through which his eyes are invisible and wearing a ragged towel as a sarong. His feet are bare, with long, dirty toenails, and a faint, sour smell exudes from his skin. I guess he is in his forties and American. He holds out his hand. 'Chuck Mendoza.' I know the name. He is a photographer and specialises in disgust, twitching at the world's conscience from leper colonies and war zones, from accident wards and slums.

I shake his hand, which is clammy, and say my own name. He crouches to help me pick up my papers, tape recorder, money, sun cream, pens, make-up, and as he drops each item into the leather bag I feel him despising me for needing them or other such symbols of luxury and wealth.

'Go on down,' he says.

I follow the path between the glossy bushes to a natural rock platform a few feet above the sea with steps leading down to water level. A huge umbrella stands on the rock, with two canvas chairs reclining in its shade. Nobody is there, but a copy of my last book is lying open on a towel.

I sit on the steps, dangling my toes in the water. Through it every stone or shell is visible, every frond of seaweed, every tiny fish. The sun beats therapeutically through the thin fabric on to my back. I put my finger into a sea anemone and feel its greedy suction.

A shadow moves over the sea bottom. A woman is swimming silently towards me, doing a stately breaststroke, her face held up out of the water. She is wearing a black costume and a huge straw hat. Her arms and legs are mahogany brown, and as she climbs dripping from the sea I observe that the exposed skin is gnarled and knotted like an old tree.

It is Celia Roget, Viscountess Blanchminster. She flaps her hand to rid it of drops of water and holds it out to shake mine. Coming into the shade of the umbrella she takes off the hat and throws it in the sun to dry.

She has short white hair, flattened to her head. Her skin is liver-spotted and wrinkled, her brown eyes stare at me without compromise. 'Anne,' she says. 'Sit down. Or do you want to swim first?'

'I didn't bring a costume.'

'Do you need one?'

'Well. Perhaps later.' I wonder whether to swim in my shirt. I do not like other people seeing the stretch marks, the inelastic flesh, the signs of over-eating and under-exercising. Even Celia? Especially Celia. The young woman imprisoned in that old body is observant and critical.

She glances from my face to the picture on my book jacket (taken some years ago and tactfully improved even then). 'You are rather like your grandmother when I first met her.'

'Other people say I'm like my mother.'

'Really?' Celia is not interested. Anxiety floods over me. Will she be cooperative, will she answer my questions? Or am I to be brushed off as other intruding interviewers have been? Her celebrity is partly due, such is the perversity of publicity, to her reticence. I hear a placatory, mannered tone in my voice as I remark on the beauty of her establishment. I gush. The view, the garden . . .

'Yes, it's pretty. Where I used to live in Santa Barbara was more so.'

'You don't go there any more?'

'No, I'm based in Europe now.'

'But you're still writing.'

'The odd piece.'

I know those odd pieces: long, sophisticated analyses of current affairs. Editors give her space. What she says matters.

'I heard you were doing a book,' I say.

'I am, but not memoirs, don't worry. I'm discussing the effect of reporting on the conduct and outcome of war.'

The right name pops into my mind. I say, 'William Howard Russell from the Crimea?'

'That kind of thing.'

'Assuming that reporting has changed the course of events, you must have been pretty influential yourself.' Do I sound creepy? Yes, but it's true. Celia Blanchminster's reports from the trouble spots of the world during the years since the last war have exerted a powerful effect on democratic electors.

Korea, Cyprus, Kenya, Cambodia, Vietnam, Malaya, Indonesia, Tibet – one would need a gazetteer to list the places from which Celia Blanchminster's spare, precise prose has stabbed the world. Words on a page . . . words that can be read again, and quoted and framed. A more permanent record than a piece of film or television.

I had found one interview in which Celia was the subject herself. It dated from 1979 and appeared in the *New Yorker*. She had said she did not want her audience to be distracted by 'visuals' or her own personality. The journalist pointed out that she seemed to avoid the word 'I'.

'Events are filtered through my sensibility but I am not writing about myself,' she had said.

The author had described Celia's technique. 'She doesn't ask questions. Her silences are a question. Her subjects find themselves forced to fill them.'

I have learned the words by heart. I sit waiting for Celia to speak to me.

She rubs her face and hair with the towel and picks up a garment that was underneath it. She steps behind me, not bothering to warn me not to look. The wet swim suit is thrown past me into the sun. Then Celia comes forward again wearing a knee-length T-shirt the colour of cinnamon with long sleeves rolled back. In this simple garment, and apparently with nothing under it, she looks like one of those legends of elegance: Colette, Chanel, Diane Vreeland – timeless, chic, defiant.

She sits down to pull on black espadrilles.

I feel like a player in that children's party game. Who will be the first to break the silence?

It is Chuck Mendoza. He creeps up without a sound again and says, 'Want to eat?'

The table under the pergola has been laid with wine, olives, bread, cheese. I sit on a wrought iron chair. Chuck stands behind

Celia. He massages and kneads her shoulders and then rests his hand on her breast. Unhurried and unembarrassed, she moves away and sits at the head of the table, pouring wine for herself and me. She looks every day of her age but sexuality exudes from her and Chuck Mendoza, intimate and taken for granted and entirely without embarrassment.

Celia produces subjects for conversation as politely as she offers me the plate of olives.

The increasing development of Corfu, here in the north-east being the last unspoilt area of the island. The dependence of the Greek economy on tourism, the standard of hotels, the preponderance of visitors from Germany, the pressure on yacht moorings. The changes since Celia's first sight of the place just after the war. The battles in the harbour of Corfu town, during which three Victoria Crosses were won. The last war: a no entry sign.

I trespass. Celia, I tell her, seems to have dropped out of the story I am writing at the outbreak of war. That is one of the gaps I hope she will help to fill.

She pushes her plate aside. Chuck gets up and begins to clear the table.

'What puzzles me,' I say, 'is the change between the career you originally wanted, with all the formality and constraints you seemed to be quite happy with then, and what you eventually achieved, as an outsider. Was it the war that changed you? I don't even know where you were during it . . . or why you left England afterwards and never came back.'

She answers after an awkward gap. 'I don't like speaking about myself. I always refuse to when they ask me . . . women's groups, graduation ceremonies, luncheon clubs.'

'But – '

'It's what you need. Let me read what you have got so far to see what requires elaborating. Did you bring your manuscript?'

It had fallen out of my bag, and now, putting it on the table, I smooth my hand over it to flatten out a crease in the cardboard cover. 'It's only a draft. Please don't think this is a final version. Anything you don't want to appear . . . ' I babble until Celia's stillness stops me.

'Come back tomorrow,' she says. 'Now it's time to lie down.'

As though he has been listening through the half-closed shutters, Chuck calls down, 'Come on, honey. I'm waiting.'

I drive back to my lonely hotel room. Unwelcoming at first, with its minimal furniture, a hard wooden bed, one table, no rug or curtains, just a stone-tiled floor and a chair on the balcony, I become fond of it as the week passes. I spend the mornings talking to Celia and the afternoons sleeping and swimming. In the evenings I transcribe what she has said from my tape recorder on to the page.

The diet suits me. The hotel staff are respectful, perhaps because I behave like a grown-up and go round half-naked only in the sea. They consider that very proper at my age, although I don't think (yet perhaps they do) the time has come for me to swim fully clothed as the village women do. Coming down to the beach in the evening, wearing their usual black dresses and headscarves, they walk straight over the shingle and into the sea without taking anything off except their black lace-up shoes.

I am wasting time. Celia parts with information sparingly, in bursts of limited confidence that alternate with silences. I do not mind that she is spinning it out. To my own surprise, having feared loneliness, I am happy. I thrive on the solitude. Why have I never stayed alone before in a strange country, in an impersonal hotel?

Nobody knows me. Nobody cares what I do. I shall never see any of the people I meet here again. I dress modestly because my skin burns easily, and for no other reason. On the third day, as I perform the invariable morning ritual – one cream to soften, three more to disguise; artful touches of colour; meticulous twitching and brushing; the artifice that helps me dare to face the world – I suddenly ask myself: what does it matter what I look like? What do I care what people think of me?

Is that what Celia asked herself? – and answered? Is that how the conformist on a career ladder turned into an iconoclastic loner? I put down the brush and the paint pot. What do I care?

I don't.

Let me never care again.

'Yes,' Celia said. 'It was the ambition of my life to be an ambassador, the first woman ambassador. I bitterly regretted giving it up at the time.'

'Did you hold it against the baby? Is that why you never saw her?'

'No, I don't think so.' She sounds surprised. 'There wasn't

much point in my going to see her. She was all right at Blanch-minster.'

'But she thought you were her mother.'

'Oh, I'm sure someone told her the truth. The old nurse or Julian himself, perhaps. It wasn't my business. I did my duty by that baby when I got her into England safely. And, as it happened, getting married was what saved me from myself. To think I might have spent years in embassies and ended up Her Majesty's envoy to Ruritania. What an escape!'

At the time, of course, Celia Roget believed she had made an enormous sacrifice. Her rescue of Lotte Silberschmidt's baby might not be a deprivation to compare with those so many of her contemporaries had suffered, but it felt supremely important then.

She and Julian Whitchurch arrived at Folkestone after a miserable journey. They had been in such a hurry to get back to England before the ultimatum expired that there had not been time to find a nursemaid to travel with them. Julian was better at soothing the baby than Celia. Somehow they managed to feed and clean it between them, but emotional tension and sleepless (though also sexless) nights exhausted them both. At Folkestone Julian hired a car so they could be driven directly to Somerset.

'Never,' Celia tells me, the old indignation vivid in her voice, 'never have I felt so humiliated as when I first met Gwendolen. She was Julian's stepmother.'

'Yes, I know.'

'Up until that moment I'd been carried along by self-sacrifice, I felt – the only word for it is – heroic. And we had been so busy organising everything, and looking after the baby, there had hardly been time to think about what I was doing once I'd made the decision to do it. When we turned up at Blanchminster it really hit me. I was bedraggled, exhausted, I felt like a refugee myself. And Gwendolen knew perfectly well that we had married to legitimise the baby. I wanted to tell her the truth but the only hope for my reputation was for our story to be generally accepted, and Julian said she was the last person on earth to tell secrets to. Gwendolen put a good face on it in public and fudged the timetable as we had planned but in private – ! She thought I was a slut, a gold digger, a title hunter, that I'd caught her precious stepson in my vulgar little toils. Me, a mere doctor's daughter. Oh, Anne, it was awful!'

Half a century later Celia still smarts at the memory. Success, distance and the passage of time have hardly soothed the sting of the late Viscountess Blanchminster's contempt.

Chuck seems to sense it from afar when Celia needs him. I am beginning to speak when he appears. Without looking up, she takes his hand and holds it against her cheek. I see his thumb make a circling motion on her palm. Almost at once it is made clear that it is time for me to go.

Celia left Blanchminster within three weeks. She and Julian never discussed divorce and she is almost shocked when I wonder why. Collusion was illegal, divorce required a matrimonial offence and shocked society. It didn't matter; neither wished to marry anyone else. 'At least, I didn't after nineteen forty-four.' Her clear, decisive voice is briefly husky. She clears her throat. 'Actually I don't think Julian was the marrying kind.'

Celia spent the war on secret operations.

'In France?' I ask.

She is evasive. 'I got around a bit. That was when I first came to Greece, among other places.'

But it was in France that she met the love of her life.

'I don't want to talk about him.'

'Of course not.'

'And you needn't go poking around to try to find out. He was killed in 'forty-four.'

'I'm so sorry . . .'

'Just so you know. Things were different after that.'

A long fax arrives from London. Viscount Blanchminster's case has been set down for action. If we are to apologise it had better be soon. If we are to plead justification, I must hurry up and find the evidence with which to do so.

I ring Celia's house and Chuck answers. 'We are still in bed.'

Am I imagining the emphasis on the pronoun?

'You can't come here today. I'm taking her to get a hair cut.'

I tell him I shall have to leave the next day and we arrange to meet that evening for supper at a beach taverna near the town. We sit on a terrace over the sea with our ouzo and mezes, with the juke box playing another generation's music and a procession of summer visitors, arm in arm or hand in hand, strolling by. On the darkening sea moving lights show where the fishing boats are setting out for a night's work.

After the meal Chuck says 'cigarettes' and walks away.

I say, 'Did you keep in touch with Julian afterwards?'

'I only met him once. In Germany after the war in Europe was over.'

'That was your first job as a journalist?'

'Yes, I got there through an American called Thaddeus Burton. I'd known him before the war. He was a playboy of the western world then, but he had a good war and then took over his family's newsprint empire. I was accredited to *Burton's Biweekly* and managed to get myself to Berlin.'

'And Julian was in the Army of Occupation, so there can't have been official doubts then about his conduct in Germany before the war.'

'Ah. It's taken you a long time to get round to that,' Celia says. 'What you don't seem to understand is this – and, incidentally, you will have to do some rewriting. Anyone who was there will know you've got it wrong. Berlin was full of Brits before the war, not only the bigwigs who turned up at the Embassy, but students, holiday-makers, commercial travellers, business men . . . Julian wasn't unusual in being there.'

'But staying with the von Beowulfs?'

'That's hindsight again. Hubertus was a Party member, sure, but don't forget that anyone who wanted an official post had to join. The point is that there was nothing politically improper about being a friend of his at the time. And Julian was never a Blackshirt, he didn't join Mosley's party. I don't think he even became a member of the Anglo-German Fellowship or Association or Brotherhood or Group or Comradeship – England was full of high-minded organisations of people who thought Hitler was putting backbone into young people and making the trains run on time.'

'Fellow Travellers of the Right,' I quote.

'Yes, and as far as I know Julian wasn't even one of them. I always thought he was a playboy with certain tastes he could gratify more easily in Germany than at home. And, of course, he adored Hubertus.'

'Sorry – do you mean Marianne?'

'That's something else that needs a rewrite. You evidently don't understand about Hubertus either,' Celia tells me. 'I don't just mean his sexuality – '

'He can't have been gay,' I protest. 'You and he, Lotte and he . . .'

Celia looks at me with an expression that says I am a poor innocent. I add hastily, 'Or a bisexual, but wouldn't you have known that?'

'He was keeping me on a string. I was too infatuated to realise that all I was to him was a private line to what the British Embassy was thinking. It should have been perfectly obvious at the time. It was, to Declan Leary.'

'He does seem to pop up in the story like a chorus.'

'You missed his significance. You have described a dull little man without showing what was beneath the facade. He was a hero. He saw what was happening and did something about it long before other more glamorous Scarlet Pimpernel figures.'

'Such as Sir Douglas Dugdale?'

'You got most of their names, I think. Peter Hoyland, Hugh Wintle, my father.'

'I haven't been able to put a finger on their leader. Do you know – ?'

She smiles at me like the sphinx, mouth closed, eyes sleepy and knowing.

I say, 'Was it Declan Leary himself?'

'Not only have I signed the Official Secrets Act, more than once, but also, Anne, I made a promise. I don't regard myself as absolved from it by the lapse of time.'

'All right. But what happened to Leary after he got the sack?'

'He stayed in Berlin until the war broke out, then he retired to Eastbourne and went into a decline. By the time I made enquiries after the war he was completely past it and I don't know when he died. His diaries were deposited at the Wiener Library and there's a memorial to him in Jerusalem as "A Righteous Gentile".'

'And he understood what Hubertus was up to?'

'Yes, he saw.'

'But wouldn't you have been able to tell yourself if Hubertus didn't mean it?' I wonder.

'Perhaps, but don't forget that girls were less well informed in those days. Even I was an innocent at the time. I hardly knew that men could be both homo- and heterosexual. Hubertus's ambivalent tastes were outside my experience. At the time I'd only had one affair, with Michael Silberschmidt.'

'My father.'

'Oh, yes. For a moment I had forgotten. Well, I learned a lot from him when I was seventeen, but not enough. In any case, the main thing about Hubertus was something else, not sexual at all. Perhaps you have never come across anyone who has that power of human magnetism. It's an attribute as objective as the colour of someone's eyes. Hitler himself had it.'

'Hubertus had that?'

'You've written pages about me and him without seeing it. I admit I went crazy over Hubertus von Beowulf, but do you think I would have done unless he had something other people don't? Charisma, I suppose one would call it now, an attraction that transcends reason. Of course, not everybody was susceptible to it. I wasn't myself at first. I have sometimes wondered since whether it could be a function of the man's will.'

'Or the woman's.'

'Oh, Joan of Arc – you're such bores, feminists of your generation, the way you can't distinguish between causes and effects. But that's not what you're here to talk about. No, that particular quality is one some people are born with and use, men like Saddam Hussein or, for that matter, Hitler. In others it is a consequence of their status. Have you ever seen a whole crowd of people bewitched, literally, as though by magic, in the presence of royalty?'

'And you were helpless?'

'It's like hypnotism, I suppose. One has to be open to it as I must have been at the time. But the experience inoculated me. I've been immune ever since from such enchanters, and God knows I have come across some. If you haven't seen a crowd of Africans in thrall to a character like Idi Amin, or I remember once in China . . . well, take it from me the power is a real one.'

'I have never met a person like that, or even seen one,' I say.

'No,' Celia replies. 'That's obvious.'

I do not ask what she means. I can guess. She sees me, as Mark Bissenden does, as a respectable woman of limited emotional experience.

Celia sits with elbows on the table, veined, wrinkled hands clasped around the thick glass. She is wearing trousers and a loose top, both pale grey, with matching espadrilles and some chunky silver jewellery.

She is a woman who has pleased herself and still does: a good example.

I follow her eyes towards the promenade, so crowded now with Greeks and holiday-makers that they walk in a kind of unison at the same steady speed. Small boys dart in and out between them. Then there is a disturbance, as though a shark were pushing through a school of smaller fish. A phalanx of young men swash-buckles along. They have shaven heads and, in spite of the heat, black leather clothes. Swastikas are painted on their backs and arms. One carries a whip. One is hand in hand with Chuck Mendoza.

Looking at Celia, I see the observer whose dispassionate reports have been a chronicle of iniquities. She sees the swastikas. She knows what their wearers are capable of. But she remains objective.

Chuck winks at Celia and calls across, 'We'll meet you at the car.'

'I must go,' Celia tells me, pushing her chair back. We move together through the tables to the exit.

'Was Julian a homosexual too?' I ask.

'Homo, hetero . . . grow up, Anne.'

'Hubertus and Julian . . .'

'Hubertus, Julian, Lotte, Marianne. Permutations, combinations. We never discussed it, but I guess Julian thought that Lotte's child conceivably – in both senses of the word – could be his.'

'Or Hubertus's?'

'Or Hubertus's. In which case he would probably have been all the more eager to take her on.'

Chuck is standing beside Celia's Land Rover with a leather-clad, white-faced, earringed boy. The three drive off into the night as I go back to my solitary room.

26

I arrive home three hours later than scheduled, in the small hours. The front door opens to the smell of cigarette smoke, the sound of Bob Marley and a volley of barks from a small black mongrel.

Flora is at home.

Gerry is not.

Our daughter emerges from the fume-filled kitchen. I try to look delighted to see her and to feel it. Here is my precious child, my firstborn, the baby I loved enough to eat, the little girl for whom I would have put my head under a fast train. This is the child I vowed to make happy. My daughter would not spend her infancy in a distant country, her childhood at boarding school. She would never wonder whether her mother really loved her; whether, perhaps, she was a changeling. Long ago, people used to remark on our similarity.

Flora is taller than I am now. Her hair, once simply brown, is cut in short, upstanding tufts and coloured inky black. She has rows of studs from ear tip up to ear top and another single one in her nostril. Her blue eyes are thickly outlined with black, but the rest of her face is very pale. A tattooed trellis with pink flowers winds up her arm and under her grey sleeve. Her laced boots have steel toecaps and around her thin waist a heavy belt is dangling. It consists of a row of brass bullets.

'Darling, how lovely to see you!' I put my arms around her, expecting a diagnostic whiff of starvation-breath but she feels marginally less skeletal than usual and smells of my scent.

Flora is anorexic. We do not mention it any more. She is dyslexic too. It was when her little brothers shot past her at school that she gave up food – or at least so I supposed at the time. Later I realised that was too simple an explanation. What is wrong with Flora is obviously me. I don't know what I did to her but the authorities have convinced me I must have done something and

205

her condition is my fault. Flora has managed to survive, apparently without consuming any food, for fifteen years. Gerry has long since ceased to worry about it.

'How lovely to come home and find you. When did you get here?' I ask, thankful, not for the first time, that the English language permits one to ask such questions without making clear whether they are in the singular or plural.

'I had to come.' Another man, I think immediately. Flora has one disastrous affair after another.

I am too tired to talk. Tomorrow I will listen to the sad, repetitive story of *him*, his failings, sayings and total impossibility. Tomorrow I will tactfully offer money and help, and even shelter for the noisy, ugly dog. I will show Flora that here at least she will always have a refuge, that she can count on my interest. Mummy's here.

But when I come down in the morning to find there is no coffee and the freezer has been left open and the battery of my transistor radio is dead, the mask of the ever-tolerant, ever-supportive mother slips a little.

Flora actually notices I am irritated and almost seems to regret it, though not to the extent of going out to the corner shop to buy some fresh coffee. She stabs ineffectually at some of the mess and I say, 'Don't bother, Mrs Carvalho will be here soon.'

I carry my unwelcome cup of tea up to my study. Flora follows. At least she has brought an ashtray. She sits on the desk.

'What are you doing?'

'I'm sorting out my notes.'

'What notes?'

I explain I am writing a different kind of story. She says, 'I read one of your books the other day.'

Flora has never read any of my work before. I do not resent it. Writing friends tell me their children do not read their novels either.

With some nervousness I ask Flora what she thinks.

'I thought it was cowardly,' she said.

I flinch.

'I'm sorry, Mum, but you did ask.'

'No, it's all right. What do you mean?'

'Well, there's not much of yourself in it, is there? I suppose you chose to set it in the olden days so you could keep clear. I mean, it was a jolly good story and I couldn't put it down and all that, but . . . '

'What I am working on now is quite different. There may be too much of me in it even to publish. Dad won't like it.'

'Tell me about it,' Flora says. She is wearing an old towelling dressing gown she found on the door of the children's bathroom. It has red, blue and white stripes. In our album we have a photograph of Flora wrapped up in it at about the age of seven, during our last family holiday in an English resort before we started heading south for sunshine in the summer. She crouches on the sand of Minehead, shivering after a swim, her long hair in wet strands on her cheeks.

Flora has had a bath and washed her hair, which now seems less improbably dark, and is drying in small, soft curls. Her face is a little flushed from the hot water, and she has not painted her eyes yet. She does not look as threatening as usual.

Yes. I feel threatened by Flora, uneasy and nervous in her company. Have I actually been afraid of her for years? This must be the first time that the sensation has crystallised into a word; the first time I have allowed myself to think it. Afraid she will eat even less, vomit more, afraid that something I say, or something I have said, causes her troubles. Afraid to displease or upset her, afraid to criticise or suggest or require anything of her, afraid the irritation, impatience, exasperation that I provoke in her will be expressed in word or deed.

'I'd really like to know,' she says.

Flora is twenty-nine years old. Gerry and I have told each other many times that she is simply taking a long time to grow up. One day she will be a nice and satisfactory adult; a friend. Is this, at last, the day?

'Well, if you're really interested.' I begin to tell her about the work I have been doing in the last few months and the disastrous broadcast that caused me to start it. She listens kindly and even asks some intelligent questions. A misquotation teeters at the back of my mind. 'My child that was lost is restored to me again . . . '

Her condition has had a curious side effect (or result) which I began to notice when she was in her teens, and although Gerry was working too hard to have much time for the children even he remarked on the phenomenon. This apparently indifferent and hostile child, who seemed to be wrapped up in herself and her friends and whose life was conducted almost exclusively outside the home, could be extraordinarily sensitive to our thoughts and feelings. 'I know what you're thinking,' she would say, and prove it. When she wanted to hurt she had all the ammunition an adolescent could desire. Now Flora says,

'I may not be the prodigal daughter, Ma, but I do care.'

'Why, now?'

More thought transference? She answers, 'Perhaps I have grown up.'

We go downstairs to the kitchen. I put a piece of bread in the toaster and she says, 'I might have some too, put one in for me.' I make fresh tea. We sit in the conservatory as we have not sat for years, facing each other across a table with food on it. I must not count on it lasting. There have been other gleams of light in the darkness of Flora's condition: once when she was in love with an Italian tennis player, once when she had a job on a glossy magazine. But she has been a freelance for a long time. She is a stylist, which means she is the person who puts together the accessories and background details of fashion photographs, deciding which handbag or pair of earrings will best set off any given outfit. I gather it is highly skilled and well paid, but like all freelances she fluctuates between being too busy and having no work.

Flora gives some toast to her dog but takes tiny bites of a half piece with a scraping of Marmite on it. I try very hard not to seem to notice her doing so.

'So what do you do next?' she asks.

'I'm not quite sure.'

'You'll have to go and see Perdita, won't you?'

'I don't think so. What I'm interested in happened when she wasn't even born, or at least she was too small to know about it. She couldn't tell me anything about Julian that I need to know.'

'I meant the other way round. Aren't you going to tell her about Julian?'

'What?'

'Well, that he probably isn't her father, Lotte was her mother, that you're her first cousin, for God's sake! I mean, listen, Ma, you can't just sweep this under the carpet, pretend you don't know about it.'

'But it isn't my job. It's not my business.'

'That's what's wrong with you, Ma,' Flora says, but the tone of her voice is quite kind; tolerant might be the right word for it. 'You'll never be able to write this new kind of book if you won't tell yourself the truth. Stop being so polite and considerate and anxious to please for a change, stop worrying about other people's reactions and whether they will hate you for it like you always do . . . I couldn't count how often I've heard you say, "But what will people think? I can't do something because of what they will think".'

'Oh darling – '

'You've spent your whole life keeping your head down. Placating, mollifying . . . You've never told me to go to hell or get out of your life or stop bugging you, not once. Not once, ever.'

'You sound as though you think I should have.'

'I do, as a matter of fact. Because it's a lie, an acted, implicit lie. I've put you through hell, you and Dad, and all you've done is turn the other cheek and pretend it wasn't happening. I didn't want your kindness and forbearance and forgiveness and that crap. I wanted honesty!'

That's what you think, I refrain from saying. That's all very fine and large, I could tell her, but I know what would have happened if I'd said any of those things. I keep my mouth shut. Flora puts her hand across the table and takes mine. Her palm is dry, bony, rather cold. 'I'm not getting at you,' she says. 'I know it sounds like it, but all I'm saying is you are so conditioned to being on your best behaviour that you don't even admit to yourself what you'd really like to say. Let go for a change. Tell the truth.'

Should I tell her of the dismay the sight of her provoked in me?

'But the trouble is I've always cared what other people think of me, darling. Even you,' I say.

'That's putting it mildly. It's become your prime motive for everything you do. It's why you write books that couldn't possibly offend anyone. It's why you stay with Dad, keeping up the public image of the perfect couple. Sometimes I've thought it isn't us you love at all, it's the image of yourself as a loving mother, a happily married woman.'

'I am a – '

'Oh Ma, must you?'

'What?'

'Must you go on pretending? You're fifty-three years old – '

'Fifty-one.'

'Whatever. Old enough to face facts. You and Dad don't have one single thing in common any more. He's away more often than he's here and if he sleeps with anyone it isn't you. I see his stuff's in Chris's bedroom now, and I should think the only time you have meals together is when you're invited out.'

'Whenever he's in London – '

'I said together. I don't mean under the same roof or cooked by you. I mean talking, sharing, behaving like people who love each other. Don't forget I've seen you when you don't think anyone else is watching.'

'Flora, I don't want to have this conversation.'

'That's right, keep it quiet. If you don't put it into words it never happened, right? Oh God, what's the use? I don't know, Ma. I came home with such good intentions, too. Something about turning over new leaves, would you believe?'

'We don't have to quarrel.'

'And the next line goes, "Some things are better left unsaid", right?'

'Well, you know that's what I do think,' I agree.

If it's not said it never happened. Gerry hasn't gone off, hasn't gone off me; we keep up a front; we are the Medlicotts, Anne and Gerry, an item, a permanence. If I am not half of that couple, what am I?

My heart is thudding uncomfortably and I feel as though I may be about to discover the meaning of the expression, 'hot flushes'.

'I'm sorry if I hurt your feelings,' Flora says unexpectedly. 'But that's always been the trouble with you and me: neither of us has ever been able to put hurtful things into words with each other. Or anyone else. But this time you've got to, Ma. You'll have to tell Perdita, since neither Julian nor Celia had the decency to do so. She has the right to be told.'

'I couldn't.'

'You must.'

'It's impossible,' I insist, and Flora, in a mature, inflexible tone that I have never heard from her before tells me that if I won't she will. By the time Mrs Carvalho has finished clearing up the kitchen, we have agreed to go to Cornwall together.

27

The lawyers are not impressed by my progress so far. They are not interested in literature. They want facts that can be given in evidence about Julian Whitchurch's pre-war affiliation to the Nazi cause and of those, as opposed to hints, rumours and assumptions, I am woefully short.

'I have read your typescript with great interest, very great interest,' Mr Paxton says. I see it lying on a table to one side of his picture window. Wootton Hardman, Solicitors, which I knew first as a small and traditional firm in perpetually dusty offices off the Strand, now employs five hundred people and occupies a modern building near St Paul's Cathedral, so magnificent in scale and design that any future archaeologist would certainly identify it as a palace. Young Mr Paxton is not much older than my son Jonathon but sounds like a man of a different generation. 'It is a rare pleasure for our usually weary task to be enlivened by such elegant prose, but I fear your labours have raised more questions than, if I may say so, they have answered.'

I nod agreement.

'Let's see where we are in legal terms. What can we prove to a court's satisfaction?' He holds up a long, freckled hand and enumerates his points on his fingers. 'Lord Blanchminster – or perhaps we should call him Julian Whitchurch, as he was known at the time in question – Julian Whitchurch was present on frequent occasions, and for long periods of time, in Germany during the Nazi era until the time war broke out.'

'They won't try to argue about that.'

'No. And there's no doubt he regularly stayed with his kinsmen, the Baron and Baroness von Beowulf. Incidentally, Baroness Marianne von Beowulf's confirmation might be helpful, though of course we don't need her to confirm the fact that her brother Hubertus von Beowulf was at the time a member of the Nazi Party and later sought but never found for a war crimes trial.'

'Check,' I say frivolously. He frowns at me over his round gilt spectacles and says severely,

'As a matter of law, our system has no such concept as guilt by association. It will take more than that to incriminate Julian Whitchurch.'

'What about the conversation Celia heard at the Olympic Games in nineteen thirty-six? Surely the inference is that Julian was putting the finger on my father. And there was his relationship with Lotte Silberschmidt . . . the fact that he seemed to be expecting her arrest in the Grünewald in August 'thirty-nine and didn't try to stop it.'

'Hmph. This comes from an eye witness: his wife. They are still married, are they not? Is it your opinion that Lady Blanchminster would give evidence?'

'No,' I say. 'I am quite certain she wouldn't.'

'Quite. And do you have anything to prove that he passed on to the enemy – though not yet the enemy – information picked up fron, his friends, Sir Douglas Dugdale and . . . ' He pauses to look at the single sheet of paper in front of him. It is the only thing on his large glass desk. 'Hoyland. Wintle.'

'No, only that he could have done.'

'But my dear Mrs Medlicott, the story you have so ably told could just as easily indicate the very reverse. How do you know that Julian Whitchurch was not himself a member of the group – perhaps even its leader?'

'I don't follow.'

'It seems patently obvious from what you have written that they had some source of information close to or even within the Nazi Party. How else could they have known – to take just one example – that Michael Silberschmidt was due to be arrested on the very day that he was whisked away from under the noses of the Gestapo?'

The facts I have assembled slide around in front of my mind's eye, like one of those trick pictures made up of tiny variegated dots which can equally obviously show one of two images at the blink of an eye. 'It simply never crossed my mind.'

'It would certainly cross the mind of counsel on the other side,' he says.

'You mean Julian could have been playing a part, acting like a frivolous pleasure-seeker and actually keeping close to Hubertus for that very reason, to pick up names and chat and hear about what was going on? It's actually perfectly possible. And then his name would have been in Professor Hahn's notebook, but for a completely innocent reason. But no, Mr Paxton, that can't be right. He would surely have told somebody afterwards. Once the war had started he'd have deserved a medal.'

'If he was in Intelligence later he wouldn't tell secrets – any secrets,' Mr Paxton told me severely. 'In any case, if what I have suggested were true – and mind you, it's only one possible explanation for the facts – then there would have been no need for him to say anything. His friends would have known already and nobody else would have cared.'

I get up to stand by the window. The view is extensive but not beautiful. The famous photograph of the cathedral during the blitz comes into my mind as I look at the degenerate buildings that filled the bomb-damaged sites. Come friendly bombs and fall on – . The insensitive quotation is interrupted by Young Mr Paxton coming across the room to join me.

'I have made some enquiries about Lord Blanchminster myself, as a matter of fact,' he says. 'He was an Intelligence officer during the war, as you know, but did you realise he stayed on in Intelligence after that?'

'No. What as?'

'I'm not sure what his official title was, if he had one at all. Ostensibly he was a director of the bank, but I've heard he was on secret committees right up until a very few years ago.'

'Who told you?'

'It's the kind of thing one doesn't say in public,' he replies, momentarily blushing like a schoolboy. I can just see him picking up hints, or dropping them, in one of the archaic gentlemen's clubs which holds out against admitting women.

'What do people say about him?'

'He's thought to be a cold fish. No girlfriends – '

'Or boyfriends?'

'Not that anyone knew of. He was described as stiff, polite, very reserved. A stony pillar of rectitude.'

I am dismayed. 'Either he changed or I've got everything wrong. In the Thirties he seems to have been more like Bertie Wooster.'

'It would have been a good cover. Perhaps he was a front man behind the lines as it were, passing information to his friends. It's a great pity there is nobody left to ask.'

I count off on my fingers. 'My father. Celia Roget's father.'

'What about your mother? You have written about the friendship between her and Lord Blanchminster. Then there was Declan Leary. Peter Hoyland – I know his brother as it happens, he's a solicitor down in Devon, an old family firm. I rang him up. I'm afraid he didn't know much though he did remember lending Peter his passport once. Hugh Wintle. Sir Douglas Dugdale.'

'He died about two years ago. I checked.'

'Sir Hans Hahn could have been one of them.'

'Hans Hahn!' I exclaim. 'You don't really think so?'

'He does crop up in so many places. And you may recall his mentioning that he last saw your father with his hair dyed black – presumably after he left England on that last, fatal journey. Was he involved? Did he even go to Switzerland too? I must just add,' he goes on, 'that I am assuming, my dear Anne – may I call you Anne? – that your tendency to, shall I say, embroider a story – '

'My dear Tony – may I call you Tony? – are you asking whether I made any of this up?'

'You are a novelist, after all.'

I assure Tony Paxton that what he has read has been the result of scrupulous research. The facts have not been improved upon by imagination.

'Well.' He shuffles his papers together. 'I don't know whether Julian Whitchurch was a crypto-Nazi or an unsung hero. But my professional opinion is that Lord Blanchminster has a case.'

28

I can tell when my daughter is lying. Flora greets Adam Ross as though his presence in his mother's house comes as a complete surprise, but I realise why she has been showing interest in my current work and why she has accompanied me to Cornwall. Now I understand the improvement in her appearance.

We have come by train to Penzance and by taxi from there, across bleak moors, to the north coast. Perdita lives in what seems to have been two cottages and a Methodist chapel, later converted into one white house. It is set above and at right angles to the road, facing the sea and the weather. There is no garden, only a pull-in big enough for one car carved out of endless hillside and clifftop.

Perdita Whitchurch does not look pleased to see us. She exudes lack of welcome and I find myself saying that we mustn't stay. Perdita's son's voice drowns hers and mine.

'Come on in, it's freezing out there. Why my mother chooses to live on a blasted heath . . .'

He is my cousin. I do not feel any sense of kinship. He is tall, with regular features and a ready smile. He wears denim jeans with the crease mark of a hot iron still on them and a white polo neck sweater, a brass-buttoned blazer and highly polished shoes, the very last type of man that I would have expected to choose my poor Flora, or would have expected Flora to choose. That is another thing I can tell about my daughter – when she is in love.

We follow Adam into a tiny lobby. There is no mirror for me to tidy my wind-blown hair and I don't even try, but leave my coat on a chair already piled with clothes and papers and go on into a sparsely furnished and cheerless sitting room. Beyond it is the studio, a vast white space without pews but otherwise little changed since it was a chapel. The tall arched window, facing north across a few fields to the wild cliffs, lets in a clear, bright light even when, as now, rain is clattering against its panes.

'English summers,' Adam Ross mutters. There is no form of heating in the studio, as far as I can see. The unvarnished wood floor is thick with dust and scraps of paper, some of them stuck down with drips of oil paint. A stained and threadbare Persian rug is rumpled in front of the easel. A canvas garden chair, with two moth-eaten tapestry cushions, is in the middle of the floor and a three-tiered wire vegetable rack is overflowing with what look like bills, private-view cards and letters. Unframed canvases lean against the walls. A few are hung up. One, I see, is not by Perdita herself but by Renoir. Its rosy delight is the only patch of comfort in the austere room.

Perdita's easel stands in front of a table laid with an orange cloth and a lustre jug of pink, mauve and blue wild flowers. On our way westwards the previous day we noticed hedgerows full of bluebells and ragged robin and other plants which Flora surprised me by identifying. Her Granny Medlicott's teaching had stuck, it seemed. Gerry's mother had been a primary school mistress before her marriage and was always irritated by my lack of interest in what she called nature study. During our children's early years she pressed instruction on them. I lived in apprehension that they might show the old woman they didn't want it but they did, lapping up everything to do with the family countryside in Yorkshire.

Perdita smokes with nervous, staccato gestures. Paint is smeared on her shirt and jeans and she is evidently in the habit of wiping her hands through her hair.

I wonder how she ever produced such a smooth young man as Adam. I wonder if he already knows why we are here.

He says, 'Flora, come and help me organise some coffee.'

I have seen my daughter kick a man on the kneecap with her heavy boots for less. Now she follows him meekly from the studio.

Perdita grins at me in complicity. 'Children!' she exclaims. 'I'm sorry, Anne. Adam somehow rubs me up the wrong way. He's so disapproving. Anyway, I'm glad you came. Is Flora going out with him?'

It is the current expression and means the exact opposite. Is she staying in with him?

'It looks like it,' I say. 'I didn't know.'

'Funny, your daughter and my son after all this time.'

Funnier, I think, than Perdita knows. She goes on:

'I shouldn't have thought she was his usual type.'

'He isn't hers either.' I am on the defensive. Other girls brought home to Mum by Adam Ross were probably well dressed and polite, with prospects and titles.

But then Flora comes back carrying some steaming mugs, and gives them to us with unprecedented solicitude. She draws a stool within reach of Perdita's hand for hers, saying to me,

'Black, Ma, exactly as you like it.'

Adam Ross perches on the window sill beside me. This window looks inland to some farm buildings. Across the hillside are the remains of a prehistoric village about which the taxi driver who brought us from Penzance told us, saying he brings his children out to play in the ruined huts. Local building methods have changed very little in millennia, for the barns and sheds are made of gigantic granite boulders heaped on each other without mortar, with vegetation growing on the walls themselves and on the low-beamed roofs. I see that one of Perdita's paintings is of such a primitive shelter. She has made it threatening, as though angry ghosts inhabited the stones.

Adam says, 'Flora and I met in London, Mrs Medlicott. I expect you were wondering about the coincidence.'

'Did you know who she was?'

He is commendably direct. 'You mean, did I know about my grandfather's libel action? Yes, of course. I recognised her name at once.'

'But you didn't – '

'Hold it against her? No. The sins of the mothers . . . ' His voice trails away as he looks at his own mother.

She says, 'Tell me, Adam, what are you actually doing here in the middle of the week. Don't they need you at work?'

'This seemed more important, just at the moment.'

Perdita turns her eyes, as though for relief, to her work in progress. At first sight it is a blur of brilliant colour; then its separate streaks rearrange themselves in my sight into the still life on the table. 'It isn't right.' She lifts the canvas on to the floor, where she props it face to the wall. It's obvious she would rather be working.

I start, 'We won't stay, Perdita. I'm so sorry we . . . '

'Ma.'

'Mother.'

Adam and Flora speak simultaneously, as though they were the parents and we two middle-aged women were their children. Adam goes on, 'Mother, Anne Medlicott has something to tell you. I think it's important.'

'It's about your parents,' I begin.

Perdita interrupts me. 'I wish you wouldn't, Anne. I realise you mean well but it isn't a good moment. Anyway, you know I don't really . . . Look, why don't you wait until the exhibition's ready?'

'Mother, this is as relevant to me as to you. I want you to listen.'

'You sound exactly like Niall. Have you met Adam's father, Flora? Adam's getting awfully like him.'

'At least that shows he is my father.'

'What?'

I say, 'Perdita, I have to tell you what I've been working on since we last met. You need to understand what happened before the war, when you were born – '

'But I told everyone when all this started. I don't care if Julian was a Nazi collaborator or sympathiser or whatever. The things that old man said on the box couldn't matter less to me. Niall and Adam only care because it affects business. The good name of Blanchminster's,' she adds, in a deep 'in quotes' voice. 'I can see it's important to you, Adam, but I wish you could understand that it isn't to me.'

'Mrs Medlicott wants to tell you something else.'

'Do you, Anne?'

'Not about politics,' Adam adds.

'It's about your mother,' I try again.

'I never knew her.'

'Your real mother.'

That catches her attention. Perdita waits for me to go on and I find it is impossible for me to put it into words. How can I, after a lifetime of never saying anything that will offend or annoy, blurt out to Perdita Whitchurch that she is the bastard daughter of a Jewish prostitute? How can I say that, whoever her father was, he must have been either a Nazi or the friend of one?

In the end Flora does the talking, which is fair enough since it is she who believes the truth must be told. Even then I find myself

218

trying to smooth things over. I begin to babble about being related, first cousins, everything we have in common.

But there is no need to smooth anything over. Perdita is not shocked or dismayed.

'I haven't seen my father – if Julian is my father – for literally years and I don't ever remember setting eyes on Celia. If she's not really my mother, I'm quite glad.' She pauses for a moment, cigarette poised by her open lips. Then she turns to me and says, 'Very glad, in fact. You've reminded me how much I used to mind that I never knew her. Imagine what it felt like to have a mother alive whom you'd never even met. Oh, I used to care, I cared like anything. I thought it must be my fault, something I'd done, something wrong with me . . . and then, when I grew up and began thinking for myself, I was angry. How could she have behaved like that? Why did she do it?' Perdita's face reddens. 'I could have killed her.'

'It always seemed very peculiar to me,' Adam says. 'I've often wondered if you knew why she had gone off.'

'I never asked. I never had a chance to ask. Who would have told me? I just felt guilty, then furious and revengeful – but not for years. It's in the past. I haven't consciously thought about her for ages.'

Not consciously; but looking round the violent paintings in the studio, I think I know where that emotion came from.

'Anyway.' Perdita pulls deeply on the smoke. 'You can see why I don't mind being told Celia was never my mother in the first place, but I don't honestly think it matters terribly who was.'

'But you must care who your real parents were,' Flora says.

'It's an overrated relationship. Parents and children don't necessarily have anything in common. Look at me and Adam.'

'But it does matter,' Flora insists. 'Heredity and family traits – it's part of the same thing. You can't pretend they don't exist. If Adam . . . if we knew his grandfather was really . . . '

Perdita says and I think, 'Ah, so that's it.' That is why our son and our daughter are interested in this old history. What a relief it will be for Gerry if Flora settles down with such a pillar of the establishment as young Adam Ross. I can't wait to see his face when he hears.

Flora is frowning and Adam puts his arm around her shoulder and says in a bossy voice, 'We think it matters, don't we, darling?'

219

'Darling', he calls her! And she looks up at him with an expression that might be called submissive. My independent, self-sufficient, rebellious daughter!

'We weren't going to tell you yet because I haven't had a chance to ask her father.'

Do young men still say such things?

'But Flora and I have decided to get married.'

Flora's eyes plead: don't tell him what my views on matrimony used to be, don't spoil it. So I say,

'Darling, how lovely! I'm so happy for you.' I step forward and hug my daughter, uninvited but safe from the usual rebuff while Adam is watching. Then I reach up to kiss him. We briskly perform the formal, double cheek-to-cheek. But Perdita does not follow suit. She is looking at a painting of trees, wild, brown, green, threatening.

'Mother?' Adam says.

'Adam. Good. Yes, do get married, excellent idea. I'll give you a picture as a wedding present.' She seizes a brush as though to start the painting immediately.

'I told you my mother was impossible,' Adam says. 'Mother, stop it. Put the brush down. Listen.'

'It's all right. I've got it. You are worried about your children's genes. Hereditary iniquity, right? I think it's a load of nonsense. Look at me. Look at you, for instance. Who would ever guess you were my son? If you weren't so like Niall they might have swapped you in the hospital. But go ahead, find out if you want to for your own sake. Not for mine, though. I gave up being Lord Blanchminster's daughter a long time ago, or anyone else's for that matter. I'm a painter. I'm myself. I don't need a family tree or a father or a mother any more than I need a husband. I stand on my own.'

We are getting into Adam's car when Perdita runs down the steps from the front door and leans in through the open window close to me. 'What did you say she was called? Your father's sister?'

'Charlotte Silberschmidt. Lotte for short.'

We go to Blanchminster on the way back from Cornwall the following day. Flora insists we should be driven by Adam. I realise it is part of their prearranged plan, so fall in without argument and watch the countryside go by in the back of his

BMW while they talk about people I have never heard of. It is a warning of what is to come: granny in the back of the car with the kids while the grown-ups sit in front hoping that both young and old will be quiet and undemanding.

Flora and Adam's conversation reveals that they met at a wedding and fell in love at first sight. It was not the sort of wedding they intend to have themselves. There were guitars and spontaneity and modern poetry. The bride wore shocking pink and walked to the altar unaccompanied.

Flora and Adam require the traditional service and the Authorised Version. Gerry is to 'give her away'. Her dress, she swivels to tell me, will be designed by a wonderful new girl recommended by the fashion editor of *Vogue*. I ask faintly whether it is to be white and she says, 'Yes, of course.'

I do not ask whether Gerry is to pay for it. I refrain from discussing the symbolism of virginity or the significance of one man giving to another the hand of a sexually experienced woman who has earned her own living for ten years. I stop myself from whining that the last part on earth I wish to play is that of the bride's mother. I realise this must be what my iconolastic daughter has been really longing for for all these years: Mr Right and a love affair that leads to the altar.

We turn off the main road between eagle-topped pillars into a wide, well-kept and overlong drive.

'We thought it would be nice if it could be here,' Adam tells me. 'A country wedding.'

Rural but not rustic. Blanchminster is a monument to generations of megalomania, starting with the man who commissioned the building in the sixteenth century and carried on by his seventeenth-, eighteenth-and nineteenth-century heirs, and even by the present owner. Rather than passing it on to a school or charity, he apparently thinks it acceptable to live in premises large enough to house every homeless family in Somerset.

This palace is the home of one derelict old man and those employed to care for him. It will be inherited by one woman who doesn't want it. When Adam told Perdita that he was taking us to see his grandfather at Blanchminster she first shuddered and then shrugged her shoulders. 'I detest the place,' she said. 'My childhood there was hateful. If I never see it again it will be too soon.'

I can see that Adam hopes to inherit it himself. He leads us through the unlocked front door looking self-confident and proprietorial. Flora stares eagerly from side to side.

The floors are polished and patterned parquet scattered with perfect oriental carpets. The walls are hung with glossy damask, crimson, golden, Wedgwood blue. There are huge portraits and landscapes in ornate frames, gilded mirrors and marqueterie furniture. I see no pictures by Perdita, which would look as unsuitable and exotic here as their painter. There are no silken ropes. This house is never open to the public.

Six vast rooms lead to a library full of leather and mahogany, globes, reading stands, drum tables, every piece of paraphernalia appropriate to a gentleman's reading room except for the gentleman reading.

Lord Blanchminster sits in a wheelchair, the lower part of his body wrapped in a grey cashmere blanket. His upper half has been clothed in a shirt, jacket and tie. He has been shaved, his sparse hair trimmed, his blue hands arranged side by side on his lap. There is a little movement in the left side of his face on which the eyelid trembles, and a muscle twitches in the cheek. Everything else is paralysed.

Adam's voice is loud and clear. 'Hullo, Grandfather. How are you today? I've brought my fiancée to see you. It's Flora Medlicott. Her father's a barrister and this is her mother. Do you remember her? You knew her when she was little. She was called Silversmith and her mother was Irene Silversmith. Flora and I are going to get married in September.' He breaks off and adds more quietly, 'The doctors think he may be able to understand.'

If he does he has no way of showing it. Is that a gleam of intelligence in the watery eye? Who knows?

'How do you do, Lord Blanchminster? I'm so glad to have the chance to meet you.' My babble trails away.

My fantasies have collided with real life.

For months I have been living with the idea of Julian Whitchurch, playboy or plotter – but whichever role he played always a vibrant, vigorous man, my subject, my preoccupation.

His younger self has been absorbed into me. I have been determined not to invent but inevitably the man I have described must be in some way my creation, at once as real and as unreal as the

222

characters in my fiction. He exists as they do, at my will; his actions interdependent with my words.

At the same time as the younger Julian Whitchurch formed himself at the end of my typing fingers, so the things he did and the things that happened to him seemed to be in the control of my brain too, at least for as long as I was writing about them.

The character in my narrative remains a man, simultaneously young and old, whose existence is at once outside me and in my control.

But even in my imagination he has been more than a character in fiction. That is why I have been floundering. For he is also, perhaps, the man who robbed me of my father. Old though he is, and infirm, he is no less responsible for the actions of his youth than Eichmann or Demjanjuk or any of the other Nazis caught late but not too late to be tried for their crimes.

But it is not until I look at the geriatric in the chair that I admit even to myself to what extent my quest has become a manhunt. I have become involved.

This shell of a man arouses emotions I cannot cope with.

I care. But I do not want to care. I hate though I only wish to analyse, I shudder when all I ever intend is to make my readers shudder. I have lost my armour of immunity.

When I embarked on this real quest I half expected to manipulate its results as I did the plots of my novels, artfully moving them forward here, giving clues to the next revelation there.

Imagination and history merge here in the still and sterile air of this luxurious mausoleum.

I look at the dying man and no longer want to know the truth about him. Villains and heroes, death and disaster, sufferers and saviours must remain in my imagination, confined within the limits of my prose. I dare not face them in real life. Or their consequences.

29

Adam Ross displays public school phlegm. He says half the boys at Eton were probably the result of the wrong man and woman getting into bed together. He thinks that breeding only matters in animals. He does not believe in inherited guilt, only in inherited wealth, privilege and stately homes.

Adam and Gerry agree on this as on much else. They form an immediate masculine alliance. Adam, however, is indulgent about Flora's attitude. Gerry finds mine irritating.

I have spoken of it only to him, not to Flora. Gerry says he will never forgive me if I spoil things for her.

'You should be on your knees thanking God that she's landed on her feet at last. You must be mad!'

'But I can't bear it. If they have children, think what they might inherit.'

'A good deal of money by the sound of it.'

'If Perdita was really Hubertus's child . . . those Prussian genes.'

'Anne. Racism, from you?'

'I know. All the same, I never thought I might be glad that it's difficult for former anorexics to become pregant.'

'Stop it.'

'I can't help it. The idea makes me sick.'

Adam's first visit to our house: Gerry is in a very good mood.

I am reserved, but have gone to some trouble to prepare the meal and the house to its best advantage.

Adam has excellent manners. He looks glossy and assured. Would I like him in other circumstances? No. He is pompous. I hate to see the humbly worshipful expression on Flora's face.

She is eating the apple pie.

Adam turns the conversation to my book. He takes it for granted that I shall be abandoning it.

'The Cavalier Press won't be a problem. As it happens my father is one of their non-executive directors, though I suppose you will have to repay your advance. What are you going to tell your agent?'

He is presumptuous.

I say, 'But I have nearly finished. Only a little more research to do.'

Gerry and Adam prove they are already on the same wavelength. In chorus they say, 'But you can't possibly publish it now.'

This time last year they would have had no need to tell me so. I would not have dreamed of exposing myself, or my family or any friend or even acquaintance. But then my own eyes would also have been closed.

My head was in the sand.

My roots were deeply buried.

Excavation, disinterment, exposure to the light – all the metaphors for revealing secrets seem to be about burial and digging.

A different image: I have stared unmasked into the mirror, or, as I used to make my poor mother say, the looking glass. My insistence on the vocabulary of the upper classes was itself a symbol of what I wanted to see and to seem.

All my life I have hidden behind it: the mask of a fully assimilated English lady, discreet, conventional, both in and under control. A girl who conformed to the expectations of society, a woman who was careful not to shock anyone.

I look down the shining mahogany at the familiar view of my husband in the foreground and behind him the plane trees outside the window in full summery leaf hiding the white stucco of the houses across the road. These are my Lares and Penates: the silver Gerry inherited along with other chattels from the Medlicott place in Yorkshire when his brother took over the farm; the topographical engravings we have collected, the Orrefors glass table-centre his Head of Chambers gave us as a wedding present, the not-quite-oblong pottery butter dish Jonathon made at his prep school. The table mats have pictures of the stately homes of England, though not including Blanchminster. Everything is just as it should be, and just as it has been for years, symbolising the life my mother wanted for me, the life I too longed for, the stability I sought and worked for.

I do not know the woman who cherished it. That is not who I am any more.

There has been a silence at the table. After a while I answer my husband and my daughter's future husband.

'Have you ever wondered why ageing women can become so critical and disagreeable?'

'Sorry?'

'I'll tell you. It's because they realise it's too late to be pretty or attractive or seductive or pleasing. It's a liberation. They break the habit of a lifetime, they stop trying and let go. They utter their thoughts instead of what other people want to hear.'

'What is your mother on about?' Gerry says to Flora. It is his familiar method of neutralising my assertions – to speak to me through one of our children. For once I carry on regardless.

'They have spent their lives being what other people wanted them to be. Then one day the trick stops working. Nobody wants them any more, no matter what they do. So what's the choice? To avoid displeasing, even if they can't please – or to break out and do what they want themselves? If they still know what it is.'

'You are talking nonsense,' Gerry says. 'What's the matter with you? Don't frown like that.'

When the actress Jane Fonda was complimented on looking wonderful for forty, she said, 'This is what forty looks like nowadays.' By the time she was fifty she had had plastic surgery. I am not frowning; but neither am I wearing the make-up with which I used to disguise the lines on my face. And I have not had a face lift.

I say, 'I'm not frowning, Gerry. This is what fifty-plus looks like nowadays.'

'What? Can't you keep to the point? We are discussing how to get you out of the book contract. After lunch I'll call Paxton and tell him to draft an apology for the Blanchminster lawyers to agree to.'

Gerry is fifty-eight years old. He is not fat because I am careful of his diet and he plays squash. He is tall, grizzled, with such hair as he has left cut by a traditional barber in Jermyn Street. His linen is starched and smooth, his suit pressed, his collar stiff. He looks as expensive and well cared for as a man can, whose wife has made herself a good substitute for a valet.

226

That is the shirt, I think, on which there was a pink mark on the collar. I sprayed the lipstick with stain remover before putting it into the washing machine and told myself it meant nothing now that men and women kiss even strangers in greeting.

We have not made love, or, to express it more accurately, had sexual intercourse for months. No: for years. Gerry comes home late – when he does come home rather than staying in the flat. He says he does not want to disturb me and goes to bed in Chris's old room.

Do I mind? Now that I am being honest, let me be honest about this too.

No.

A passing phase? Perhaps; there have been others such, after childbirth, after quarrels, after illnesses. But it is only in contemporary mythology that lust is a universal, inescapable, invariable motive force.

I don't miss it.

With whom does Gerry make love?

Whom does he love?

Not me.

I remember the moment I realised that Amy Swift, the companion of my imagination, had taken wing and left me, faded into the invisible distance.

Suddenly the material facts with which I have always described my life take on a similar evanescence. The husband, the house, the home, the persona of a physically attractive woman who loves and is loved seem equally illusory. Or perhaps they were the chrysalis of a new, a different Anne.

'Ring Paxton. Feel free,' she says. 'But I have made up my mind.'

'Mummy . . . !' Flora wants her fiancé to see the mother she knows, the good mother who has nothing in common with his bad one. I remember what she said to me the other day. I've put you through hell all these years. Yes, Flora, you did. But that is over too.

30

The Peruvian novelist, Mario Vargas Llosa said: 'If you write fiction lying is perfectly moral and acceptable. You don't expect to write a novel telling only truths.'

Or telling any truths?

In the words of the first Queen Elizabeth: 'They say. What say they? Let them say.'

They do say; and without any prompting from me.

Marianne von Beowulf's death is announced and so is Adam and Flora's engagement, in three daily papers, the Somerset local weekly and the Blanchminster's Bank *Bulletin*. Flora has posed for unrecognisable portrait photographs, wearing pearls. They have decided on wedding present lists at the General Trading Company, Peter Jones and Divertimenti. The wedding is to be put off until Christmas so Christopher can come. His girlfriend is pregnant. They got themselves married one morning in Arizona and wrote a fortnight later to say so. Her baby is due in September. I shall be a grandmother.

I look like one.

I have seen Gerry eyeing my changed appearance. He has not commented on it yet.

It seems Marianne Beowulf was a celebrity and there were obituaries in most English newspapers. She had spent some years as a member of the West German Parliament. At first a Socialist, she had later joined the Green Party and in her old age was treated by modern young feminists as a kind of role model.

I gaze long and hard at her photograph, wondering whether I can really trace in it the hungry face of the woman who had called on my mother when I was a small child. In middle and old age, Marianne had become strong-boned and gaunt, her white hair

228

scraped back in a bun or a bunch, with no vanity in the eyes which stared, open and candid, into the lens.

She never recanted her left-wing views; so at least it says in the articles about her printed after her will was published. Nonetheless, at some point during the last months of her life and after the reunification of the two Germanies, Marianne von Beowulf, heir by survival of its previous legal owner, staked her claim to ownership and possession of her family's ancestral home and lands at Heorot.

She had designated two heirs.

Marianne Beowulf left her estate in equal shares to: The Honourable Perdita Ross, née Whitchurch, daughter of Julian, Viscount Blanchminster, and Professor Sir Hans Hahn of King's College, Cambridge.

Hans Hahn gave many interviews and said the same in each.

His father had been the land steward for the von Beowulfs, and Hans had grown up in a small house at Heorot. The family, though baptised, was of Jewish descent. After the Nazis came to power in 1933 the Hahns left Heorot and settled in the Saxon town of Chemnitz, now known as Karl Marx Stadt. Hans escaped to England before the war, expecting to be followed by his parents, but they had not emigrated in time and died in a concentration camp.

He had never published his precise place of birth before.

Why not?

'You have to understand what British society was like when I arrived in England. Do you suppose this bloody foreigner would have been accepted at a Cambridge High Table, or have been given the acting rank of major in the Control Commission after the war? Could I have become what I am now if people had known I was working class?'

When had he renewed contact with Marianne Beowulf?

Never. They had not met since he left Heorot.

Then how did he explain her legacy?

Hans Hahn assumed that Marianne von Beowulf, half a century too late, was making amends. A kind of atonement, perhaps. An apology.

What about the other beneficiary?

'How should I know?' Sir Hans Hahn said. He had no idea why

Marianne Beowulf should have made Perdita Whitchurch her heir. He had once met her on a TV programme, that was all. 'Ask her, not me. She can tell you herself.'

So they did; but she didn't.

An article by one of Marianne's disciples, printed in the *Neue Züriche Zeitung*, was sent to me by Mark Bissenden who had seen it when he was in Zermatt looking at wild flowers.

In her last years Marianne had become interested in her own family background. She was returning, on a more personal level than before, to her first academic interest, the quest for an explanation of what happened to Germany in the twentieth century. In old age she began to believe that events which she once supposed were entirely the result of historical forces and economic pressure had been at least equally shaped by individuals nurtured and educated in a certain direction.

She used her own relations as a paradigm, but the more she learned about them the more respectful she became of their achievements having, for most of her life, repudiated the connection. Blood will out, she was heard to mutter, and began to draw up pedigrees and mention family traits.

The young journalist implied that Marianne regretted her own childlessness. The von Beowulf name would die with her.

To me it is obvious why Marianne left Heorot to Perdita. She believed her to be the daughter of Hubertus. She believed Adam Ross to be his grandson. His blood runs in their veins.

Is it in Hans Hahn's too?

I am telephoned by an old acquaintance from the British Council, at whose behest I have occasionally performed such cultural chores as speaking about crime writing in Milan or reading aloud from my own work in Madrid.

'I hear you're writing something very exciting.'

'I wouldn't say that.'

'I met Mark Bissenden. He's full of it.'

I did not realise Mark had started talking the book up. The thought of Gerry's reaction, and Adam's and Flora's, makes me hesitate. Then I say,

'That's nice of him. I hope he isn't overselling it. I haven't even finished it yet.'

'That's what he said. You've got a research trip to eastern Germany still to do. What I was thinking . . . '

The British Council is laying on a festival in Dresden. It will include art, drama, books: all the paraphernalia of cultural diplomacy to show the former East Germans the British culture they have been missing.

Will I do a reading from a published book and speak about the one I am finishing now?

I will think about it and let him know.

But I do not mention it at home.

Flora has colonised the dining room for wedding preparations. A new list is added every time Adam comes to stay. The whole thing sounds more like a military campaign than a marriage of two ordinary young people.

I try to feel sorry for Adam. Uncertainty about one's true identity should be unsettling for anyone, and especially for a man who supposed himself to be the scion of an aristocratic English line.

He must be disorientated and anxious, but I can feel sorry only for myself.

How can the daughter of Michael and Irene Silversmith reconcile herself to an alliance with the descendant of Hubertus von Beowulf?

So far, she cannot.

I am intensely polite to Adam. I chat and smile and enthuse. I cook and smile and attend.

'You don't like him,' Flora says. 'I can tell.'

In August Gerry leaves, as usual, for a month in Scotland. Adam and Flora are to cruise with friends around the coast of Turkey.

I sound vague about my plans. I might go to the writers' retreat in Wales, I say, or perhaps I'll just stay at home and get on with some work.

Thinking about a new novel, Gerry supposes approvingly. That's more like it.

I pack my luggage. It is the first time I have done so without worrying about its contents and weighing them down with things brought 'just in case': in case I have to meet smart people, go to elegant restaurants, keep my end up.

Don't you care about the impression you make on other people? I asked Flora once. No, she said. That's their problem.

I leave out the high-heeled shoes, the restricting underwear, the flattering, impractical fashions in which Anne Medlicott used to make her good impression.

I pack notes and files and an old photograph album, once my grandmother's. Here, in sepia or faded black and white, is the Silberschmidt house in Berlin, its front view and back view, its garden, its verandah with a table set for tea. Here is the country house in Thuringia, the picnic hut in the Grünewald, with unidentifiable relations grinning in striped bathing costumes.

Into my smallish bag I throw tennis shoes and trainers, jeans and sweat shirts. Will other people disapprove?

That's their problem.

31

Mrs Carvalho forwards my mail. In Germany I receive what is known as a 'dear John' letter. Why is it not called dear Jane, dear Jean, dear Joan?

Dear Anne.

Gerry has been having an affair. His girlfriend is pregnant. He is going to leave me, live with her, divorce me, marry her. The baby is due in February. It is to be kept secret until after Flora's wedding.

I am surprised by my lack of surprise. I am pleased by my own pleasure. Gerry is welcome to spend his old age retreading the familiar circuit of sleepless nights and anxious adolescence.

Mine will lead along new paths.

First, to Berlin.

I expect it to be fateful for me. Images built up by an overweight of meaning and threat run through my mind; of the black and scarlet power of the Nazi era, of the flattened, starving ruin of the nineteen forties, of a persistent later metaphor, a forest clearing, its inhabitants huddled round the light of a fire, as the wolves circle in the communist dark outside.

Instead I find new, unevocative streets, their buildings massive and unglamorous, and people who are brusque and unyielding. This is just another foreign country. I feel a twinge of personal involvement only once, dining in the Hotel Berlin, when a middle aged couple comes in with a tiny, old, crippled man, bent double, his fingers hooked into claws, his face scarred, to whom the menu is shouted. He is helped to eat. I wonder whether he was a victim, or a persecutor. And there is no way of telling.

If it had not been for Hitler I would be as German as I am English and feel as at home here as I do in London.

A slightly drunken Scotsman, on his way out of the grill room, greets me as a compatriot. 'Can you stand the place? I can't stand it,' he says loudly. 'We should have razed it to the ground in 'forty-five and sown the ground with salt.'

The next day I find the site of my family's home, of which no trace remains, and see the Silberschmidt clinic. It is still a sanatorium, now for mentally handicapped children and called Sonnenschein, which means sunshine.

On to Potsdam. I walk slowly along an eighteenth-century street and try to admire the pretty architectural details in spite of their coating of grime and decay.

I am reading in my guidebook that these degraded buildings have been tastefully restored when a man's voice says, *'Voulez-vous souper à Sans Souci?'*

I recognise Frederick the Great's famous cryptogram, which should be written

$$p \qquad a \qquad ci$$
$$\text{voulez vous} \qquad\qquad 100$$

but cannot remember Voltaire's reply. The man who spoke is prepared, holding an artist's sketch pad at the ready. With charcoal, he scrawls,

$$G\,a,$$

and says,

'J'ai grand appetit. Do you understand? *G-grand*, capital G, *A petit.'*

He is about forty, gaunt, tall, fair. An Aryan. When I meet his eyes he gives a small, jerky bow, and says, 'Bruno Heinemann, at your service. Are you going to Sans Souci now? May I walk along with you?'

He picks up my right hand, although I have not held it out to him, and kisses it, staring into my face as he does so. Then he walks beside me with an anxious, archaic courtesy, dodging on to the traffic side of the pavements as we cross roads. He is like a man who learned his manners from a book, and so he probably did, having grown up in a time and place where such capitalist falsities must have been forbidden.

He guides me through the park and palace talking good, well-rehearsed English. When we reach the tea room I ask him if he would like to join me. He drinks coffee and eats cake with delicate greed. I suddenly understand that this is how he lives: rich foreign visitors to this austere land of unemployment buy him food. In exchange he guides them, acts as courier – and as gigolo?

The practised, insincere gallantry is curiously seductive.

Shall I abandon myself to my own pleasure, not faking it, nor caring whether he is satisfied?

What if he thinks me old, flabby, wrinkled, past it?

That's his problem.

The complete scenario flashes before me.

Above, below, behind, between.

Not Anne, not Bruno: any man and any woman. A woman who lays herself bare.

The familiar litany of caution pops up like a stop sign in my head. Rape, theft, extortion, ransom money, sexually transmitted diseases. Embarrassment, shame, prudishness.

There are still more habits of Anne Medlicott's circumscribed lifetime to be discarded.

He sees me watching him and smiles, holding my eyes with his own, concentrating on me. His seduction technique is good. Better fed and more confident, he might have the capacity to enchant.

Not me.

I buy him more coffee. He eats my cake.

I have paid him off.

The roads are bad and the hotels unwelcoming. The Thuringian forest is dying. Pollution has killed the conifers. Bare trunks lead upwards to sparse, browning vegetation. The air is acid, harsh; my eyes water, my nose and throat feel raw.

At the Silberschmidts' country place nothing is left of the castellated mansion but uninhabitable dereliction. Shall I stake a legal claim to it?

Am I Michael's heir? It is the first time, since discovering my parents never married, that I realise there could be legal consequences of my illegitimacy.

I stand in what was once an orchard. Some wizened plums dangle from the trees, though most are worm-eaten and attracting a swarm of wasps. I find one that looks edible and suck at the sour, tough skin.

I do not want this house.

Over the years of being a part-time writer and a Good Wife, I have undertaken numerous time-filling activities appropriate to the image of Mrs Gerald Medlicott. Many the charitable committee of which I have been a member, many the cultural society and conservation group. I have dabbled in foreign languages, pottery, wine tasting and 'Better Bridge'.

One year I did picture restoration for beginners. As I drive southwards towards the Saxon mountains, I remember a vast, dim canvas on which the expert demonstrated his technique. At first sight it was of a gruesome carouse, showing merry peasants flourishing pewter tankards over a rush-strewn floor scattered with mongrels and toddlers. As we examined it more closely we saw the ghostly traces of the picture on which a later painter had overlaid his own. As the chemicals took effect, earlier details showed up amidst their disfiguring later surroundings. An exquisitely painted hand with rings and a dangling cuff of lace emerging in a thicket of ruddy cheeks, a cerulian sash in a puddle of ale.

Now I am reminded of that picture by the few traces of an older Saxony that stand out in the recent uglification. I am jolted along in my hired Volkswagen behind dusty trucks and rusty, put-putting two-stroke cars in sallow shades of grey or ochre. The way leads through industrial wastelands. There are traces of the countryside Celia remembered: arable land, grazing cows, an unimproved village street fossilised in antique simplicity. With my pre-war maps and a copy of the 1936 edition of Baedeker I find my way to the area once known as Heorot. It is called Freistadt now, and is a chemical works. The sporting estate has disappeared under factories and ranks of grim apartment blocks, square, uniform, with corrugated plastic tacked on to balconies.

To the south the mountains still loom, and here is the house Celia described: a immense frontage, not white but dirty brown with many of its windows filled with sheets of wood or cardboard. On all sides of the once isolated mansion other buildings have been added, some single-storey huts that may, a generation ago, have been called temporary, others new blocks of concrete already stained and slummy.

In the front of the house shabby cars and bicycles are parked in orderly rows. I back neatly into a space. This place may not be tidy but it is regimented.

Nothing is left of the planned landscape except scrubby grass and some vestigial hedges. I walk past the broken remains of a fountain and the boggy traces of an artificial lake, past plinths that no longer bear statues. I decipher a dragon rampant under a splash of spray paint.

On the far side of the expanse of bare earth and weeds that was once a terrace and lawn I perch on a piece of broken stone. There are others lying on the ground around me, some carved with single words: Thor, Fido, Spitz. This was the site of the pets' cemetery. Somewhere in this ground Hubertus's mother lies unceremoniously buried. Small pits have been excavated in the dry earth. The family treasures must have been dug up long since.

It is hot and sultry. I cannot tell whether the sky is overcast from thunderclouds or pollution. The few people I see are either excessively thin or flabbily fat. Their clothes are not as drab as they might have been five years earlier – rather they are in glaring, garish colours – but the materials are poor and the faces above them stressed and sallow. They are slum-dwellers, and it shows. Nobody speaks to me. But far away I can hear the international sound of children playing.

I look back at the house. It is identifiable although no longer like the photograph I found in the memoirs of a Princess of Pless who stayed there in 1915. She snapped opulent, huge-hatted ladies, arrogant men, ranks of servants and huntsmen, a cavalcade of coaches.

Above the main door a broken stone shows where the proud Beowulf shield was broken.

So much for their thousand-year reign.

An exotically large and clean car draws up by the steps. A man in a light linen suit and Panama hat and a woman, young-seeming and lithe with bobbed hair and a flowered dress, get out and go into the house. I walk back slowly and follow them in, up the shallow front steps and through an unlocked door.

The entrance hall is still pillared. It is piled with cardboard boxes, plastic rubbish bags, old, discoloured newspaper. Background music, with a heavy, insistent beat, sounds everywhere through wall-hung speakers. There is a powerful smell of sauerkraut.

A door to the right is open. It shows a vista: room after room, dusty, partitioned, with clumsy, flimsy furniture. A man has walked purposefully through, leaving the doors open behind him. He has reached the far corner of the house. He is standing beside a red-laminated table on angled metal legs. A dusty gleam of light falls on his white hat. It is Sir Hans Hahn.

I follow him, my footsteps clicking against the dry, chipped floor, through rooms that smell of drains.

This house is still a dwelling place. I wonder whether more people live here now than when the house was full of the von Beowulf family and their retainers.

A snotty-nosed child wrapped in a grey blanket and seated on a low bed is staring at me. She draws in her breath to wail, and I pass on quickly to the end.

Perdita Whitchurch is standing by the window with black grime on her hand. She has rubbed it over the glass to look out on to a courtyard where two men are stacking planks of wood. The far wall is high, raw concrete with spikes and rusty wire on top.

Hans Hahn is wiping his forehead and neck with a pristine handkerchief. Then he uses it to clean the seat of a plastic chair before sitting down.

'Anne,' he says. 'We thought we might see you here. Sticky weather, isn't it?'

A sticky situation. I defer it. 'Have you come to check over your inheritance?'

'We're combining it with the British Council affair,' Sir Hans replies. I had forgotten that among the many other public appointments he holds is a directorship of the British Council. His posts are listed in *Who's Who* by date of appointment. This one comes between the Arts Council and the Royal Commission on Historical Manuscripts. His life since the war has been utterly respectable and conventional; utterly English. He married the daughter of a rural dean in 1970 (d. 1981), had no children and devoted his spare time to public and voluntary work. He is part of the Establishment.

'Are you involved with the British week?' I ask Perdita.

Hadn't I read the programme? That was the exhibition she was trying to get ready when I went to see her in Cornwall. It shows paintings by her, sculptures by Rosenthal and photographs by Susanna Thomas. The theme is the English landscape. Not, Perdita says, that she had any intention of coming to Germany herself when she last saw me. But they had been advised, she and Hans, that they should have a look at Heorot and to her own surprise she was keen to do so. She thinks it is grim. Grim and creepy. 'Where has everyone gone?'

'They are working,' Hans Hahn says absently. He is tracing a pattern on the table top with his forefinger, round and down and up and round. He stops to feel in his waistcoat pocket for a small phial of pills, one of which he puts under his tongue. His face is still sweaty and very pale.

'Are you all right?' Perdita asks.

He closes his eyes and whispers, 'I will be in a moment. This is all a bit of a shock.'

'He remembered Heorot as beautiful,' Perdita says to me. She puts her hand on his wrist. 'That's funny,' she says. 'Look.'

We look at their hands: hers is brown, with roughened skin and dirty nails. His is almost mauve with big liver spots and thick, ridged oblong nails. On both the two middle fingers are of equal length.

I say, 'A family trait.'

'It was I who had his hands,' Hans Hahn says. 'Not Hubertus, not Marianne. I inherited them.'

'The old Baron? Your father?'

'This is where he sat. His desk, his lamp . . . one saw him through the darkened rooms, illuminated. The master.'

A tall, hatchet-faced man in a grey suit comes into the room and speaks angrily in biting, clipped words. 'He says we have no right here. We must leave,' explains Hans Hahn.

'My mother was a chambermaid. She was married to the estate factor before I was born.'

'Were they really Jewish?'

'My foster father's maternal grandmother was.'

'You needn't have emigrated.'

'I didn't think it would be for ever,' he says.

We have driven in Hans Hahn's BMW to the site of the house in which he had grown up. It has completely disappeared, its position in the scrubby trees marked only by a thicker growth of nettles and brambles. Nearby is a hen run made of corrugated iron and barbed wire. We sit in the car and speak against a background noise of cheeping chicks.

'You were von Beowulf's spy in London,' I say. 'When Michael met you on the cross-Channel ferry you were on your way to report to Hubertus.' His silence is assent. I continue: 'It didn't work that time, but you betrayed my father. You followed him, that last journey. You wanted my mother for yourself.'

239

'Your mother was a very attractive woman, Anne, but she had no eyes for anyone but her husband, believe me. It was not until he was long gone that she turned to me.'

'That's why you pretended to have heard Lotte needed him. To get him out of the way.'

'Lotte? What are you talking about?' Perdita says.

I tell her how Michael Silversmith was decoyed back into German territory, and how he was never heard of again. 'Except by someone who met a man using his name at the end of the war. A woman who conveniently died after she had spoken to you.'

I find myself stymied by uncertainty about what to call him. By the knightly title, by his first name?

I want him to know I am not his friend. I must keep my distance, as I did in childhood when I sensed but did not recognise the intimacy between him and Irene.

He puts another pill in his mouth. It seems to give him a little vigour. He says, 'You had better know. What harm can it do me now? It's true. When Hubertus took a false identity at the end of the war I did make sure his secret was safe. I even helped him to escape. I and Julian Blanchminster.'

The moment of truth, at last. 'So Julian's name really did belong on that list!' I exclaim.

'Don't be silly,' Hans Hahn says. 'Surely you have worked out that Julian Whitchurch was the instigator of the escape route?'

'But the notebook . . . '

'Shows how well he played his part.'

'You must have had it all along. Why produce it now?' I ask. His doing so has changed my life. I should not be surprised if he realises that.

He shakes his head. 'No, it was sent to me, as I said. By Marianne.'

'So that was another of your lies. You were in touch with her.'

'Anne . . . ' Perdita is protective of the old man. Her uncle, not mine. As I have hardened, she has mellowed.

'It's all right,' he says. 'No, Anne. We met only once after the war, when I went to see her at London University and we quarrelled. She couldn't accept that we were both victims of our times. She insisted we were equally guilty. But all Marianne had done was remain an ignorant girl who did what her big brother told her. She was here during the war, you know. She ran the farm and kept the house going, but afterwards she wouldn't forgive herself. Or me. She must have changed in recent years, for about eighteen months ago she sent me the notebook to keep as a historical document. It could no longer do Julian any harm since he'd had a stroke.

My suspicions are not allayed. 'Where did she get it?'

'It was returned to her with Hubertus's belongings. She was never told he survived. She might have betrayed him.'

'While you and Julian Whitchurch wouldn't! You betrayed us instead.'

'He was still my brother.'

'And Julian's lover.' My voice is thin with bitterness and disgust. Hans Hahn puts his hand on mine and I snatch it away.

He says, 'That was long since forgotten. None of us had any love for Hubertus by 1945, least of all Julian Blanchminster, believe me, he had put all that far behind him. I realised that after the war when we became acquainted in Berlin. He was the sort of man to think of homosexuality as an indiscretion of his wild youth, a rite of passage on the way to respectability. No, Julian maintained his relationship with Hubertus and Marianne so as to carry on with his pre-war work of rescue.'

'In that case why did he help Hubertus to get away, why didn't he want him to be put on trial and punished, hanged like the other war criminals?' I demand.

'None of us wanted Hubertus to tell what he knew. I was afraid for myself, I don't deny it, he had already talked about me to Celia, I knew what he would say to the British authorities. But Julian was simply thinking of Perdita. The last von Beowulf would hardly be a father for her to be proud of. We needed to keep him quiet.'

'So what happened?'

'When Celia Roget recognised Hubertus in the camp in Berlin she told Julian.'

'I suppose she wanted to keep her relationship with him quiet too.'

'No. Not that. Julian persuaded her that this would be her second and last service for the child whose life she had saved.'

'For me,' Perdita says. 'Why did she care? Why did he? Neither of them had given me a thought for years.'

'Remorse? Responsibility?' The old man's voice takes on a harsher bite. 'Take it on face value, why don't you? Yours was one of many lives Julian saved before the war. What's wrong with saying it was all pure bloody altruism?'

Rain has started to beat on the roof like a xylophone, a tinkling monotone. 'So what did you do?' I ask.

'We got hold of papers with a more suitable name than Michael Silberschmidt's. In the prevailing chaos, an army intelligence officer and an official in the Control Commission could arrange for a man to disappear. Which we did.'

'Where did he go?'

'Eventually, to the Argentine, but he died not long afterwards. I never saw him again.'

'Why didn't you go with him?'

'Then? In 'forty-five? My dear Anne, I was a quite different person by that time.'

'A turncoat.'

'Yes, I accept that,' Hans Hahn replies with a dignity that reminds me of what he has, in a worldly sense, achieved. 'People do change their minds. I realised that I had been wrong, just as most of my contemporaries who joined the Communist Party in the Thirties did. When I came to England as a spy – I don't deny it, as a spy – I still believed in my country right or wrong.'

'Until you saw it was losing.'

'No, long before that. I repudiated the Fatherland in the middle of the war.'

'When?'

'I can tell you exactly. It was in December nineteen forty-two when I, along with the British public, first learned of the extermination camps and the whole House of Commons stood silent in tribute to the suffering Jews.'

The rain is heavy now. There is thunder and then distant lightning. Perdita turns on the car's engine and puts it into forward gear. The wheels spin. Just audible through the roaring engine, Hans Hahn whispers, 'By then, you see, I was in love with a Jew.'

We sit in silence as Perdita tries to go forwards or backwards, sinking ever further into the suddenly sodden ground.

Hans Hahn and I eventually get out and try to push the heavy car from the rut. Half a minute in the open air and we are wet through. My hands slip on the metal, my feet in the mud.

I am beginning to realise that we cannot possibly do it when Hans Hahn slumps forward over the slippery metal, and then slides to the ground. Without even turning the engine off, Perdita leaps out and crouches beside him. His face, as wet as everything else by now, has dark blotches and his eyes are closed. I can't tell whether he is breathing until we have somehow managed to heave him on to the back seat; he is. For the time being.

I don't know what to do. I know nothing about medicine or first aid. I have never seen death. I have only imagined it.

I feel in Hans Hahn's pocket, where I find his bottle of pills. Wincing, cringing from the contact, I put two of them under his tongue.

Perdita takes her coat, and Hans Hahn's, from the boot and edges them under the rear wheels. Then she manages to back the car up and out.

By the time we reach the house, where my hired car is parked, Hans Hahn has come round. His eyes rest on me. He is experienced, knowledgeable, wily; a survivor. Do I wish he had died?

He carries on where he left off, gasping between the words. 'Haven't you ever had to admit your mistakes? Don't judge me, Anne. Not unless you have been infallible yourself.'

32

Dresden's old centre, once the 'Jewel of Europe', was devastated by bombs that caused a firestorm. What remains is blackened by acid rain. The roads are pot-holed, the tenements crumbling and a soupy haze smudges the view across the River Elbe. The rubble of the Frauenkirche has been left as a memorial to the air-raid victims. Along its fence, home-made wooden crosses and banners carry the words, '1945 Dresden, 1991 Baghdad'.

The delegates and performers at the British Cultural Festival have been booked into a utilitarian hotel. I lie down for a while and am changing into clean but still inelegant clothes, which seem entirely suitable here, when the telephone rings.

It is Hans Hahn. He has been listening to the BBC World Service and has heard the news that Julian Whitchurch, Viscount Blanchminster, died in his sleep last night.

'That's the end of his libel action,' Hans Hahn says.

'You could have stopped it before it began, if you had just told me – '

'If I had you would never have done the research of the last few months. You would have spent the rest of your life hiding your eyes. I always told your dear mother you would look up one day.'

'She didn't want me to know.'

'She did, but not until you wanted to as well.'

In the hotel lobby I am met by a young university lecturer, who takes me out to his rusty car. As he closes its door, an irrelevant thought flashes into my mind. My daughter will become a viscountess. How pleased I would once have been. Now it means nothing to me. I have grown out of snobbery too.

My escort tells me that things are very bad. Forty percent of the population is unemployed. Outsiders take the Germans' jobs. It is like the nineteen twenties. 'And we know what happened next,' he says.

The British Festival is taking place in the Palace of Culture. It is a debased modernist building decorated with a gigantic mural about the history of the working class.

The exhibition is well attended, but the visitors' behaviour in public gives no clue to their feelings. They are quiet and solemn and smile very little.

Perdita's pictures are supposed to represent the English landscape. I pause by the biggest, a vehement, thickly-coloured canvas.

A wood, a pond, a fallen tree, a baby. But this is not a pleasant pastoral scene. In the corner is a woman, her two hands raised, mouth open in a dark oval of horror.

'It's my latest,' Perdita says.

'What is it?'

'It's called "Lost Lotte".'

In tiny print are the words 'Property of Viscountess Blanchminster'. I am surprised. 'This belongs to Celia?'

'I did it for her. It's a present.'

We go towards the hall where the English writers are to perform. A woman approaches and says to Perdita, 'Mrs Medlicott, I have so looked forward to meeting you. Will you give me your autograph?'

'I'm Perdita Whitchurch. This is Anne Medlicott.'

'Pardon me, please! But you are so alike. One would take you for sisters.'

We sit together at the back of the hall while Sir Hans Hahn welcomes this German audience to a British cultural festival. He looks tired but speaks with authority, introducing, in English and then in German, a Chinese Glaswegian called Gordon Wong who then reads from his latest book. It is about guerrilla resistance in a totalitarian state. The audience is attentive. When he finishes his English reading, another man stands up to read the same chapter from the German translation.

Perdita doodles on a pad. With rapid, nervous strokes of a soft pencil, she sketches a thin man with a great beak nose, his body averted, and another sketch, and another. He is always turning away. It is Julian Blanchminster as she remembers him.

During the applause for the actor she says,

245

'I'll go to the funeral. Will you come too? When are you going home?'

I have always known when I would be home; when, where, how, with whom. Why or whether were never in doubt.

The reading is followed by the usual questions about message, methods and manipulating one's material. Do the characters take on a life of their own? Is fiction autobiography?

Gordon Wong says that he works from a detailed synopsis. Every paragraph is preordained. He begins each book by writing its last page first: it is a mistake to embark on a journey without being sure of its means of conveyance and destination.

I did not manipulate my material. It has manipulated me. And now I do not know where I am going.

I step on to the platform and am introduced by a stout woman who wheezes as she speaks; she is a professor of English at the University. She reads from a typed sheet on which she has evidently copied out the entry about me in *Twentieth Century Crime and Mystery Writers*.

Anne Medlicott: born in London, educated at public school and Cambridge. Wife and mother. Books mannered, logical, unemotional. Elegant prose and neat plots. In the cosy English tradition of the ladylike mystery writer.

I open the book I am holding, and read aloud from the adventures of Amy Swift for twenty minutes. The same passage is read in German. Then the professor speaks again. She poses the familiar question.

Why do respectable Englishwomen choose to write about murder? Are they trying to neutralise the terrors of real life? Are the conventions of their genre an armour against self-revelation? Whodunnits provide satisfactory answers. Do they imply that all other problems have solutions too?

The professor has studied my work. Anne Medlicott's fantasies, she says, always have a happy ending.